G-S.

# MURDER
# AT THE
# VILLA BYZANTINE

# MURDER
# AT THE
# VILLA BYZANTINE

# R. T. RAICHEV

Constable • London

Constable & Robinson Ltd
3 The Lanchesters
162 Fulham Palace Road
London W6 9ER
www.constablerobinson.com

First published in the UK by Constable,
an imprint of Constable & Robinson, 2011

First US edition published by SohoConstable,
an imprint of Soho Press, 2011

Soho Press, Inc.
853 Broadway
New York, NY 10003
www.sohopress.com

A copy of the British Library Cataloguing in Publication
Data is available from the British Library

UK ISBN: 978-1-84901-476-2

US ISBN: 978-1-56947-914-8
US Library of Congress number: 2010037142

Printed and bound in the UK

1  3  5  7  9  10  8  6  4  2

To Chitra, in gratitude for the second murder motive.

# Author's Note

This is a work of fiction. All the characters are imaginary and bear no relation to any living person.

R. T. R.

# Contents

*. . . a hundred swords*
*Will storm his heart, Love's fev'rous citadel . . .*

John Keats

# 1

# Peril at Kinderhook

Major Payne said, 'We have had our share of murders and disappearances at grand houses, we unmasked the killer of the high-class hooker on the subcontinent and of the baronet at the exclusive retreat in Dulwich, but one thing we don't seem ever to have tackled is the kind of mystery that is unremittingly suburban. I was thinking about it only the other day. Silly thing to think, but there you are.'

Antonia put away her lipstick and examined her face in the mirror. 'Do people like reading murder mysteries set in the suburbs? Won't that be too boring? *Peril at Kinderhook* . . .'

'You suspect some devilry will happen at Kinderhook tonight?' Payne's left eyebrow had gone up.

'I suspect nothing of the sort.'

'You said *Peril at Kinderhook*.'

'I thought it would make a good title, that's all. You need *so* little encouragement.'

'Is there perhaps something you know and I don't?'

'There isn't. OK, it's an odd name and it's an odd-looking house and Melisande Chevret has definite possibilities, but that's all. To tell you the truth, I am not at all wild about going.'

'Would you rather we stayed at home and watched the box? Or we could play canasta. You are getting awfully good at it, you know.'

1

'I am not at all keen on the box either, but at least I won't have to talk to people I don't know.'

'Hell is other people, eh?'

'I wouldn't go as far as that . . . I believe I am shy.'

'Your social manner is impeccable. You possess enviable poise as well as ease.'

'It's all an act . . . I don't feel like playing canasta tonight. I suppose we could do the *Times* crossword. Or we could have an early night and read in bed . . . Oh, I hate it when I am indecisive! Don't you hate me when I am indecisive?'

'I love you in any and every state you happen to be in.' Payne kissed her.

'No – we must go. We've got the flowers and everything. Of course we'll go. It's only down the road anyway.'

'Where did you say you and Melisande Chevret met? At the local Women's Institute?'

'At Wild Oats. We keep bumping into each other. Whenever I go in, she is there, or if I am already there, she suddenly makes an entrance. She is the kind that makes an entrance, yes. She is very dramatic. I must say she is always extremely charming to me.'

'Perhaps she's managed to engineer these meetings somehow? Perhaps it's all leading up to something? Perhaps tonight is the night?'

'The night for what?'

'Some hair-raising outrage. *Kinder* sacrifice? Soul-bartering? Incidentally, what *is* wild oats in this particular context – *not* what young men sow?'

'The local organic shop. You know that perfectly well.' Antonia gave him a sideways glance. 'I hope you won't be saying silly things when we get there. Please. Don't show off. Especially not in front of Melisande Chevret. *Please.*'

'I am not entirely familiar with the local topography,' Payne protested. 'I don't go shopping as often as you do.'

'Perhaps you should.' Antonia draped a scarf round her neck and patted her hair. 'Melisande Chevret enjoys attention. The man who owns Wild Oats treats her like royalty. He is always dancing and bowing and scraping and tugging at his forelock when she is around. I think she likes that.'

2

'It seems to be our lot, meeting people who are in the middle of some impossible drama, or else on the brink of perpetrating some terrible thing, have you noticed?' Payne stroked his chin with his forefinger. 'Or who are in some way desperate.'

Antonia said she didn't think Melisande Chevret was desperate. 'It's her birthday.'

'For some people that's cause for desperation. How old is she? Seventy-eight? Eighty-three?'

'I don't think she is eighty-three. Don't be silly.'

'Sixty-six? The number of the beast.'

'I don't think anyone is *meant* to know her age. I suspect she is a little older than me, though of course she looks younger than me. I am not sure we should mention the word "birthday" at all. It is a *cocktail* party we've been invited to, don't forget.'

'I've never been to a birthday party masquerading as a cocktail party before. Did you say she had an older sister? So these are the people who bought Kinderhook. Two sisters. Chekhovian, almost.'

'Melisande pointed out that she and I were the only celebrities in the area. I am not really a celebrity, am I?'

Payne said that Antonia was what was known as a 'minor celebrity'. 'You have written five detective novels. There are a number of blogs devoted to you. You were on the box last Friday. That was quite a performance,' he went on reminiscently. 'You tore strips off that play.'

Antonia had appeared on *Friday Review*.

'I don't think I was particularly horrid, was I?'

'You used phrases like a "masterclass in pure theatrical torpor". You said there was an almost epic scale to the play's dullness. You said the sets were so horribly huge that even Fritz Lang would have considered them some-what de trop. You were devastatingly witty. You made everybody laugh. If I were the playwright,' said Payne, 'I'd shoot myself with my old army revolver.'

'Oh nonsense, Hugh. It's a well-known fact that play-wrights thrive on controversy, infamy, censorship and disgrace. As it happens, that particular playwright is

3

already dead – has been dead for more than three hundred years. We are talking about Thomas Middleton.'

'Middleton? Really? I must have dozed off.'

'It was the direction and the production I criticized.'

'In that case, it's the director and the producer who should shoot themselves with their old army revolvers,' Payne said smoothly.

'Have you got the flowers?'

'Here they are. Should I kiss Melisande Chevret's hand?'

'Certainly not. It will give her ideas. Purple roses – why purple?'

'I thought purple appropriate for the mistress of Kinderhook somehow. Is my tie straight? I could have toddled along in my dressing gown and slippers ... It's acceptable in suburbia, isn't it? Neighbours don't stand on ceremony and so on.'

'That would definitely give Melisande Chevret ideas.'

'I must say you paint a somewhat disturbing picture of Melisande Chevret. Is she really a man-eater? I am scared now. I am not sure I want to go.'

They went out. Payne locked the front door. It was a warm evening in early August. The sun was sailing low in a pink and gold sky.

'One can easily imagine an actress being called Melisande Chevret. It's a jolly striking name,' Payne went on. 'Would you describe her as the kind of woman whose manner is normally faintly histrionic and often more emphatically so?'

'I would. She likes to strike attitudes.'

'The kind that either gets terribly excited or terribly upset about things and finds all that is in between sort of *beige*?'

'That wouldn't be a bad way of putting it.'

'Perhaps you will make her the anti-heroine at the very heart of your next novel. She sounds just right for the kind of murder mystery you write,' Payne said portentously. 'Is she divorced or widowed?'

'Divorced, I imagine.'

Payne gave his man-of-the-world nod and said that actresses were always divorced and, in that respect, minor actresses were the worst offenders. Hadn't Antonia noticed?

Five minutes later they stood inside the drawing room at Kinderhook. Their hostess had gone to the kitchen to have a word with the two hired waiters.

'I hate arriving first,' Antonia whispered.

'I thought it was being ushered into a crowded room you didn't like ... I have actually seen her before. She drives about in a cerise-coloured two-seater. She always wears a scarf round her head and dark glasses, even when it is far from sunny. The Garbo touch. Her nose is a perfect shape. She is the *diva divina* type. She seems in a febrile state – is she always like that?'

'I believe she gave you the glad eye.'

'I am sure you imagined it.'

'I didn't imagine it.'

'You are notorious for your writer's imagination. The roses were a hit. She *adores* purple roses. I believe she meant it. I promise to try not to say anything remotely funny,' said Payne firmly. 'We don't want another Bee Ardleigh kind of situation, do we?'

'She seems worried someone might not turn up, it's the way she keeps glancing at her watch.'

'I bet it's her newly acquired toy-boy who's causing her anxiety—'

'Keep your voice down.' Antonia cast a nervous glance at the door. 'Terrible manners, standing around whispering!'

'Golly, she was Joan of Arc – look at those photos!' Payne pointed to the wall. 'I'd say that photo was taken about thirty-five years ago. Theatrical make-up is a great giveaway. I must say she's holding the sword most expertly – like a real pro. And there she is with a cocktail shaker, looking adventurous in taffeta – what play would that be?'

'Some drawing-room comedy. William Douglas-Home?'

5

'It could be an Agatha Christie . . . *Spider's Web*? I wonder if she was Clarissa . . . D'you think she'd make a good murderess?'

'Do you mean on stage or in real life? I can't imagine her having the patience to plot and premeditate . . . Clarissa didn't murder anyone, did she?'

'No. She only told a lot of lies and tried to conceal a dead body. If Melisande Chevret did commit a murder,' Payne said, 'it would be in a fit of extravagant passion, which she would later regret—'

'Shush – she's coming.'


'You'll never believe this, but my sister has decided to put in an appearance. That in itself should be a cause for celebration.' Melisande Chevret brought her hands together. 'This morning she threatened she would lock herself in her room.'

'I didn't threaten anything of the sort.' Melisande's sister smiled.

'You refused to come down to breakfast, darling.'

'I didn't "refuse". I was extremely busy. I simply *had* to finish that book—'

'I'd go blind or mad if I read as much as my sister, but Win is so terribly disciplined. My sister lives in organized rigour. I am the complete opposite. The light in this house is *awful*. So sorry, I'm forgetting my manners – Antonia and Hugh Payne – my sister Winifred.' Melisande Chevret turned on Payne a gaze of embarrassing brilliance – the kind that 'projected' across footlights, he thought.

'How do you do?' Winifred extended her hand. 'I don't think your house has a name, has it?'

'No, only a humble number,' said Payne.

'I hate houses with names,' Melisande said.

'I believe you have a cat?' Winifred said.

'Yes. His name is Dupin,' said Antonia. 'Do you like cats?'

'I *used* to like cats. I have mixed feelings about cats.'

'This must be the worst-lit room I have ever been in. I believe we all look like drowned people floating at the bottom of a lake.' Melisande sighed. 'For some reason nothing seems right tonight – or is it just me?'

'I have heard about you of course, Antonia, but I'm afraid I haven't read any of your books,' Winifred said. 'I read *all the time*, but rarely for pleasure these days.'

'You aren't by any chance a publisher's reader? A small independent publisher?' Payne suggested.

'Yes . . . How did you know?'

'I told you Hugh was frightfully good, didn't I? I said he was bound to astound us all. Well, I was right!' Melisande grimaced enigmatically at Payne. She laid her hand on his arm. 'Do not be alarmed. I do not dabble in the dark arts. I tend to hear things, that's all. I believe "Hugh" means "bright in mind and in spirit", correct? I used to have a boyfriend called Hugh, that's how I know.'

'Would it amuse you to know that in Pig Latin "Hugh Payne" is "Ughhay Aynepay"?' Payne avoided Antonia's eye.

'This is one of the funniest things I have ever heard in my life!' Melisande laughed and clapped her hands.

'I used to enjoy my job. I try to like the books I read, I really do, but slush piles are depressing things,' Winifred said. 'I'm afraid bad writing leaves me completely demoralized.'

'I have never regarded acting as a "job",' Melisande said. 'Actors are the opposite of people!'

'I read a review of one of your books, Antonia. It was in the *Telegraph*, I think. The plot was described as "flowing with the fluid precision of the Changing of the Guard".'

'That was a bit silly,' Antonia said quickly.

Winifred smiled. 'The whole book was "cunningly conceived, satisfyingly shaped and enormously entertaining". I'll certainly get some of your books now that I have met you.'

'You needn't bother, really.' Remarks like that always threw Antonia into an agony of embarrassment. At the same time she decided Winifred would be more interesting to talk to than her sister.

'I love detective stories. Always have, since I was a girl. Nobody seems to take any care over plotting any longer, do they? Most modern crime writers seem obsessed with – *issues*. Commendable but tedious.'

'I love stories that deal with the destruction of innocence and the corrupting effects of great wealth.' Melisande spoke in a serio-comic voice.

She can't bear not occupying the centre-stage, Payne thought.

'Who is your publisher?' Winifred asked.

Antonia told her.

'I understand they don't pay large advances.'

'They don't.'

'I am no longer interested in money,' Melisande said. 'I intend to spend the next thirty years of my life educating my emotions. One doesn't need money for that. If everything else fails, I'll go into a nunnery.' She glanced at her watch.

Does she ever mean anything she says? Antonia wondered.

Although their features were not dissimilar, one wouldn't have been able to tell at once that Winifred and Melisande were sisters. With her demure chignon, virginal bosom and restrained, somewhat wistful manner, sensible dress and shoes, Winifred Willard might have stepped out of the pages of an Anita Brookner novel. Melisande, on the other hand, was highly strung, restlessly temperamental, brittle and 'young'. Her eyes were a curious yellow-brown colour. She had good cheekbones, but clearly that was not enough – her face was heavily made up, her hair had been dyed copper; it was short and swept back boldly. She wore a little black dress, an Etruscan-style necklace and high heels.

More guests were expected to arrive at any moment, though not an awful lot, Melisande said. No other neighbours, no. She didn't really care for the people who lived on either side of Kinderhook, she had to admit. They had made overtures, they seemed good, decent people, one saw them in their landscaped gardens at all times, building rockeries or hunting for moles, even in the foulest weather, but they were not *her* sort of people. No, no luminaries from the theatre world either – she was sorry if Hugh and Antonia were disappointed – it would be an intimate gathering – her fiancé, her agent and a playwright friend, whose one-woman show *Tallulah* Melisande had performed a couple of years back, to spectacular acclaim.

'Drinks! Do let's have drinks – and something to eat. I hope you like pheasant pâté? It's organic. We look awfully solemn – awfully static – or is that the light? The light is all wrong tonight.'

'I don't think there's anything wrong with it,' Winifred said.

'I'm afraid I am too temperamental. I seem to be one of those unfortunate human beings on whom fairy god-mothers bestow moods rather than qualities. This is supposed to be the happiest day of my life. I should be in a blissful, glowing, untouchable kind of state, only I am not! There's plenty of crushed ice, thank God. I don't think I could have survived without crushed ice.' Once more Melisande laid her hand on Payne's arm. 'Hugh, would you be an angel and open one of the windows? There isn't enough air in the room. Am I being neurotic?'

'You are being neurotic,' Winifred said good-humouredly.

'I do feel awful. I may need an oxygen mask soon— Oh! That must be James!' Melisande exclaimed as the front door bell rang. 'Thank God! At long last! I'll never forgive James for making me wait, never! One thing I hate more than anything else in the world is *waiting*. I forgot to mention it, but James is bringing some people I've never met before, he told me at the eleventh hour. Hope they won't be too boring. I have no idea who they are.'

## 2

# The Uninvited

'Whatever took you so long, darling? I was getting really worried. I thought something truly dreadful had happened. Why don't you answer your mobile? My fiancé, James Morland.' Melisande introduced him somewhat huffily. She was holding on to his arm.

'So sorry, Meli. We were held up.'

'*Held up*? You mean you were set upon by men with guns?' She opened her eyes wide.

'No, not by men with guns. Wherever did you get that idea? The traffic was quite appalling—'

'Oh dear. *Must* you always explain in such detail? Why is everything so difficult tonight? That was a joke, James. A *joke*. But I did say, didn't I, be here before the Leviathan could swim a league. And you said you would be.'

'I am so sorry,' Morland harrumphed.

'No, it doesn't matter one little bit, darling. It's just that I needed you here *earlier*. That's all. I did tell you to come as early as possible, didn't I? I wanted you to do something for me.'

James Morland was most certainly not a toy-boy. He looked every inch the prosperous merchant banker he turned out to be. Late fifties, Payne imagined – pink-faced, fattish, baldish, dullish, resplendent in a Savile Row suit with a subtle stripe but sporting a flamboyant-looking tie, which seemed to have been knotted in a hurry and was a bit askew. Bluff and blissfully uncomplicated. The kind of chap who wears braces rather than a belt, Payne decided. Might turn out to be a pillar of the Weybridge Rotarians. A man of a conventional mind and limited imagination. Or was he doing him an injustice? Was it possible that a chap like Morland could have hidden depths?

'You told me once you liked to keep your promises,' Melisande said.

Morland asked what it was she had wanted him to do.

'Oh, nothing, nothing. It doesn't matter a row of pins, darling. Not any longer. It was nothing important. It's just that you *promised*. Where *on earth* did you find that tie?'

'Don't you like it?'

'What does it matter whether I like it or not?' Melisande gave a light laugh. 'I must admit I get a funny feeling each time I am confronted by a Paisley pattern or what *looks* like a Paisley pattern. Don't you think it's a little too – vertiginous?'

'What do you mean?'

'Do be an angel and get Antonia a drink. Antonia's been very brave, very stoical. Antonia has been displaying extraordinary powers of patience and fortitude. I have an idea Antonia and Hugh are the cleverest people in this room. The kind of people who have more ideas in one morning than the rest of us have in a week. There are canapés – sandwiches – venison vol-au-vents – pheasant pâté – *amuse-gueules* – all sorts of naughty little things. Hugh, would you care for a nibble?'

So far Melisande hadn't so much as glanced at the couple Morland had brought with him – a matronly woman in her mid-forties and her black-clad teenage daughter. He felt compelled to introduce them a second time, in a louder voice. 'Stella and Moon. Friends from Bulgaria. They were at something of a loose end, so I took pity on them. Ha-ha. They didn't really want to come but I insisted. Ha-ha.'

Melisande went on smiling. 'You insisted? How extraordinary.'

11

Morland explained that Stella had been extremely helpful to him in Sofia. 'Stella knows Sofia like the back of her
hand.'

'How kind. How overwhelmingly touching. Poor James
hates being on his own, don't you, darling? I wish I were
as gregarious as James. Tillie, is it? And – Lenya, did you
say? Or is it Loon? I am sorry. I am terrible with names.
Positively pathological. You mustn't think I do it on purpose. I don't. Please make yourselves at home.'

Melisande managed some semblance of graciousness but
it was more than clear she could have done without the
Bulgarian matron and the Bulgarian matron's daughter.
Her eyes, Payne noticed, rested speculatively on the shawl
the Bulgarian matron was wearing. It was of a vaguely
Paisley pattern not dissimilar to that of Morland's tie. Was
the colour co-ordination a coincidence? It couldn't possibly
be a statement, could it? Had the Paisley tie been a present
from Stella, perhaps?

'I have very bad headaches,' Stella informed Antonia.
'The English weather makes my headaches worse. I am not
used to it. My friends warned me. Everybody said to me,
you will hate the English weather, Stella. You will be ill all
the time.'

Stella had mournful eyes, a prim mouth and vague hair
the colour of hay. In addition to the Paisley shawl, she wore
a frilly blouse, a long chocolate-coloured skirt and shiny
brown shoes with buckles. In shape she rather resembled
a plump partridge. Hers, Payne thought, was a ripe kind
of femininity. Did Morland fancy her? Was Stella more than
a mere friend?

'Look, Stella – all the cocktails have name tags!' Morland
waved his forefinger.

'Yes, James, this is very amusing.'

'Such an awfully clever idea! Ha-ha. What's that?
Modesty Blaise? Battle Royale? That's the kind of thing that
makes a party go with a bang, Payne, wouldn't you say?'

'Most decidedly,' Payne agreed.

'So today is Mrs Chevret's birthday,' said Stella. '*Mrs*
Chevret, yes? Not Miss?'

'It is Lady Chevret, actually – though I never use my title.'

'You were married to a Lord?'

'Something like that. Long time ago. I never talk about it.'

'There is a birthday cake, yes? With candles? A birthday cake is not a real birthday cake if there are no candles. The birthday cake comes at the end, yes?' Stella paused. 'I like cakes with lots and *lots* of candles. Isn't that what you say? *Lots*?'

Morland harrumphed a warning.

'May I have some crushed ice? I need more ice.' Melisande's smile remained frozen on her lips. 'Hugh, would you be an angel? The light in this room is awful. I feel a little disoriented. Thank God for Hugh! Hugh strikes me as the kind of man who would be indispensable in a crisis.'

'Would you like a Brief Encounter, Stella – or how about a Perpetual Passion?' Morland asked.

'I would like Perpetual Passion very much, thank you, James,' Stella said gravely.

Melisande declared she would have a Tomb Raider. 'Hugh, would you be an angel?'

Antonia congratulated Stella on the excellence of her English.

'I speak English very well,' Stella agreed.

Antonia asked her if she knew any other languages.

'French and Russian and German, a little Albanian and a little Hungarian. I have a degree in political economy and a degree in linguistics. I held a very important job, you see. Isn't that what you say? *Held*?'

Antonia said, 'Most English people are very poor linguists.'

'English people expect everybody to speak English. One of James' friends told me the other day – do you remember, James? It was very funny. Oh, it was so funny.' Stella covered her mouth. 'He said that my English was so much better than his Bulgarian, but, you see, *he did not speak any Bulgarian*. I didn't think that was a compliment at all. It was just something polite to say.'

'You have met James' friends?' Melisande said.

'Someone called Chambers or Gibbs. And someone called Rutherford? That is correct, isn't it, James? I liked Rutherford. Rutherford was very funny.'

'Rutherford is one of the most boring men who ever lived,' Melisande said. She glanced round. 'He divorced his wife and then married her again.'

'Stella used to work for King Simeon.' As James Morland handed Stella a cocktail, their hands brushed. 'The rightful heir to the throne of Bulgaria, you know. Can't get higher than that, can you? Ha-ha.'

Stella explained that until not so long ago King Simeon had been Bulgaria's Prime Minister.

'King Simeon is in *The Guinness Book of Records*. Under "youngest" and "first",' Stella's daughter said. 'When his father Boris died, he became the youngest European monarch. He was six. And then he became the first former monarch to get involved in politics.' The girl spoke with an American accent. She was chewing gum and gazing at Payne with the liveliest interest.

'Are you interested in politics?' Payne asked.

'Nope.'

The girl's name was Monika – spelled with a 'k', apparently – but her mother and Morland addressed her as Moon. Although it was a warm evening, she had refused to take off her long black coat, which, she informed them, was a *shinel* that had once belonged to an Albanian soldier whose head had been blown off by shrapnel. She insisted on showing them the bloodstains on the lapel. Payne found her good-looking in a rough, dangerous kind of way, but then most teenagers of either gender nowadays struck him as dangerous.

'Balkan politics have always been terribly complicated,' Payne said diplomatically.

'Each time I hear the word "politics", I want to curl up and die,' Melisande said. 'Or to go on drinking Tomb Raiders till some kind of conflagration takes place.'

'My country has a very tragic history,' Stella said after a sip of Perpetual Passion. 'No one understands Bulgaria – *no one*. It's a land soaked in sunshine and sorrow. We

14

believed the Russians understood us, our big brother, we called them, but we were wrong. We made a big mistake.'

'I hate Russians,' Moon said. 'And I simply hate Muslims.'

Winifred asked Stella if she and her daughter were in England on holiday.

'No, not on holiday,' Stella said.

'My mother is in England on a secret mission,' said Moon. 'My mother is a spy. She'd never admit it.'

'Are you really a spy?' Payne entered the spirit of the game.

'I am not a spy.' Stella gave an awkward laugh. 'My daughter is joking. Please, Moon, do not say such things!'

'I told you she'd never admit it.'

'My daughter is joking.'

'The Cold War is mercifully over,' Payne said.

'I am *not* joking,' Moon said. 'My mother is an under-cover agent.'

'I am the secretary of the Bulgarian Monarchist League. It was so difficult to get that job, but if I decide to get some-thing, I get it.'

Melisande raised her glass to her lips. 'Something or someone?' Payne heard her murmur.

'I am sorry, but I have a headache. I need to take a tablet. Please, excuse me.' Stella opened her handbag. 'Sometimes my headaches are so bad, I need to lie down.'

'My mother thinks she has a tumour on the brain,' Moon said.

'I am afraid of having a scan,' Stella told Antonia.

'I don't think scans are at all scary,' Antonia said brightly. (Why oh why was it so hard to keep the conversation neutral?)

'I don't suppose you are aware that we have a real writer in our midst?' Melisande waved her hand dramatically in Antonia's direction. 'I simply adore stories in which novice nuns succumb into lust, paranoia, despair and psychosis, as the convent environment at first rejects them and then violates them.'

15

Stella said, 'I write a little too. Articles on the future of the monarchy, and poetry . . . What kind of books do you write, Miss Darcy? Detective stories? Who is the killer, let's suspect everybody, there's arsenic in Aunt Wilhelmina's tea, yes? Very amusing, very English. But it is more difficult to be a poet than to write detective stories, I think.' She placed her hand at her bosom. 'Poems come from the heart.'

'Detective stories come from the mind,' Payne said.

'Poems come from the soul. It is very hard to explain to people who are not poets. Poets in Bulgaria are regarded very highly, especially in villages and in small towns, where poets read their poems aloud at parties. Poets expect no financial rewards.'

'Poets are losers,' Moon said.

'Poets are exceptional human beings. Poets represent the best of every nation,' said Stella.

Morland frowned. 'The child is father of the man – what's that supposed to mean? The boy stood on the burning deck. My love is like a—' His eyes rested on Stella. He raised his glass. 'The cocktails are top-notch, Meli. Well done.'

'Do you think it would be a good idea if Bulgaria became a monarchy again?' Payne asked Stella.

'Oh puh-*lease*, do not start my mother on the monarchy,' Moon groaned.

'It would be a very good idea. Yes. The monarch's role is moderation, something we lack in Bulgaria,' Stella said. 'The monarch is above parties and politics. The monarch's role is to calm people and lessen frictions and tensions and—'

'Advise, encourage and warn? I see you know your Bagehot.' Payne nodded. 'That's Bagehot, isn't it?'

But Stella didn't answer. She had covered her mouth and her nose with her right hand. She seemed distressed. It looked as though she was about to burst into tears. Payne was taken aback. It couldn't have had anything to do with his introducing Bagehot into the conversation, could it? He saw her rummage frantically in her bag, then mime imploringly in the direction of their hostesses. A handkerchief, she needed a handkerchief. A sound, like the blowing of a raspberry, was then heard and the mystery was resolved.

Stella had had a sneezing fit. They should pretend they hadn't noticed a thing, that's what good manners dictated. As Payne helped himself to a Rum Collins, he heard Moon laugh raucously.

Stella's thanks were profuse when a handkerchief was handed to her. She would wash it, she would iron it and send it back, she promised.

'Political parties cannot be trusted, but the monarch imparts a sense of permanency and continuity,' Stella was saying a couple of minutes later. 'The wisdom of a monarch is to be treasured. *Control your rage and do not give offence.* Do you know who said that?'

'Groucho Marx?' Melisande suggested. 'Lord Haw-Haw?'

'No, no—'

'Cicero? Liberace?'

'It was Louis XIV who said it. I like clever maxims,' Stella said. 'I have a notebook full of maxims—'

'And I have extremely fond memories of Maxim's.' Melisande raised her cocktail glass. 'Shall we drink to it? To Maxim's! I mean the one in Paris. The one and only.'

'This must be the very first time the Sun King of France has been quoted under this roof,' Winifred whispered to Antonia.

It was all perfectly absurd and rather droll, yet, for some reason, Antonia was filled with a curious apprehension.


Stella's preoccupations with poetry and the monarchy had converged in a poem she had written entitled 'The Return of the King'. She had composed it in a state of quiet exaltation, she said, but by the time she had finished writing it, she had been in floods of tears.

'Won't you recite it for us?' Payne urged.

'No, no.' Stella shook her head. She had written the poem in Bulgarian. A spur-of-the-moment English translation would destroy any beauty, significance or deeper meaning the poem might possess. Sometimes translations changed poems *beyond recognition*.

They were familiar of course with the famous experiment? When a poem was translated from Finnish into English into French into Russian into German into Mandarin Chinese into Swahili into Danish – and then back into Finnish? No? The author of the poem – a Finnish poet of some distinction – had been unable to recognize it! He had written a light-hearted allegory about a lonely clown at a circus who falls in love with one of the two performing bears, *not* about a divorced woman contemplating suicide in a Tunbridge Wells antique shop.

In the silence that followed, Moon asked if there was any Red Bull.

'What is "red bull"?' Morland asked amiably.

'I am not talking to you,' Moon said. 'You didn't let me take a puff at your cigar, so I am not talking to you.'

'Would you care for a glass of *Coke*?' Winifred might have been referring to some outlandish concoction.

The front door bell rang again and Melisande flounced out of the room.

'Why can't I have vodka?' Moon was heard asking her mother.

'Because it contains alcohol.'

'What a dumb thing to say. Vodka *is* alcohol.' Moon sighed. She turned to Payne. 'If you ever want a quick buzz, pour some neat vodka over your eyes. It's called "drinking through the eyes".'

'I'll bear it in mind,' he said with a curt nod.

'Ladies and gentlemen, this is Arthur, my agent!' Melisande had reappeared with a small grey-haired man, dressed in a bookmaker's checked, three-piece suit, who raised her hand to his lips and declared he had been hopelessly in love with her for most of his life.

'Why hopelessly?' Moon asked.

'How are you, Win?' Arthur waved his hands in the air. 'Have you read any good books lately?'

'I'm afraid I haven't.'

'Why *do* people bother to write books? Has it ever occurred to you to wonder?'

'Frequently,' Winifred said with a rueful smile.

'Arturo, darlink, do help yourself to a *lee*tle drinkie,' Melisande said in a Ruritanian accent.

'Shame you never did *Zsa-Zsa*! I can't remember the exact reason, what *was* it? You were born to play Zsa-Zsa! What happened?'

'Oh, I don't know. It's all lost now in the mists of time. I believe you persuaded me not to, you faithless man.'

'No! I always said you were born to play Zsa-Zsa!'

'I dain't knair,' Moon said in Melisande's voice. She had sidled up to Payne. 'You faithliss min.'

'It's very rude to mimic,' he pointed out.

'Arturo looks very camp. Don't you think he looks camp? He sounds very camp. I don't like camp men.'

'There are some things you can think but not say,' Payne said didactically. Moon laughed.

The front door bell rang again.

# Wild Thing

'The Return . . . of the King!' Melisande delivered in mock-heroic tones. She mimed the placing of a crown on her head, assumed a solemn expression, then made a neighing sound and pretended to ride a horse. Her mood seemed to have improved considerably. Well, Antonia reflected, she was starting on her third Tomb Raider.

'Shades of Tolkien . . . Does King Simeon ride? I suppose all kings ride. At one time it was considered a sine qua non in regal circles.' Payne was getting bored. Perhaps they could bowl off soon? He stole a glance at his watch, then tried to catch Antonia's eye.

'Bravo!' Arthur clapped his hands. 'Bravo! How about an encore?'

They had been joined by a morose-faced man – Stanley Lennox, the playwright and author of *Tallulah*. He was accompanied by an anonymous blonde in tinted glasses.

'Is there any water? I can't drink anything but water,' the blonde in the tinted glasses said.

'I have a big surprise for Melisande tonight,' Arthur whispered in Antonia's ear.

'You've got her a part?'

'Yes! Coward. Don't breathe a word. Not yet. She'll be delighted. She's been resting for – um – quite a bit. You aren't an actress too, by any chance?'

'I am not.'

'Are you sure? You possess a certain indefinable *something*.'

Antonia smiled. 'You don't really mean that, do you?'

'I do mean it.' He lowered his voice. 'I don't say these things lightly.'

'But the King is already in Bulgaria!' Stella was heard crying triumphantly. 'He was our Prime Minister, now he leads his own party.'

'What's the party called?' Payne asked.

'The King's Party.'

'How intoxicatingly witty,' Melisande said. 'How inordinately original. We *must* drink to the King's Party.'

'I believe the King styles himself Mr Saxe-something-or-other, doesn't he?' Morland said. He was smoking a cigar. 'Quite a mouthful.'

'Saxcoburggotski,' Stella said. 'His advisers persuaded him to take on a name that was the closest to a Bulgarian name. His family name is Saxe-Coburg-Gotha.'

'*Sex*coburggotski,' Moon said, casting a meaningful glance at her mother, then at Morland.

'Pleasant sort of chap,' Morland said. 'Or so everybody says. Unassuming, though of course he never lets anyone forget who he is. Not particularly effectual, perhaps. Too much of a gentleman. Bulgarians don't seem to understand him.'

'They used to execute kings.' Moon squashed her empty Coke can, producing a crack that might have been a gunshot. 'My mother used to believe all kings and queens were parasites. My mother was brainwashed by the Communists. She became a "pioneer" and kissed the red flag and then she became a Communist. *And* she married a Communist. My father was a Communist.'

'We didn't have much choice, Moon!' Stella protested.

'Now my mother is a Monarchist. My mother is a turncoat. Turncoats should be executed.'

'Those were *such* difficult years. My parents struggled, how they struggled. If you wanted to have a successful career, a happy home life or travel abroad, you had to be a

21

Communist. We had no choice! We had to do what we were told. We had to spy on our neighbours.'

'So *that's* where you learnt how to spy.' Moon nodded. 'My mother spies on me all the time.'

Moon's American accent was explained by the fact that she had been attending high school in America, in the state of Pennsylvania. She had had to give it up because her mother's funds had run out. 'Stolen money goes fast totally, I guess,' she said. She then turned to Payne and tried to get him interested in something called Hammers of Hell.

'What's that? Not a story by Chesterton? Some sort of an electronic game?'

'Yep. The coolest game there ever was.' It had been her American boyfriend who introduced her to it. Elimination by numbers as well as ingenious ways of killing your enemy seemed to be at the heart of the game and one had to be 'like totally ruthless' to achieve one's goal. 'I like beheadings best. I guess I am a bloodthirsty kind of person.'

Arthur said, 'I read somewhere that the brain of a severed head continues functioning long enough for the executed person to see the body from which his head has been detached. Then the person dies of shock. It is a scientifically proven fact, or so it was claimed.'

Her father, Moon informed the company, was in jail in Bulgaria. For bribery, corruption, falsifying documents, money-laundering and general abuse of power. Only dumb people managed to get themselves sent to jail, she said firmly. 'If I were to commit a crime, they would never catch me.'

'I like your coat,' Arthur said. 'It could do with a wash, or is that how you like it?'

'This is *not* a coat. It's a *shinel*. I bought it on eBay for fifty dollars. This is real blood. I am not kidding. I don't want it washed.'

'I am told Liza Minnelli sold her Oscar on eBay.' Arthur lowered his voice. 'It seems she's completely bonkers now.'

'Do you really write murder mysteries? That's so cool.' Moon addressed herself to Antonia. 'Like Mrs Fletcher in *Murder, She Wrote*?'

Antonia admitted she hadn't seen a single episode of *Murder, She Wrote*.

'Is there a lot of blood in your books?'

'No, not much.' Antonia gave an apologetic smile. What an alarming girl, she thought.

'Blood is kinda interesting. Pure red liquid. Gallons and gallons of it. Our bodies are full of it. If you cut someone's throat, blood will gush out like a fountain. It will be so powerful, you will have to jump away.'

'Do you enjoy reading?' Antonia asked politely.

'I read all the time. When I was a kid, I used to be mad about the Marvel comics. I used to imagine I was Rina Logan, the daughter of Wolverine and Elektra. You know Rina Logan?'

Antonia said she didn't. It occurred to her that most of her responses to Moon's queries had been negative.

'Rina Logan is an extremely dangerous character, kinda loopy, so many heroes avoid her. I used to believe I possessed a set of "psi-claws", like Rina Logan. Psi-claws do damage on a mental rather than on a physical level,' Moon explained.

'I thought cyclones did damage on the physical level,' Morland said as he helped himself to another cocktail and a handful of peanuts.

'Psi-*claws*, not cyclones, James. *Psi-claws*. Have you never heard of psi-claws?'

'What books do they do at American schools?' Payne asked. 'Nathaniel Hawthorne? Mark Twain? Arthur Miller? Have you read *The Crucible*?'

'Yep. It's about witches, isn't it?' Moon cast a meaningful glance in the direction of Winifred and at Melisande. 'We read a story called "The New Mother". At first I thought it would be dumb, kids' stuff, but it was so cool. It's about two innocent children who are encouraged in their naughty behaviour by this strange and charming young woman who may or may not be an evil spirit. The children's mother threatens to leave them and send home a new mother – a mother *with glass eyes and a wooden tail*.'

Payne was intrigued. 'And what happens?'

'Not telling you! It's by a woman called Lucy Lane Clifford. Get it and check it out, then you'll see how it ends. It's really weird stuff. Oh, do you know what they call Rina Logan?'

'What do they call Rina Logan?'

'*Wild Thing.*' Moon made a snarling sound, which she accompanied by a clawing gesture in Payne's direction.

Stella and her daughter had arrived in England some ten days earlier. The reason for the visit, Stella explained, was her collaboration with an English biographer, Tancred Vane. Tancred Vane was engaged on writing a 'life' of Prince Cyril, King Boris' dissolute younger brother, who, after a misspent life, had been executed by the Communists in 1945.

Stella had answered an advertisement placed by Tancred Vane in the *International Herald Tribune*. Payne thought the biographer's name rang a bell. It was a distinctive enough name. Obscure royalty seemed to be Vane's speciality. Stella's grandmother, it transpired, had operated the switchboard at the royal palace in Sofia during the war. An insatiable eavesdropper, she had become privy to a great number of secrets, which she had revealed in diaries and letters, some of which had survived and were now in Stella's possession.

Moon said, 'Tancred Vane wanted to give her fifty pounds for the letters and the diaries, but my mother wouldn't sell them for less than five thousand.'

Stella's face turned red and she said something in Bulgarian, which made Moon laugh.

'I guess Tancred Vane is a crook. He's the sort of guy who wants something for nothing. He looks kinda weird. Show them the photos!' Moon tugged at her mother's sleeve. 'Come on, show them the photos. Let them see what a weird guy he is and what a weird house he lives in.'

'I am in the grip of an intolerable restlessness. I believe I am unhappy.' Melisande leant towards Payne. 'Wouldn't

24

it be wonderful if something marvellously unexpected happened?'

'Mr Vane is a very nice man. Very educated, very cultured.' She had already paid Tancred Vane two visits, Stella said as she produced her mobile phone and squinted down at it. 'I like to take photographs of interesting buildings and interesting people. My friends in Bulgaria will be very interested.'

'What friends?' Moon said. 'You have no friends.'

'This is Mr Vane's house. It is called the Villa Byzantine. It is very interesting, isn't it?' Stella held up her mobile. 'Very unusual. It is baroque, I think.'

'Golly,' Payne said. 'No, not baroque. Where's this monstrosity?'

'In St John's Wood.'

'Really? I've got an aunt who lives in St John's Wood.'

'The house looks like a lunatic asylum,' Moon said. 'I bet this guy Tancred is a homicidal maniac. Or a necrophiliac. Be careful he doesn't steal your grandmother's diaries,' she warned her mother.

'And this,' Stella said, 'is Mr Vane.'

Melisande laughed. 'Such an *earnest* look. Rather sweet, actually. What a pet. I bet he speaks hesitantly without finishing his sentences? Reminds me of someone I used to know—'

'Mr Vane is a *young* man,' Stella said with an odd emphasis.

Payne caught a look of unadulterated hatred on Melisande's face.

Winifred's expression on the other hand was hard to interpret. She looked as though she had had some kind of revelation. 'Are these church bells?' Her voice shook a little. 'Can you hear them?'

The next time Major Payne heard the Villa Byzantine mentioned was precisely six weeks later – on the day of the first murder.

# 4

# Fire Walk with Me

This is what happens in bad dreams. Somebody you think you know becomes a stranger. No – a stranger turns out to be someone you know.

As I think back to my terrifying encounter at the Villa Byzantine, I start shivering.

Why does Fate insist on buffeting me? Is there any particular reason why I, Stella Markoff, should be made to pass through so many strange fires? Don't I deserve to be happy? If there is a cosmic design behind it all, I fail to see it. Have I not suffered enough?

I haven't told James about the incident at the Villa Byzantine. Why worry him? He will probably say I imagined it. He is very nice to me, very considerate, very gentlemanly, though sometimes I wish he weren't so gentlemanly. I wish he were more demonstrative when we are alone together. I wouldn't mind.

I am extremely susceptible to bad vibes. Something happened that day at the Villa Byzantine when she – the old owl-faced woman she pretended to be – looked at me through those glasses – a terrible pain cut *right* across me – I haven't been myself since – have I been given the evil eye?

She looked like Baba Yaga. When I was a little girl I feared being spirited away and devoured by Baba Yaga more than anything in the world.

I knew who she was at once, the moment our eyes met. Did she imagine I wouldn't recognize her?

I am sitting in James' car, James' old Harris tweed jacket lies on the seat beside me, everything seems familiar and reassuring, but this is no ordinary journey, oh no.

Once more I am on my way to the Villa Byzantine, but it is not to see Mr Vane. Mr Vane will not be there. But for Mr Vane's Chinamen and other precious objects, the Villa Byzantine will be empty.

As I remind myself that I am about to commit a crime, I clutch at my knees to prevent my hands from shaking.

A crime, yes. I can't quite believe it. I, Stella Markoff, am about to commit a crime.


I glance at my watch. Each tick of the second hand aches like the pulse of blood behind a bruise. I can hardly breathe. How dark the sky is. There is going to be a storm.

Never for a moment does the Great Fear leave my side. Darkness at noon. That is a bad omen. I am extremely nervous. I have a headache. No, I can't change my mind. It is too late to go back.

But what if Mr Vane has decided to stay at home? Well, I would tell him that I had made a mistake, that I'd come on the wrong day. I intend to ring the front door bell three times, four times – no, till my finger starts hurting! Only then shall I start unlocking the front door.

My headache is rooted behind my eyeballs and seems to cast a spell on every nerve of eye and ear. Perhaps something *is* there, some terrible growth, some entity, delighting in torturing me, feeding off me, sucking in my vital energies, causing me to make wrong decisions, unsettling my sanity? I don't want to go for a scan. I dread what they might discover.

But what if Mr Vane suddenly comes back and catches me red-handed? Mr Vane may call the police, then I'll be put in handcuffs and all the English newspapers will write about me. *Villainy at the Villa*. English people like to make jokes like that. English people are very childish. I will be ruined, destroyed. I won't be able to survive the shame.

It is now as dark as the darkest night. This is all wrong. I feel ill. My head throbs. Each breath becomes pain. A meteorite pounds into my heart. There is a clap of thunder, then another.

I am doing all this for my daughter. This is a mother's sacrifice.

I want my daughter to love me.


The car moves along the drive, slowly, *slowly*, under the tunnel of trees. As we come out of the tunnel, I see curtains of rain, deep purple, almost black, pierced by gold shafts of sunlight.

I have no idea why I pick up James' jacket and bury my face in it. I am silly and sentimental. I feel insecure. All my life I have craved reassurance. I shut my eyes and I breathe in the now familiar smell of James – expensive cigars, Polo aftershave, the special mints he claims he can get *only* at Harrods – James calls it the 'Good Life'—

What is this? Something in the pocket. I open my eyes. Papers – letters? Yes, a bundle of letters.

I hold the letters in my hand. No envelopes. The same handwriting on all of them. I tell myself I mustn't read the letters, James may not like it, but then I recognize the handwriting . . .

Suddenly I feel hot. I start shivering.

I gasp—

The car is stopping. We have arrived. We are outside the Villa Byzantine. My eyes are blurred with tears, but I can't tear them away from the letters. I feel as though I have run till my lungs have burst.

No, this can't be true – it is absurd – monstrous – a cruel joke!

I look up and see my reflection in the car mirror. My face is pale and disfigured by shock. It does not look pretty. It does not look like my face at all.

I scream – but no sound comes out of my throat.

# 5

# The Worst Crime in the World

It was seven o'clock on a mild evening in mid-September. There had been a storm in the morning but all was quiet now. The air felt fresh.

'So they think she bumped off her mama—'

Major Payne broke off. Mustn't be flippant, he reminded himself. The trouble was he tended to view life, even when at its most appallingly tragic, as comedy. Made him appear inconsiderate, insensitive and damned superficial – which he was not. Antonia thought it was a defensive reaction of sorts.

He pressed another scotch on James Morland.

'Thank you, Payne. I didn't mean to drink, but this is a terrible business. Yes, that's what the police think. I'm afraid they regard Moon as their number one suspect. Complete nonsense of course. Um. It helps me, being able to talk about it. Most decent of you to listen to me.'

'Don't mention it, my dear fellow.'

'I hardly know you, Payne, but I felt you'd be the right person to come to.'

Major Payne found himself wondering why he hadn't called Morland 'old boy' but 'my dear fellow'. He tended to employ the latter address with men he didn't quite take to. Morland had a haunted air about him and, unless it was Payne's imagination, a somewhat guilty look. Morland gave the distinct impression he was holding something back . . .

'She has been "helping them with their inquiries" – that was how they put it – that's how they always put it, don't they?'

'How old is she? Fifteen? Sixteen?'

Payne remained standing by the 1930s cocktail cabinet, which had been a present from his aunt. Lady Grylls had at long last managed to sell her country estate and move to a house in St John's Wood, which had always been her dream. Chalfont Park was now a conference venue, managed by some super-rich industrialists who, Lady Grylls insisted, were in fact members of the 'Russian mafia'.

'Sixteen and a half, nearly seventeen.'

'Did you say you bailed her out?'

'Yes. Money's not a problem. I know she's a difficult girl, but I feel responsible for her, Payne . . . In a *loco parentis* kind of way . . . Stella and I were about to get married . . . I'd have been Moon's stepfather.' Morland spoke haltingly. 'Melisande has no idea I'm here . . . I don't want her to know . . . She took it rather badly, you know – our breakup . . . My fault . . . Couldn't be helped . . . One of those things.'

'Yes, quite.'

'Look here, Payne, I'd be grateful if you didn't mention to Melisande that I'd been here. I mean, if you bumped into her or something.'

'My lips are sealed.'

'I'm sure they – the police – will realize they're on the wrong track soon enough and start looking for the real killer . . . Though when *is* soon enough?'

Payne gave another sympathetic nod. Morland seemed to have got himself into a pretty mess. It was the kind of complicated emotional drama one wouldn't have associated with him. By no stretch of the imagination could Morland be said to represent high romance, but there it was, no accounting for taste. When they had first met him, Morland – middle-aged, widowed, with grown-up children – had been about to marry Melisande Chevret.

30

Melisande had introduced him to the gathering as her fiancé. Morland had then become secretly engaged to the Bulgarian matron, Stella Markoff, with whom he appeared to have been having an affair for some time. And now Stella Markoff was dead – mysteriously murdered!

Morland sat slumped in his armchair, looking dejected. 'I wonder what Moon's doing now. She didn't like it when Julia told her she had no Sky. That's my sister,' he explained.

'You left her with your sister?'

'Yes. In my sister's flat in Kensington. She wanted to come with me here, actually. Moon likes you. She said you were "cool". She said you say funny things. She likes that. She wants to know about the murders you and your wife have investigated.'

'Isn't she upset?'

'Of course she's upset. Terribly upset. Distraught. She's not as tough as she appears. It's suddenly hit her she'll never see her mother again. She's frightened. She knows it's serious. She's no fool. My solicitor's doing his best, though he advises caution . . . I don't think he took to Moon . . . Not many people do . . . Stella . . . My God, I can't believe Stella is gone!'

'When was the last time you saw Stella?'

'This morning. We made plans for tonight. I had tickets for Covent Garden. Stella loves opera – loved . . . She was delighted, awfully excited, really looking forward to it . . . I've still got them somewhere . . . I mean the tickets.' Morland took out a fistful of papers from an inside pocket, but his hand shook and some of them scattered on the floor. Puffing, he picked them up. 'Here they are.' He waved the tickets in the air.

'What were you going to see?'

(Why did Morland think it necessary to show him the tickets?)

'*Battered Bride*. No, Moon wasn't coming with us. There were going to be only the two of us. Covent Garden, yes. I mean *Bartered Bride* – sorry.' Morland gave an awkward laugh. 'Moon hates opera.'

'Did she hate her mother too?'

'I wouldn't say "hate", that's too strong a word, but they didn't get on too well. Moon is keen on doing her own thing. She's wilful, headstrong . . . She wants to go back to America. I don't know what to do, Payne . . . I really don't . . .'

Battered bride, eh? A Freudian slip? Had Stella been battered to death then? The manner of her demise was yet to be revealed to Payne.

'Stella used to say all of Moon's problems sprang from the fact that she'd never had a proper father figure in her life. I've been wondering whether I could adopt Moon. Not a terribly good idea, perhaps? Not sure it would work. It might prove to be a disaster.' Morland spoke distractedly. 'Moon doesn't really like me, but she knows no one in England. She doesn't want to go back to Bulgaria. She refuses to give me the names of any of her relatives in Bulgaria. Says they are all peasants.'

Would a man planning a brutal battering buy expensive opera tickets? When he knew perfectly well they would be wasted? Well, yes – the tickets constituted an alibi of sorts. Money was not a problem for Morland.

'Is her father really in jail?' Payne asked.

'I believe so. Yes. He was one of those Communist apparatchiks. That's all I know. Poor Stella didn't like talking about it. It embarrassed her. She managed to get a divorce. She'd had a terrible life. Terrible. And now – now she is dead!'

'Did the police question you?'

'They did. All sorts of idiotic questions. Made me feel like a criminal! You used to work in the police, didn't you?'

'Not the police. Intelligence. That was some time ago now.'

'Melisande said you and your wife were experts in murder.'

'I don't know where people get such ideas.'

'Melisande said you told her you always carried the Police Code and Procedure with you and you tried to memorize seven pages a day. Oh. Is that a joke? The story's bound to be in tomorrow's papers. People are such ghouls. The way poor Stella died is sure to attract attention—' Morland broke off. 'Where did you say your wife was?'

'America. Signing tour. It ends the day after tomorrow . . . How did Stella die? Where did it happen?'

Morland's hand went up to his forehead. It looked as though he was checking whether he had a temperature. He then loosened his tie. 'She was found at the Villa Byzantine. Tancred Vane's house. The royal biographer fellow. It was Tancred Vane who discovered her body. It was in the drawing room. If the police had any sense at all, they'd see at once why Moon couldn't have done it. You see, Payne, Moon broke her wrist only a couple of months ago. She can hardly use her right hand. It – it would have been too heavy for her—'

'What would have been too heavy?'

'The—' Morland broke off. 'Stella was – she had been—' Payne leant forward eagerly. 'Yes?'

'No, it's too horrible.' Morland made a breath-catching sound like a sob. 'I can't say it. No, I can't.'

The next moment he did. He blurted it out. There was a pause.

'Golly.' Payne stared back at him.

# 6

# Blithe Spirit

'This is the best thing that's happened to me in a long while, you are absolutely right, so I should be happy. Only I am not.' Melisande Chevret raised the champagne glass to her lips. 'Oh, don't look like that, Win. You do think I am being unreasonable and spoilt, don't you?'

'As a matter of fact I do. You have been "resting" for quite a while. I'd have thought you'd leap for joy at any opportunity to act again.'

'Leap for joy. You do say horrid things. You make me sound like one of those desperate ageing actresses for whom anything is better than nothing. Listening to you, one might be excused for imagining my career has entered the tundra-like wasteland stage. My bone structure is *not* yet obscured by pouches and jowls.'

'I never said it was ... I wouldn't call Madame Arcati "anything".'

'It's a wonderful character part, I do agree – Coward at his most comically inspired and so on – but I simply can't make the transition that easily.'

'What transition?'

'I was Elvira *not such a long time ago*. Unpredictable, wilful, capricious, irresistibly attractive Elvira. Bursting with erotic energy – dangerous – destructive! I *enjoy* being destructive,' Melisande added in a reflective voice. 'Can

34

you see Elvira transmogrifying into Arcati? I mean –
*can* you?'

'I can. Why not? Isn't that what being an actress is all
about?'

'I would have thought such clichés were beneath you,
darling.'

Pale sea-water eyes – seductively asymmetrical – a carefully made-up, predatory kind of face – a flat sheep's nose
– black velvet dress, cut low at the neck – long sleeves – a
single row of black pearls – aiming at an intriguing *triste*
effect. At one time, Winifred reflected, men had been mad
about her sister.

'D'you remember my Joan of Arc?' Melisande asked.

Winifred said she did, vividly. 'You were twenty-one.
You were terribly good. Was that Anouilh?'

'One critic wrote he had feared for the safety of my
fellow actors! His exact words were that he'd been surprised heads hadn't rolled on the stage!' Melisande gave a
reminiscent laugh. 'Ah, that sword! It was a *real* sword of
course.'

'You declared you couldn't get into the part if you were
to hold a papier-mâché one.'

'I took fencing lessons. Did some special exercises to
strengthen my wrists. They provided me with my own
personal trainer. Such a charming boy – so agile. Ah, how
they indulged me! D'you remember the party they gave
after the play? A thousand white cymbidium orchids flown
in from New Zealand and suspended from willow
branches on sterling silver thread! Then – then I appeared
in that modernist medieval morality play, which I couldn't
understand at all, but the critics unanimously agreed I was
brilliant in.'

'Oh dear, yes. What a curious amalgam of antique meta-
physics, harsh Calvinism and contemporary absurdism
that play was . . . What was it called? They invariably sink
without trace, plays like that . . .'

'But don't you see? If I did accept Arcati, there would be
no going back – I'd have reached the point of no return –
don't you see?'

'See what exactly?'

'The die, darling. The die would be cast.' Melisande shut her eyes. '*I'd be entering the dreadful dimension of typecasting.* No-nonsense nannies – Valium divas. Character parts, darling! Dipso dolly divorcees on the verge of a nervous breakdown.'

'The dipsomaniac divorcee is a particularly Anglo-Saxon phenomenon,' Winifred said thoughtfully. 'In French films, I have noticed, women excel in a kind of existential hysteria without need for a whiff of alcohol—'

'All right, there are some good dramatic parts, perhaps, for, to employ your pet phrase, *women of a certain age*. I wouldn't mind playing Mrs Stone in her Roman spring . . . Blanche Dubois – don't tell me I am too old to play Blanche! No, not Bernarda Alba – I have pledged never to play matriarchs . . . I wouldn't mind Florence Lancaster either, or Livia in *Women Beware Women*.'

'How about morose Mrs Alving?'

'I am not sure . . . I have a soft spot for Ibsen, true . . . But it would mean patting the cheek of some sallow, sweaty, syphilitic Oswald night after night after night . . . A most definite no to Miss Havisham and Aunt Betsey Trotwood, or to any other Dickens woman, for that matter. Most Dickens women are *such* bores.'

'Lady Dedlock and Rosa Dartle are not bores.'

'I haven't really done much comedy, have I?'

'You did Miss Prism last year.'

'Miss Prism was an exception. I did it as a special favour to Neville. I wouldn't have done it for anyone else.' Melisande lowered her eyes. 'I believe I was a little in love with Neville. I wore pince-nez! How ridiculous people in pince-nez always look!'

'You made Miss Prism recite a limerick, which is not in Wilde. "The Young Lady of Clare".'

'That wasn't too awful, was it?'

'No, not at all. It struck the right note. It was hilarious. You brought the house down. Your comic timing was perfect.'

They were sitting at a corner table at the Savoy Grill. The service, as could have been expected, was impeccable, the food delicious, if a little too rich for Winifred's taste. She regretted having plumped for roast Anjou pigeon with sautéed Jerusalem artichoke and *pommes Anna* after the pan-fried *foie gras*. She should have had the veal cutlet with root vegetables. Melisande had insisted that they have dinner together. Melisande had hinted she might have important news to impart . . .

'Actually, Win, I would love to play *you* one day.'

'Me?'

'Yes. One of those ladylike, rather repressed Rattigan-esque Englishwomen, passionless in a cloche hat.' Melisande sketched an amorphous shape above her head. 'The kind of woman who haunts the Riviera in the low season, having taken advantage of reduced rates, not minding the discomforts of her small *pension,* her excessively composed manner hinting at latent hysteria. One sees her reading a novel after dinner, or merely immersed in maiden meditation – having ordered a small pot of black coffee in perfect French.'

'Is that how you see me? How very amusing.'

'No, *not* passionless. Seething with suppressed emotions behind her fastidious and aloof exterior – disguising her true feelings from everyone, even from herself. I'd insist on a scene where she takes off her hat and brooch and disrobes herself to reveal some really *outré* underwear.'

'Why *outré*?'

'That would convey the idea that she has a startling fantasy life,' Melisande explained. 'Do you remember how Papa Willard used to say that you would make a good actress? He refused to even *consider* the possibility of *me* becoming one.'

'On that count Papa Willard was wrong.'

'As it happens, Papa Willard was wrong on most counts.'

They had always called their late father Papa Willard.

Melisande peered at her. 'You look a bit wan, Win. Grey and withered. What's the matter? Or is it the light?'

'Must be the light. I am fine, really. A little tired, perhaps.'

'What have you been doing to tire yourself? I know you've been up to something.' Melisande spoke in teasing tones. 'I never know what you do or what you think. You look as prim as a prawn, but I am far from convinced that's the real you. I haven't the faintest idea what goes on in your head. No one would think we shared a house!'

'It's a large house,' Winifred said lightly. 'We have our separate quarters.'

'I have been feeling *trop troublante*,' Melisande said after a pause. 'The truth is that I have been occupying an emotional cul-de-sac. I have been conforming to a pattern of existence only the most desperate human being would have chosen for themselves. You see, I haven't recovered yet. The perfidy of my *cavalier servante* still haunts me.'

Winifred's face remained blank. When it came to putting on a display of histrionics, her sister had no equal. 'You mean James, don't you?'

Melisande covered her eyes with her hand, as though to protect them from the glare of a merciless sun. 'I still can't believe he left me for that woman. Isn't it incredible that I should have been deposed by a bulky-bottomed Balkanite? Isn't it grotesque? Well, perhaps now he'll reconsider. Perhaps now he'll come to his senses.'

'What do you mean – *now*?'

'I know that I hated James and I wished him dead and I wanted to cut his Savile Row suits and ties into strips and raid his cellar and smash all his bottles of vintage port and pour paint all over his Porsche – but that was because I loved him so much.'

'You said that James' conduct, by any standards of civilized behaviour, was despicable.'

'I am sure you think me inconsistent and irrational, but I am quite prepared to give him another chance. I believe it is not too late for me and him to find mutual flowering in each other.'

'You swore you'd never give him another chance.'

'It is a woman's prerogative to change her mind. There will be some conditions of course. He will have to apologize. He will have to show genuine remorse. He will have to give me his word of honour that nothing like that would *ever* happen again.'

'You said you didn't want to see him for as long as you and he occupied this world. You said he deserved to be buried alive.'

'Oh dear. Such colourful denunciations! Such pyrotechnics of verbal dexterity! I believe I was in a Medea mood. I remember alternating between rage and despair. When one is upset, darling, one says all sorts of things one doesn't really mean. Try not to look so disapproving. The poor waiters will think there's something wrong with your Anjou pigeon. They are so horribly sensitive here.'

'It would be a mistake to have James back.'

'You talk like this, because you were always a little in love with James yourself – you think I don't know? No, it isn't nonsense. Whether we like it or not, Win, we are both at an age when our cells and tissues start to impart unwelcome information, when the tick-tock of our body clocks becomes as loud and insistent as a church bell—'

'I don't think it would work. I really don't.'

'I wish I had your uncompromising spirit. Unfortunately, I haven't.' Melisande dropped her starched napkin on the table. 'Furthermore, I am not ashamed to admit my weakness. James and I had something very special. Still have – these things don't change overnight.'

'But he is engaged to be married – I thought that was as good as settled. You said he told you they'd be leaving for Bulgaria early next month. They've bought the plane tickets, rings and practically everything, haven't they? Stella's moved in with him. Stella wants to be married in an Orthodox monastery, so they even contacted a priest—'

'Oh, how I wish I didn't tell you everything!' Melisande cried. 'Why am I such a fool? You even use the priest against me!'

'Don't be absurd.'

'You've never wanted me to be happy. Never! Not even when we were children. Remember Blue-Eyes and the Turkey? Remember Miss Rossiter and the Glass-Eaters?'

'I remember Miss Rossiter and the Glass-Eaters. I don't think *that* was my fault.'

Melisande took a deep breath. 'As a matter of fact, darling, there has been a development. The status quo has changed. You are, as they say, a bit behind with your facts.'

'What facts?'

'By the most incredible quirk of fate, James' fetters have been removed and he is now what is known as a "free man". He is in a state of shock, of course, though that will pass soon enough.'

'Why is James in a state of shock?'

'There is something you don't know. Stella is dead.'

'*What?*'

'She died today. It was a ghastly kind of death, apparently. I mean – ghastly. A veritable Grand Guignol. But do let's try to be positive and rational about it.' Melisande tugged at her pearl choker. 'Don't you see? *This seems to me a blessing of an extremely obvious kind.* These are Miss Prism's words, *not* mine. I am going to have a crème de menthe now. Sorry. I suppose you will say I am flippant and heartless?'

'How did you know Stella was dead?' Winifred asked quietly. 'How did she die?'

# 7

# Lethal Weapon

'She was – *beheaded*?'

Major Payne felt his skin crawl – a vibration – a pale terror like the mist on an old-fashioned photographic plate.

'Yes. I still can't believe it. It's incredible. It's an abomination. An outrage. It makes no sense.' Morland shook his head. 'What kind of person would want to do a thing like that?'

'What indeed . . . Let me get you another drink . . . You poor chap . . . Would you like something to eat? Sorry, I should have suggested it sooner. I'm not much good without Antonia, I'm afraid, but I could rustle up something – an omelette, perhaps?'

'No. Nothing to eat. Thanks awfully, Payne, but I couldn't touch a thing. I'd be sick if I did.'

'Do go on, if you don't mind . . . She was lying on the drawing-room floor at the Villa Byzantine? It was Tancred Vane who found her?'

'Correct. She'd been to the Villa Byzantine twice before, you see. I know she rather liked it, but it's a damned peculiar place—'

*Villa Byzantine.* Without the definite article, Major Payne reflected, it could be the name of a nightclub singer, a racehorse or a secret wartime operation. It was the kind of name that conjured up the intrigue and mystery of oriental adventures.

'I thought it looked like a miniature Albert Hall,' he said, remembering the photo on Stella's mobile phone. 'Is the interior awfully sumptuous?'

'A Carrollian staircase. Lots of curios and draperies and antiques on every possible surface. Curved daggers and glass cases full of giant butterflies on the walls. Silver and crystal. A harmonium, if you please . . . Stella – her body – was in the drawing room – on the floor – between the french windows and the fireplace. Her head—'

'Yes?' Shouldn't be ghoulish, Payne chided himself.

'Her head was on the floor – near the window – it had almost rolled *out* of the window.'

'The french windows were open?'

'Yes . . . Such a bloodbath – it must have pumped out with great force from the neck. The rug in front of the fireplace was soaked with blood. There was some on the curtains too, I think, unless that was the pattern—' Morland broke off. 'Oh God – it was terrible – terrible!'

Payne wondered what he knew about beheadings. The Queen of Hearts in *Alice* – Salome kissing the head of John the Baptist – Islamic terrorists – Charles I – the Lord High Executioner in *The Mikado* – Polanski's *Macbeth* – Marie Antoinette. Wasn't there a detective novel by Ngaio Marsh called *Off With His Head*? About a beheading during some kind of rural dance? He seemed to remember a mildly comic German folklorist character called Mrs Bunz. Actually, Ngaio Marsh's victims often came to gruesome ends . . .

Major Payne hated violent crime stories. Antonia's never were. He had never been able to understand the great following bloodthirsty authors enjoyed. Patricia Cornwell – Mo Hayder – Val McDermid – all women, as it happened – but, he believed, it was the creepy Thomas Harris and his cannibal chronicles that had started the trend . . .

'No signs of struggle, the inspector said. Nothing broken. None of Tancred Vane's *objets* seemed to be missing either,' Morland was saying. 'They asked him to check.'

Royal biographers, Payne reflected, tended to be a rum lot. And hadn't Tancred Vane wanted to buy Stella's precious letters and diaries for fifty pounds? Moon had referred to Tancred Vane as 'weird' and a 'crook' . . .

The obvious suspect of course was Moon. Moon had said that she liked beheadings. Moon had displayed an unhealthy obsession with blood. Moon had also boasted that if she were to commit a crime, she would never be caught . . .

'What was the murder weapon exactly?' Payne asked. 'Sword of some kind?'

'A samurai sword. Twelfth-century, I think. It was lying on the floor by the body. It had been hanging on the wall beside the fireplace. One of Vane's most treasured possessions, apparently. A single chrysanthemum in a vase on a table had also been decapitated – as well as one of the curtain tassels.'

'Really? How curious . . . One possible explanation is that the killer decided to test the sword's sharpness before delivering the lethal blow,' Payne mused aloud.

Had the killer *played* with the sword perhaps? *Swoosh-swoosh*. Again, the kind of thing a maladjusted demi-adult would do.

'What's Tancred Vane like?'

Morland frowned. 'Youngish . . . mid-thirties, I imagine. I found him perfectly civil, though he was in a bad state. Shaking like a leaf . . . Extremely spruce . . . Wore a bow-tie . . . Described himself as a "scattergun collector, but one of the utmost discrimination". Chinamen are his passion.'

'Chinamen?'

'Porcelain figurines. He collects them. Has a cabinet full of them in his library. All an inch high. Smooth, luminous, smiling – something inhuman and sinister about them. I found myself puzzling whether the ferocious pleasure in their expressions was really the oriental artist's idea of unqualified good humour, or whether the Chinese were not, after all, rather a cruel breed.'

Payne wondered whether what he had just heard revealed something about Tancred Vane – or about

43

Morland. Morland, judging by this latest observation, wasn't such an uncomplicated chap after all . . . Ferocious pleasures, eh?

'Vane produced some brandy. Good high-quality stuff. I needed it,' Morland went on. 'We sat in the library. He was white as a sheet. Kept tugging at his bow-tie. A bit hysterical. Insisted on showing me the owl he'd bought that morning.'

'A real live owl?'

'No, no, not a live one. A Victorian doorstop fashioned like an owl – wrought iron – he'd got it at some antique shop, he said. Rather a comic face. He said it reminded him of Miss Hope, that's why he bought it. He kept saying mad things like that. He said he was terribly worried about Miss Hope. He kept looking at the clock. He said he expected Miss Hope to turn up at any moment.'

'Who is Miss Hope?'

'No idea. Never occurred to me to ask.'

'Did she turn up?'

'No. Not while I was there. She might have done later on.'

'How did the police know where to contact you?' Major Payne asked after a pause.

'They checked the numbers on Stella's mobile. The inspector asked if I was a friend of Mrs Stella Markoff. I thought at first Stella might have got lost – or that she'd had her handbag stolen or something. I explained that Stella and I were engaged to be married . . . The inspector then said that there'd been an accident . . . They sent a car to pick me up—'

'Where is the Villa Byzantine exactly?'

'St John's Wood.'

'My only remaining aunt lives in St John's Wood. Bought a house there quite recently.'

Morland took another gulp of whisky. 'I've been trying to remember something Tancred Vane said. I don't think it matters one little bit, but for some reason I can't get it out of my head. Oh yes. He had the idea that Miss Hope had recognized Stella.'

'Stella had met Miss Hope before?'

'That's the impression Vane had. Or was it the other way round? No, can't remember. Sorry, Payne, hate to waste your time. None of this could possibly be of the slightest importance. Don't know why it keeps nagging at me. Hope I'm not going mad.'

'Could Miss Hope have had something to do with Stella's death?'

'No, of course not. Ridiculous. Sorry I mentioned it. It – it all feels like a dream now. Poor Stella was killed by some maniac, wouldn't you say? She was in the wrong place at the wrong time. Or it might have been someone who'd been trying to burgle Vane's house – and she intervened. That strikes me as the likeliest explanation.'

'How did Stella come to be inside the Villa Byzantine?'

Morland sat very still, gazing into his glass. 'All the police said was that she'd had an accident, that she'd been hurt. They didn't tell me she was dead, Payne. They didn't. Then – then they took me into the room and showed me the head. Just like that. Damned insensitive . . . Sorry, Payne, what was it you said?'

'How did Stella come to be inside the Villa Byzantine?'

'How? No idea. No idea at all. Some misunderstanding. At first I assumed she'd had a call from the biographer fellow. Tancred Vane always made his appointments with her by phone. Only this time he didn't. He said he couldn't possibly have wanted to see Stella this morning since he needed to go to the British Library rather urgently. He'd mentioned it to her—'

'She knew he wouldn't be in?'

'That's what he said. He left his house at about ten thirty. He had made arrangements for an interview with Miss Hope at three o'clock in the afternoon. He came back home about two thirty. He said he found the front door unlocked—'

'Is he certain he'd locked it before leaving?'

'No. He couldn't swear to it. He admitted to being the absent-minded professor type. When he discovered Stella's body lying in the drawing room, he got the shock of his life. Had to sit down. He then called the police. He referred to the police as "the Law" – I thought it odd – not many people say "the Law", do they?'

'I imagine not. Only as a joke, perhaps. The Law. That much-invoked abstraction,' Payne murmured. 'Where was Stella's daughter while all of this was happening? At which point does she come into the picture?'

'Moon was arrested on the underground. At Baker Street station, I believe. She'd been travelling without a ticket and apparently she was jolly rude when they challenged her. She refused to say who she was and had no papers on her. She was taken to the local police station where they found she answered the description which I'd given the police.'

'You said she was their number one suspect. What grounds do the police have for suspecting Moon of her mother's murder?'

'When the police asked her if she knew where her mother was, she said her mother was dead. She later explained she only said it so they would leave her alone. She had no idea her mother was really dead.'

'I see. That all?'

'Not quite. A handkerchief was found lying beside Stella's body. It was drenched in blood. The police believe that it is Stella's blood. They haven't had the blood analysed yet. The handkerchief has the initials MM embroidered on it.' Morland shook his head. 'They believe Moon dropped it there after she killed Stella. MM. Moon Markoff.'

'Is it her handkerchief?'

'Of course it isn't. Moon has never been to the Villa Byzantine. She has no idea where the Villa Byzantine is!'

'You can't be certain of that.'

'It's just one of those idiotic coincidences that the initials on the blood-drenched handkerchief should be the same as Moon's. You must see that. I can't say I like Moon, but I believe in being fair. I've never seen Moon use a handkerchief, Payne. She hates handkerchiefs.'

Payne gave a little smile. 'She thinks handkerchiefs are "uncool"?'

'She thinks handkerchiefs are "dumb". She only uses tissues.' Morland spoke impatiently. 'She likes things rough. You saw her. Can you imagine her holding a silk handkerchief to her nose?'

'Did you actually see the handkerchief, Morland?'

'I did. The inspector showed it to me. It's their Exhibit A. It's made of silk. Very fine silk. Gossamer thin. Impossibly "ladylike". Moon would never use a hankie like that. *Not* her style, Payne.'

'Was there any blood on her clothes when the police arrested her?'

'No. Of course the police took her clothes away. They propose to run tests.'

'She wasn't wearing the blood-bespattered *shinel*?'

'As it happens, she wasn't.'

'She may have got rid of her bloodied clothes and then bought new ones,' Payne said thoughtfully.

'They were the same clothes I bought her last week. Bomber jacket, jeans, sports top, trainers. She had been pestering her mother, saying all her clothes were rubbish. She said she needed new clothes. Poor Stella asked me if I would take Moon shopping, which I did. I took her to Oxford Street. Shop called Top Girl, some such name.'

'Back to this morning – did you actually see Stella leave your flat?'

'No. I saw her at breakfast, briefly, then had to rush off. Had an important board meeting to attend. Stella seemed all right. A bit quiet, perhaps. She said she had a headache. She was never at her best in the morning, but then who is? I never saw Moon.'

'How did Moon spend her morning? Did she say?'

'She said she left soon after her mother. At about eleven. She said she got on the tube and went to Tottenham Court Road. She wanted to look at the CDs at Virgin Megastores. Something like that.'

'She might have followed her mother instead . . . All the way to the Villa Byzantine . . .'

'If she'd wanted to kill her mother, she'd have done it in a different way. That's what she said. *Not* with a samurai sword and most certainly *not* at the Villa Byzantine. She said she wasn't a fool. Nor was she a psycho.'

'I never thought she was a fool,' Payne said.

There was a pause. Morland glanced at his watch. 'Well, at least I'll know I've done my best. Thank you very much for listening to me, Payne. Awfully decent of you.'

'Try to get some sleep tonight.'

'Perhaps – perhaps you could look into the matter? If that's the right way of putting it?' Morland rose to his feet. 'You said you had an aunt in St John's Wood, didn't you? Sorry. That's neither here nor there.'

'I might look into it,' said Payne cautiously, 'though I can't promise anything.'

'I must admit I don't have much faith in the Law. Nothing but a bunch of bureaucrats. Somebody did behead Stella and it wasn't Moon,' Morland said firmly. 'I do hope you have a crack at finding the true culprit.'


After Morland had gone, Major Payne produced his pipe.

The true culprit, eh? He had to admit he enjoyed being flummoxed by intricate riddles, though perhaps this one wouldn't prove so terribly intricate.

The idea of a teenage girl committing matricide, while indubitably shocking, was not unique. Teenagers delighted in delinquent demeanour. Teenagers enjoyed perpetrating outrages. They had their ears pierced and studs inserted into their tongues. They made no attempt to control their emotions. They tended to bear grudges. They 'experimented' with things, namely sex and drugs. They listened to the most appalling music imaginable – hardly *music*. Teenagers could be violent and indeed often *were* violent. He remembered the sense of danger he'd had the moment he'd clapped eyes on Stella's daughter ...

Well, Stella's daughter seemed indicated – she was the most obvious suspect – but there were questions that needed answering.

Not so long ago Payne had bumped into the Prime Minister at a private gathering in Notting Hill and been told to expect an OBE – *for elevating the powers of rational thinking to the point where they became positively shamanistic.* The PM had spoken off the cuff and he hadn't been entirely serious of course. (He and Payne had gone to the same school and, as it happened, they could both trace their ancestry back to William IV, so the waggishness had most certainly not been de trop.) Payne knew that if he did get an OBE, it would be principally in recognition of his intelligence work in Afghanistan in the eighties.

Reaching out for the tobacco jar, Payne started filling his pipe. Questions, yes. How did Stella enter the Villa Byzantine? Had the front door been left unlocked, perhaps? Had she been instructed to go in and wait? Could Tancred Vane have set a trap for her? Was the mono-grammed blood-soaked handkerchief so conveniently left on the scene of the crime a bona fide clue or a plant? As a device – if this had been a detective story – it would have been considered awfully passé.

He struck a match and held it to his pipe. A samurai sword was the kind of weapon Stella's daughter *would* have chosen. The girl was loopy. She seemed to identify with some highly dangerous comic strip character, who went about under the sobriquet of Wild Thing. Moon liked beheadings, she had said so herself. She clearly despised her mother. At Melisande's party she had done her best to make Stella look a fool ... Though, of course, so had Melisande ...

What if the handkerchief was part of somebody's plan? Perhaps the intention was to incriminate Moon and use her as a scapegoat? Well, in that case, Payne reflected, we are looking for somebody with no particular knowledge or understanding of young people. Someone elderly and hopelessly old-fashioned? The kind of person who didn't see that a rough teenage girl would be unlikely to have an elegant silk handkerchief in her possession. A woman rather than a man – yes – a woman – an unmarried woman of a certain age? An elderly spinster ...

That was an ingenious theory, actually. The culprit was an unmarried elderly lady who was behind the times and had no idea at all what Moon was like, only knew her initials. One could buy initialled handkerchiefs – or have them specially made. Had the murder of Stella Markoff been carefully premeditated, then?

But did such an unmarried elderly lady exist?

It couldn't be the mysterious Miss Hope – could it?

Payne smiled at the idea.

# 8

# Hide My Eyes

It was the following day.

Tancred Vane sat at the desk in his study, writing.

*When a monarchy is gone, there is a sudden emptiness, an eerie silence – as the crowned head rests on the sandy ground of the executioner's pit – or on a Côte d'Azur beach.*

The Côte d'Azur had at one time been the favoured exile destination of deposed kings. Well, he reflected, modern readers seemed to like it when royalty were treated with irreverent flippancy.

His phone rang.

'Tancred?'

'Oh, Miss Hope – Catherine! At last! Where have you been? I've been worried sick!'

'Have you? My dear boy!'

'Why didn't you come yesterday? What happened?'

'I am so sorry. Something cropped up. I got a phone call from my niece – no, you don't want to know! Too tedious for words!'

'I tried phoning you – several times!'

'Didn't charge the damned object – mislaid the – what do you call that thing? The *charger*. Goodness. *Mobile* phones indeed. Whatever next? I am afraid I am hopelessly old-fashioned. I am quite the wrong age for that sort of nonsense. Lamentably behind the times! So sorry. The truth of the matter is I have been extremely preoccupied.'

'Why – what happened?'

'My niece – no, you don't want to know! A calamity! Young people nowadays! I must admit I find young people impossible to understand. A closed book, as they say. Nothing compared to *your* calamity, of course.'

'I suppose you saw the newspapers?'

'I did. It's on page three of *The Times*. I couldn't believe my eyes! *Murder at the Villa Byzantine*. Are you all right?'

'I am fine. I am fine now. I didn't sleep too well last night. I lay awake till five in the morning . . .'

'Yes? Go on, go on. I want every single detail!'

'I couldn't stop thinking about the murder. Then – then a great weight of numbness began to pull me down. I believe I fell asleep because I had a dream – a terrible dream! It all seemed so real. I saw her – Madame Markoff – Stella – pale and haggard-looking, her hand stretched out before her in an imploring gesture – no – accusingly!'

'*Whose horrid image doth unfix my hair* . . . Sorry, Tancred – most tasteless – couldn't resist it!'

'She was stiff and immobile – her eyes were wide open, glazed and staring. Suddenly I realized she was not real. She was made of wax. It gave me such a jolt that I woke up. I felt awful, really ill. My heart was pounding—'

'My poor boy!'

'I read somewhere that – that dreams are misleading because they make life seem real. That's a paradox I don't understand but for some reason I felt chilled thinking about it. Does it make sense?'

'No, it doesn't,' she said robustly. 'Paradox – bah! You *must* take your temperature. I don't suppose you slept in your house?'

'No. I was with a friend . . . I came back about an hour ago.'

He expected her to ask which friend he meant exactly, she seemed to take an interest in everything he did, but all she said was, 'I am glad. A friend in need is a friend indeed. What are you doing now?'

'Writing. Working on the biography.'

'That's the spirit! Work is the best remedy for a troubled

52

mind. Work and more work and then more work! That was the splendidly Puritan ethic of my dear late father. The police have gone now, of course? Did they leave a mess behind?'

'I don't think they bothered to wipe their shoes,' he said in a rueful voice.

'Pigs! Who do they imagine they are? The Pope? I think you should complain,' Miss Hope said firmly. 'Don't let them get away with it. They didn't break anything, did they? None of the Chinamen? I've been worried about the Chinamen.'

'No, nothing's broken. The Chinamen are intact.'

'I am so glad. Rivers of blood everywhere?'

'No. It wasn't *too* bad, actually. Still, it was pretty horrible. I never thought – I never imagined I'd come back and find—'

'No, of course not! You poor thing! You have had the curtains changed, of course? All that magnificent brocade!'

'How did you know there was blood on the curtains?'

'Mere guesswork. I am notorious for my morbid imagination. Sometimes I *see* things – my Scottish ancestry, you know. But I shouldn't keep nattering away at a time like this. I do believe you need a little rest? How about a nap?'

'Actually – Miss Hope – I was wondering whether you—'

'Catherine,' she reminded him. '*Catherine*. We agreed, didn't we? You promised! You gave me your word of honour! You want me to come? Are you sure you don't feel like taking a nap?'

'No. I don't feel at all sleepy at the moment.'

'In that case I will come. And we'll talk. About the murder, yes! I want you to get the whole thing out of your system. It will release the tension. It will exorcize the demons. You must tell me everything – how you found her, where the body lay and so on. It was you who found her, wasn't it?'

'Yes . . . You won't be bored?'

'Not at all. I must confess to a certain degree of vulgar curiosity. I lead *such* a drab life.' Miss Hope sighed. 'I hope you'd be able to elucidate at least *one* of the mysteries surrounding Mrs Markoff's dreadful demise. How on *earth* did the woman manage to gain entry into the Villa Byzantine? You didn't by any chance give her a key, did you?'

# 9

# Hearing Secret Harmonies

An hour later they were sitting on the ottoman in Tancred Vane's green-and-gold study, drinking coffee out of large snow-white cups and eating the delicious cake Miss Hope had made herself and brought with her. It was one of her very special walnut cakes that had a don't-you-dare-cut-me-with-anything-but-a-silver-knife sort of air about it. Tancred had been only too happy to bring a silver knife from the kitchen. He had no great appetite but she urged him to eat. He needed to eat! She was treating him like a growing boy.

'The police took the sword away—'

'Ah – the sword! That noble sword! It was a samurai sword, wasn't it? *What can ail thee, knight at arms, alone and palely loitering?*'

'They need it for fingerprinting and – and blood analysis, I believe they said.'

'Keats' knight of course would have been carrying a different kind of sword altogether,' she said thoughtfully. 'Not a samurai one. I told you, didn't I, that there was a samurai sword at the royal palace in Sofia?'

'No, you didn't.' The way she sprang the most fascinating information on him! 'Wait a minute.' Tancred Vane produced his little notebook and pen. 'Was the sword Prince Cyril's?'

'His brother's. It belonged to the King, but Cyril couldn't keep his hands off it. The sword was a present to Boris III from Hirohito, the Japanese Emperor, you know. The Japanese were to become allies. Fellow fascists, you know. Rome, Berlin and Tokyo. The notorious Axis. Those appalling POW camps! The way they treated our boys! Such beasts, the Japs. That's what my dear father used to say—' She broke off. 'Sorry, I was telling you about something else. What was it?'

'Cyril and the samurai sword.'

'Oh dear. Yes. He would pick it up and brandish it from left to right and then from right to left, looking gleeful – *swoosh-swoosh* – around the Salle de l'Ambre – the Amber Chamber – *swoosh-swoosh* – making those ferocious "Japanese" noises . . . *Aaargh*! It drove the Queen mad! Giovanna couldn't *stand* her brother-in-law.'

Tancred Vane reflected that many readers would be more interested in Prince Cyril and the sword than in, say, Prince Cyril's Nazi sympathies and treachery, or the account of his kangaroo trial and summary execution.

'I believe I tried to pick up the sword once or twice, didn't I? I mean *your* sword. The murder weapon. So my fingerprints would be on it? I don't think I was wearing gloves, was I?' Miss Hope frowned. 'Would that get me in trouble? Would the plod come pounding after me?'

'Actually the inspector asked for your phone number. I'm sure it's only routine. I gave it to him. You don't mind, do you?'

'Not in the least,' she reassured him. 'I'd be happy to talk to the plod, though of course I wouldn't have much to say. How did my name crop up?'

'I said I was expecting you. I kept looking at the clock. I told them you might come any moment – only you didn't.'

'I suppose that made them suspicious?' The familiar dry laugh. 'Did they take your fingerprints?'

'They did. I also had to write a statement – um – explain how long I'd known Stella Markoff, the reason she'd been coming to my house and so on.'

'How fatiguing for you!'

'I can't believe any of it happened.'

'Neither can I! This *murder yet is but fantastical*.' Miss Hope spoke in grave tones but there was an air of impish gaiety about her.

'Isn't it considered unlucky to quote *Macbeth*?'

'Nonsense. The Scottish Play can only affect *actors*. Which, my dear boy, you and I are not.' For some reason this made Miss Hope laugh till tears sprang from her eyes. 'Can't abide actors!' She blew her nose with her handkerchief. 'Detest the theatre!'

This was odd, Tancred Vane reflected, since Miss Hope seemed to know an awful lot about the theatre. Only a couple of days before she had quoted from Terence Rattigan's *The Sleeping Prince*. Prince Cyril, she explained, had talked to British embassy officials in a manner similar to that employed by the Regent in the Rattigan play. She had also told Tancred how at the age of thirteen she had been taken to see an amateur production of *Murder in Pupil Room*, William Douglas Home's very first play. Douglas Home had written the play while he was a pupil at Eton.

By a strange coincidence Tancred Vane had always called his study Pupil Room. Strange coincidences seemed to be happening all the time with Miss Hope, from the very moment his collaboration with her had started. Objects she saw at the Villa Byzantine, or something she heard him say, seemed to trigger off the most extraordinary memories. It was almost as if they had been *meant* to meet and collaborate on this project.

She had entered his life a month before, completely unexpectedly. She had answered his ad. Was it only a month? It felt as though he had known her all his life! He felt at peace when they were together. They moved in perfect harmony. He adored her. She had become indispensable. She was now part of his life.

Miss Hope wore a sensible tweed skirt and a heather-coloured blouse. She sported a hairnet over her carefully arranged white hair and an anachronistic rimless pince-nez on a black ribbon. She sat very straight. She was the English nanny par excellence, the last of a vanishing breed, yet, he reflected, there was something *archetypal* about her. The wise woman – the fairy godmother – the white witch – the eternal aunt figure – one of Barbara Pym's excellent women. Eccentric, faintly preposterous, yet kindly and reassuring and spouting sound no-nonsense advice.

'You are a funny colour, Tancred.' She reached out and held him by the chin. 'Show me your tongue – say aah – wider – wider! This looks all right, but when I leave, I want you to go to bed. Promise you will. Pull the blinds down, let your head hit the pillow and start counting – no, not sheep – *coronets*. That would be more your thing. Envisage peers. A sea of peers in ermine cloaks – each with a coronet on his head. Say you promise?'

'I promise ...' A curious happiness, a contentment, a warm glow crept over him.

'Good! No, don't move. Your tie is a bit askew. Your terrible tartan bow-tie! Let me—' Once more she leant towards him. 'There! The perfect butterfly effect.'

'Is my bow-tie terrible?'

'An absolute fright, but then there is no accounting for tastes, is there? Why the long face now? Vane by name, vain by nature! All right, you silly boy, your bow-tie makes you look like an auctioneer at Christie's! That better?' She patted his cheek.

He reached out for his notebook. 'One thing I wanted to ask you. What was the colour of Prince Cyril's eyes exactly?'

'Cyril's eyes? I am sure I have told you. You've started asking me the same questions twice, Tancred!' She laughed. She wagged her forefinger at him. 'I hope you aren't *testing* me, are you?'

'No, of course not. It's just—'

'Windsor blue. Cyril's eyes were Windsor blue. There!'

'I've been reading Chips Channon's diaries and Chips refers to Prince Cyril's "dark satanic gaze". Apparently Prince Cyril's were the only dark eyes among the royalty that attended George V's funeral in 1936. Chips Channon is usually quite accurate over little details like that.'

'I do believe Cyril's eyes changed colour,' she said slowly. 'They were like the sea. On a "good" day, that is when he hadn't drunk the night before and didn't have a hangover, his eyes appeared *much lighter*. This does suggest, doesn't it, that he must have been drinking heavily the night before George V's funeral? I must say Cyril drank an awful lot, like the proverbial fish. Now *you* must tell me something.' She leant forward. 'How *did* this Stella manage to get in?'

'I have absolutely no idea. Perhaps I forgot to lock the front door. I never gave her a key.'

'She might have stolen one of your duplicate keys from the hall the last time she was here . . . How about that?'

'Why should she want to do any such thing?'

'I don't know, Tancred, but, to tell you the truth, she struck me as a bit odd. I wouldn't say "unhinged", but she reminded me very strongly of—' Miss Hope broke off. 'No, that's awfully unfair! All right, but you must promise you won't laugh at me!'

'I promise.'

'Well, she reminded me very strongly of a woman who stole my poor father's umbrella at an open-air event in Sofia in August 1941. The same soulful eyes, the same prim mouth, the same vague hair. There was thunder and lightning and it looked as though the heavens were about to open. The woman stopped us and asked the time, then she suddenly grabbed my father's umbrella, just as he was about to open it, and skedaddled. She vanished into the night. We never saw her again.'

'She stole your father's umbrella?'

'It all happened in a flash. My father was not amused! Now then, your three duplicate keys are prominently displayed on that wall board in the hall, correct? And as though that were not enough, you have actually attached tags with *Front Door* written out on each one of them! Most invitingly, if you know what I mean.'

'As a matter of fact one of the keys is missing,' he said sheepishly.

'Are you serious? Goodness.' She put down her coffee cup. 'Did you tell the police?'

'I did.'

'You are too good, Tancred, too trusting. Too full with the milk of human kindness!'

'But why should Stella want to come into the house while I was away?'

'Why indeed! Well, one's name is often an indicator. *Stealing Stella*. It would be different in Bulgarian, of course. No, no, we shouldn't assault the integrity of someone who was destined to remain a stranger. Still, your house is full of treasures. Something may have caught her fancy. Not inconceivable, is it? One of your bibelots – or even the sword?'

'Now that you mention it, she did ask to look at the sword the last time she was here.' Tancred frowned. 'She said her little girl would find it interesting – she's got a daughter, apparently – but she wouldn't try to *steal* the sword, would she? It's too big!'

'Where there's a will, there's a way,' Miss Hope said firmly. 'Shame you haven't got a security alarm. Culpable carelessness, my Tancredi!'

Sometimes, when in one of her 'Italian moods', she addressed him as 'Tancredi'.

'I ordered a security system this morning.'

'Being wise after the event, my Tancredi!'

There was a pause.

'That day – when she met you – Stella Markoff behaved rather oddly,' Tancred said. 'She stared at you, did you notice?'

'I did notice. Hard not to! Such big eyes! I thought it bad-mannered of her, but then Bulgarians do tend to stare, poor souls, even the so-called "better-class" ones.'

'She seemed somewhat agitated – asked a lot of questions about you after you left.'

'I know one mustn't speak ill of the dead, Tancred, but she gave the impression of being a little peculiar – as well as of being a singularly unfulfilled woman. But what an awful way to die! To be deprived of one's head! I believe the sword was in what they call "good working order", wasn't it?'

'It was. It was extremely sharp.'

She shook her head. 'The whole thing brings to mind a *not* very good detective story, if you know what I mean. Incidentally, Prince Cyril was terribly fond of *Englische Kriminalgeschichten*. Cyril adored Edgar Wallace. He had quite a collection of Edgar Wallace's books, all in German translation. German was the language he spoke best. *Not* a congenial language, my father used to say. Designed for barking out orders and cracking crude jokes.'

Tancred picked up his pen. 'I had no idea Prince Cyril liked Edgar Wallace.'

'He *adored* Edgar Wallace. On one memorable occasion Cyril missed a dinner party at the Romanian embassy because he needed to finish Edgar Wallace's *Das Gasthaus an der Themse*. He actually wrote a fan letter to Edgar Wallace in English and had it despatched to London through diplomatic channels.'

'Did he receive a reply?'

A strange faraway light came into Miss Hope's eyes. 'I believe he did, yes. Edgar Wallace sent Cyril his autograph. The Guesthouse on the Thames, that's correct. Well, few writers can resist the allure of royal patronage and second-rate writers are particularly susceptible. All of Edgar Wallace's books are quite ghastly. I don't suppose you have read any?'

'No.'

'He apparently boasted that he could write a book in a week! Well, let me tell you one thing – *it shows*! He had three secretaries, I read somewhere, sitting in the same room – he would walk about and dictate a different book to each one.' She watched Tancred Vane as he scribbled in his notebook. 'I hope you are feeling better?'

'I am much better. Thanks to *you*.'

'Jolly good.' She beamed at him. '*Jolly good*.' Suddenly she rose from her seat and smoothed down her skirt.

'What's the matter?' He blinked. 'You aren't – you aren't going, are you?'

'I'm afraid I am. Don't look so disappointed! I'm sure you will find sleep more salutary than my silly old yarns.'

'I won't! Must you go?'

'Ah, Lady Antonia Fraser's memoir. I've been reading it. What a terrifying creature the late Pinter seems to have been. Unfortunately, my answer, unlike hers, will have to be, yes, I *must* go. I am sorry, Tancred, but I've *got* to go. So much to do! All kinds of unresolved problems. My niece – my *great* niece, actually – an absolute calamity—' Miss Hope broke off and shook her head. 'Young people nowadays!'

'When – when will you come again?'

'Soon.'

'When exactly?'

'Soon.'

'When is soon?'

'Soon enough.' She adjusted her hat and pushed the pince-nez up her nose. 'Tomorrow afternoon, perhaps. At half-past three? We'll have tea together. We'll have a proper powwow then. And now – now you must go to bed.'

Tancred protested that he did not feel in the least sleepy.

'You need to make an effort, my boy. All great artists need to die for a few hours in order to live for centuries. You wouldn't want to develop into one of those insomniacs who get sent to a *kurhaus* in the mountains, would you? Have you ever been to a *kurhaus*? Such strange places! Staffed by werewolves and vampires, or so everybody said. Sinister sanatoria, my mother called them. They have them in the Balkans. Or used to.'

'I'll go to bed later,' he prevaricated.

'No. Now.'

'*How happy is he born and taught,*' Tancred quoted sullenly, '*that serveth not another's will.*'

'*Whose armour is his honest thought – and simple truth his utmost skill.* See? I know my Sir Henry Wotton!' She patted his cheek. 'Come on, let's go. Chop-chop.'

'Five more minutes?'

'Chop-chop.'

'Three minutes – please!'

She remained adamant. 'Chop-chop.'

He sighed. She held the door open. She accompanied him to his room.

Tancred wondered whether a casual onlooker might not find their relationship a trifle on the odd side. Miss Hope had already suggested – as a joke, no doubt – that perhaps she could move into the Villa Byzantine and keep house for him. It was not inconceivable that a casual onlooker might get the idea that Miss Hope had a crush on him. He smiled. Ridiculous – impossible – at her age!

As he reached for his pyjamas, she turned round primly and faced the wardrobe. A minute later he lay in bed and she kissed his forehead lightly, then stepped back. Before she shut his bedroom door, she whispered through the crack, 'Goodnight, sweet prince, and flights of angels sing you to sleep.'

# 10

# Vie de Château

The story of how Miss Hope had become involved with the Bulgarian royal family in the early years of the war, how she and her parents had idled in the wilderness while the face of Europe was being changed, was quite remarkable, to say the least.

Tancred Vane found himself thinking about it, going over details, as he lay in bed in his darkened room, unable to sleep. It had been such a vivid account. He now felt the irresistible urge to listen to it again. He wanted, nay, *longed*, to hear Miss Hope's voice once more.

He had actually recorded her story on tape and the cassette recorder stood on his bedside table, so all he needed to do was to reach out, locate the button and then press it – *voilà*.

'It was back in 1941. My father was appointed Head of Chancery at the British legation in Sofia. Mother had the gravest doubts about living in Bulgaria and so did I, if I have to be perfectly honest. A girl at school had told me Bulgarians were cannibals. She said Bulgarians were grim, gnome-like and extremely ferocious and that they liked nothing better than drinking blood. I think she must have been thinking of Borneoans.

_____ mother dreaded becoming marooned in a
_____ ng people with whom she'd find no
commu__.        ' she might be made to feel like
Keats' Ruth. That ,          ·ite poet, yes – fancy you
remembering! *The sad hea_ . _     '. when sick for home, she
stood in tears amid the alien corn.*

'Well, we'd been warned that life in these parts of the
Balkans lacked the choreography and grace of Western
civilization, that wealth was rare, and either impossibly
ostentatious or hidden – that no sponsoring of arts and
letters or any form of cultivated living ever took place.

'Glory and prosperity were said to have eluded Bulgaria.
Bucharest had acquired a pseudo-Parisian sheen and
Athens a Levantine cosmopolitanism, which is better than
no cosmopolitanism, but Sofia – alongside Belgrade and
Tirana – never amounted to more than a dull, quasi-
oriental provincial capital, lacking aristocracies of the
blood or the spirit.

'The reports, however, turned out to be inaccurate and
Sofia came as a most pleasant surprise. It was a thoroughly
decent place, you might say. We were given a fine house
made of yellow stone and hordes of servants. There was a
marvellous well-tended garden with roses proliferating
like a tapestry of Burne-Jones! We were befriended by the
ruling elite, whose members, my mother discovered soon
enough, had been educated in France, Germany and even
in England. And immediately my parents started receiving
invitations to the palace – to luncheons, soirées, garden
parties and charity galas.

'Well, in a couple of months, as you know, Bulgaria was
to abandon its neutrality and join the war as Germany's
ally. Consequently, all the British subjects living on
Bulgarian territory would leave and the British legation
would close – but that time had not come yet.

'Officially at least, we were not yet *the* enemy.

'The third of August was the anniversary of King Boris'
ascension to the throne. That was when the annual garden
party took place at the royal palace in Sofia. My parents
were certainly invited and on that occasion they decided to

take me with them. I was just fifteen – a very mature fifteen, I must emphasize.

'Dr Goebbels had come from Germany especially for the occasion. I have the most vivid recollection of him limping nimbly through the glittering throng. Although temperatures that day couldn't have been higher, an icy wind seemed to blow as he passed me. It was as if an evil, solitary, cruel god had clambered down among the bustle of pleasure-seeking, cowardly, pitiful mortals!

'Prince Cyril had with him his *maîtresse-en-titre*, a cabaret singer of Magyar extraction called Victoria Kallassi, and their infant son Clement, known as Clemmie. To bring a bastard baby – what they used to call a badling – to the King's anniversary garden party was not the done thing of course, but Cyril enjoyed being outrageous. Cyril had a talent for getting away with things.

'That poor badling! He died five years later – fell in Lake Garda and drowned, or so I heard. I vividly remember the swan-shaped white pram and his corpulent and rather peevish-looking Austrian nanny. Her name was Fräulein Guldenhove.

'The mistress, Victoria, was a tempestuous beauty. She had flashing eyes, raven-black hair and sculpted scarlet lips. Her complexion exuded a rose-and-amber glow. She wore a scarlet dress that day. *Very* tight in the waist. Elbow-length gloves but *bare legs*. She sported a diamond necklace that had once belonged to Princess Clementine, Prince Cyril's Bourbon grandmother.

'Someone – the wife of the Austrian chargé d'affaires, I think – drew a parallel between Victoria and Sylvia Varescu, the heroine of *The Czardas Queen*. The Kalman operetta, you know. It's on the joint subject of misalliance and true love. It was enjoying a tremendous success at the local musical theatre at the time. It was, as they say, all the rage.

'Victoria was the proud owner of a bed that had once belonged to Napoleon's mistress Josephine, complete with fragrant linen and pillows of unparalleled softness. I liked to sit on that bed when she was not around – but that was later, when I became their nanny. Sorry – mustn't jump the gun!

'Prince Cyril strutted about in a white mess jacket. He wore the Grand Cross Collar and Badge that went with the Order of the Bath. The decoration had been awarded to his late father, King Ferdinand, by Edward VII. My mother took rather a shine to his well-trimmed moustache, much to my father's annoyance. My mother thought Cyril looked like a character out of *The Chocolate Soldier*. In my father's opinion he looked like a bounder.

'The presence of the badling – poor little Clemmie – was causing particular tension. The Queen, puritanical, Catholic, Italian-born Giovanna, had been driven to distraction by her brother-in-law's indiscretions. She cared an awful lot what Sofia high society might be saying. Rather *suburban* of her to mind, I remember my mother saying. Well, Sofia high society, like most enclosed high societies, had more than its fair share of busybodies, gossips and intriguers. I imagine little else was being discussed that day but the mistress and the badling.

'Giovanna sported a sort of redingote of pale moth-coloured chiffon with a pelisse covered in solid sequins, a big pearl and diamond necklace and tiara. She only needed a wand to fly to the top of a Christmas tree! But her expression was sour – oh so sour – not fairy-like at all! She was said to be controlling and manipulative and to demand absolute conformity to her narrow views.

'Hundred of photos were taken that day and they later appeared in various illustrated Continental magazines. I cut them all out and pasted them in my scrapbook. All gone now, alas, vanished without a trace!

'What was King Boris' reaction to the badling's presence? Well, in characteristic style he pretended he hadn't noticed anything amiss. He went on walking about rather stiffly, smiling, shaking hands, making small talk.

'The King was a thin, mild-mannered man with a high balding forehead, and, like his younger brother, he sported a well-trimmed dark moustache. He was a decent chap, but scarcely an entertaining one. His two much-publicized passions were for steam trains and Bavarian cream, but he was best known for never telling people what he really thought.

'The King was dressed in a white general's uniform and had white gloves on. He was covered in glittering decorations and had a sheathed sabre at his right thigh. Good thing too – otherwise he might have been mistaken for a bank manager taking it easy at some Continental spa!

'The palace was adorned with flags of all sizes. Brightly coloured tapestries hung from the windows and the balconies. There were flowers everywhere – white freesias, lilies of the valley, parrot tulips, pansies, morning glory and roses. A hussar band played a pot-pourri of Viennese waltzes and polkas. Trays of chilled champagne were carried round by footmen in splendidly frogged silk coats and silver-buckled shoes.

'The food was scrumptious. I remember something called *norde pole* – extra-special vanilla ice-cream on a pedestal of clear ice – and an "architectural" cake with ramparts fashioned after the bastions of the palace of Darius! I remember the great glazed slabs jewelled with scarlet cherries glistening on fine porcelain plates . . .

'The next day the Sofia papers were to describe the event in the most gushing of terms. "A scene of profuse hospitality and festivity . . . a most elegant repast . . . a brilliant display of loveliness, beauty and style".

'I believe it was the kind of saccharine prose that was churned out on every grand occasion of the time.'

# 11

# Smiles of a Summer Day

'It was a sweltering hot kind of day. The thermometer had climbed to eighty-six degrees! I don't think anyone was really surprised when Fräulein Guldenhove groaned, clutched at her bosom and pitched forward in a dead faint, like some felled oak. There was a commotion. People rushed towards her. I think someone pushed the pram, causing Clemmie to start crying.

'It was no ordinary crying, Tancred. You've never heard anything like it. The badling was bawling – screaming his tiny head off. The badling was notoriously sensitive – might have been a baby oyster, was how the Austrian military attaché put it – I believe he suffered from colic – I mean the badling, not the Austrian military attaché. Various flunkeys and ladies-in-waiting tried ineffectually to calm him down, but they only managed to make matters worse.

'I was standing nearby, sucking iced lemonade through a straw. I saw Clemmie's face turn the colour of a Seychelles sunset as he was passed round like a parcel from one pair of arms to another. No one seemed to know what to do with him. They put him back into the pram, but then he started making a noise as though he were breathing his last – gasping, gurgling, coughing, spluttering. Really, it was most alarming.

'The band had been playing the *Merry Widow* waltz. They hadn't stopped when Fräulein Guldenhove prostrated herself on the beautifully mown lawn, but now all the musicians leapt to their feet.

'Victoria had disappeared a couple of minutes previously. She was seen storming out of the garden and stomping towards the lodge where she and Clemmie lived, following some acerbic remark made to her by Giovanna. I can't say what remark exactly. The Queen always spoke in a low, flat voice, thinned by resentment.

'Poor Clemmie's face started turning a German-plum kind of blue. King Boris stood by, glumly contemplating the scene, tugging at his moustache, looking indecisive. (He frequently looked indecisive.) I surprised an expression of pure *schadenfreude* on Giovanna's face. Giovanna would have rejoiced if the badling had swallowed his tongue and choked to death!

'Prince Cyril's eyes were terribly bloodshot. He flew into a rage and started swearing in German. His moustache bristled. He cut a fearsome figure.

'It was at that point that I stepped forward. I stood beside the pram and picked Clemmie up. It was something I felt I *had* to do. What happened next was quite extraordinary. You have heard about horse whisperers, of course? Somebody told me afterwards I must have the same kind of "touch" where babies were concerned!

*'Clemmie stopped crying at once.*

'In a few seconds he was his normal colour once more. A smiling semicircle formed round me. Then the clapping started. Really, it was most embarrassing. I hate fuss. Fräulein Guldenhove was still lying on the ground, moaning, wretched woman, but I fear she remained unheeded. In later years she was to write a colourful account of life at the palace. I believe it became quite a bestseller in Liechtenstein.

'What did I do next? Well, I took out my handkerchief and wiped Clemmie's face with it. Clemmie smiled back at me. He then began to coo. He waved his hands in the air and laughed! His fingers brushed my chin.

'That poor badling.

'Sorry, Tancred – this always makes me a little emotional – no, I'll be all right. Let me blow my nose—

'Prince Cyril marched up to me. (He must have been wearing stays because he creaked.) He shook my hand and patted my cheek with a gloved forefinger. He told me I was a gift from a kindly Providence. I had saved his son's life and words could not express his gratitude. He then said that I should consider myself employed as his son's nanny. I was to take over from Fräulein Guldenhove without a second's delay. All boring formalities would be taken care of by his aide-de-camp, so I needn't worry about anything.

'He had always known English nannies were the best in the world, English nannies were legendary, it had been madness employing an Austrian one. That, he explained, had been his sister-in-law's tomfool idea. He should never have listened to Giovanna. "You are fired. No nanny should be so fat anyhow," he then barked at Fräulein Guldenhove, whom four people had just, with considerable difficulty, managed to pull up to her feet – causing her to collapse on the ground once more!

'No, Tancred, it never occurred to me to say no . . . Funny, isn't it?

'What did I do? Well, I felt thrilled, but I managed to keep my presence of mind. Don't forget that I'd been impeccably brought up. I curtsied and I addressed Prince Cyril very correctly as "Your Royal Highness". I then said I was greatly honoured – but would His Royal Highness mind if I consulted my parents first?'

Tancred Vane had fallen asleep, but at some point during the afternoon he stirred and woke up with a start.

The room was dark and very quiet. The fluorescent hands of the bedside clock said six o'clock. He'd slept for quite a while. What was it that had awakened him? He lay still and listened. He heard furtive noises, the squeak of a pressed floorboard, dragging footsteps, a scraping sound, as though a stealthy hand had removed the metal owl doorstop from Pupil Room – but he knew it was all his imagination.

Something was nagging away at the back of his mind. He had a vague sense of . . . danger.

He had had a dream. He had seen Stella again. Stella was anxious to impart some information to him urgently – to warn him – time, for some reason, seemed to be very short. She kept pointing to her mouth and he saw that her lips had been sewn up crudely with black wire. She only managed to emit a series of inarticulate mumbling sounds. Realization then dawned on him. *Stella had been silenced.* Stella had been killed because she knew someone's guilty secret.

I am imagining things, Tancred Vane thought. It's just a silly dream. My nerves are in a bad state. I need to start taking exercise.

Stella Markoff had been extremely curious about Miss Hope. She had asked him questions. How old was Miss Hope? Had he known Miss Hope long? Where did Miss Hope live? What exactly was Miss Hope's connection with the Bulgarian royal family? He had had the distinct impression that Stella had met Miss Hope on some previous occasion – or imagined she'd met her – that she had *recognized* her.

But Miss Hope said she'd never before clapped her eyes on Stella!

Tancred Vane held his breath. He had remembered one of the questions Stella asked him that day. Did Mr Vane know a woman called—?

Now, what *was* the name? It was rather an unusual, rather an *actressy*, sort of name—

12

# The She-Wolf

Melisande Chevret had had a mental picture of James dropping on his knees, bowing before her and begging forgiveness. She had envisaged a passionate reunion – James covering her hands with kisses, then rising and burying his face in her bosom, mumbling that he was sorry, so terribly sorry, he had been mad to turn his back on her, he had no idea what had possessed him – would she take pity on a miserable sinner? – would she give him a second chance? – would she have him back?

But of course nothing of the sort happened. James was stiff and formal and far from demonstrative. He shook hands with her, then, as an afterthought, gave her a peck on the cheek, near her left ear – as far from her lips as possible.

She was wearing her immaculately cut pearl-grey peignoir with blue ribbon bindings along the edges, with several long gold chains strung from her neck. She had had a massage and a facial in the morning and thought her face looked particularly smooth and luminous, like that of the Dresden shepherdess on her dressing table. She was whippet-thin now – exactly the way she wanted to be. The ayurvedic diet seemed to have worked. No red meat and nothing but liquids after 6 p.m. She'd hated it, but now she looked at least fifteen years younger. *Il faut souffrir pour être belle.*

She led the way into the drawing room and sat down on the sofa. She patted the place beside her and gave him her most seductive smile, but he chose to sit in one of the armchairs.

All right. Suit yourself, buster, she thought. Perhaps she was expecting too much. Perhaps it was too soon. It was only three days since Stella had been separated from her head. James was pale and tense and he too seemed to have lost weight. His habitual bulging orb seemed to have diminished somewhat. He kept avoiding her eye.

No, nothing to drink, he said – thank you so much, but nothing to eat either. So much for her carefully prepared dinner à deux. (Asparagus soup, chicken in aspic, green salad, figs in strawberry sauce, Stilton, black coffee.) Why had she bothered? Why had he come? She pressed him to have a drink and eventually he said he would like a cup of tea. Tea! She'd always despised people who asked for a cup of tea, but this – this was particularly bad.

James was wearing a black suit, black tie and black shoes. *And* black socks. For heaven's sake, she thought. All he lacked was a black armband! The disconsolate widower! He looked quite absurd. Maestro, the Death March, please, and don't spare the violins!

Melisande felt the urge to laugh aloud, blow a raspberry, neigh like a horse, but she managed to exercise self-control. She still believed she had a chance with him. Having handed him his cup of tea, she poured herself a large brandy. This was not how she had imagined their reunion, most certainly *not* the way she had contemplated the evening ahead.

'Kind of you to come when you clearly have so much on your mind, James,' she said softly. 'How have you been?'

'Not awfully well. I've been sleeping badly.'

'I am so terribly sorry. Have you seen your doctor?'

'I'm afraid I haven't had a chance. Too busy.'

'Poor darling. Would you like one of my sachets? They reduce you to the most delicious kind of coma and no headaches afterwards, just a pleasantly treacly sensation. I am quite addicted to them.'

'No, thanks.'

'Would you like me to massage your poor neck and shoulders? It would release the tension. You know I can do it really well.'

'No, thanks.'

Melisande pursed her lips. She had only been trying to be helpful. Did he fear she might try to seduce him? He used to love it when she had massaged his neck and shoulders in the past, couldn't get enough of it, the greedy pig.

She thought the atmosphere in the room had become charged with wariness and potential conflict. *I see the world through a shroud that is as clammy as it is dark.* Who said that? One of those middle-aged women characters Winifred was urging her to play? Was it Carlotta in *Song at Twilight*?

She took a sip of brandy. Perhaps she should get roaring drunk?

'Have the police released the body?'

'No, not yet. I don't know when exactly that will be. They keep their cards very close to their chests. We've been trying to contact Stella's relatives in Bulgaria.'

'What a bore. Who's "we"?'

'Moon and I.'

'That awful girl.'

'She is very young.'

'Ghastly manners. Quite shocking. I don't believe she gives a fig for her mother, dead or alive. Where is she now?'

'At my sister's place in Kensington.'

'That's the flat next door to yours, isn't it? There is a communicating door, if I remember correctly. Poor Julia. How I pity her. What an ordeal. How is she coping?'

'It hasn't been too bad, actually.'

'Make sure the girl doesn't cut your throats as you sleep,' Melisande murmured.

'Sorry?' How ridiculous he looked, cupping his ear and thrusting his head forward.

'I said, make sure the girl gets enough sleep.' Melisande raised her voice. 'Sleep at that age is so very important, James.'

75

'I know it is.' He sighed. 'Moon's been under terrible strain. We've been trying to contact Stella's relatives in Bulgaria, but the whole communication business has been a nightmare.'

'Well, darling, what else can one expect when one goes exploring the unknown rather than exploiting the assured? If people fall below something called a certain standard, they are asking for trouble. No, I am not in the least angry with you, darling. It's just that I don't quite see why you should be going out of your way to accommodate that girl. It's more than clear it's affected your health. It breaks my heart to see you looking so ill.'

He harrumphed. 'I'm not as bad as I was.'

'I think this whole thing was nothing but a ghastly mistake from start to finish. The sooner you realize that, the better. It is my firm belief that once Stella has been buried, and her daughter goes back to Bulgaria or America or wherever, you will start seeing things in a totally different light.'

'I'm not sure I will.'

'You're still in a state of shock, darling. I don't imagine you've been thinking rationally. You really have been your own worst enemy, you know.'

'What the hell do you mean?'

'The impulse to destroy oneself is among the most ancient human impulses. It is the *crux* of most of Shakespeare's greatest tragedies. The moment of madness – when a great man makes a single decision that sets his downfall irreversibly in train. Macbeth allowing the witches to plant ideas in his mind. Lear preferring his wicked daughters to his good, loving one.'

'I don't think I understand—'

'Clearly insane decisions,' she said firmly. 'It is almost as though some bacillus has infected your entire physiology and unbalanced your judgement!'

'What bacillus? What are you talking about?'

She took another gulp of brandy. I am going to drink myself into scintillations of self-pity, she thought.

76

'Remember Malvolio suckered into wearing yellow cross-garters as a supposed aphrodisiac to his employer, Olivia?'

Looking at his blank face, it occurred to her that she might not be adopting the right approach. James wasn't the least bit artistic or intellectual. Theatrical allusions weren't exactly his thing. Witty parallels between life and high literature were all but lost on him.

Rising from the sofa, she went up to him and perched on the arm of his chair. 'I feel for you, James. If you only knew how much I feel for you. My heart bleeds for you, darling. You can kiss me, if you like.'

'I'd rather I didn't – sorry, Melisande. I don't feel terribly well—'

*He'd rather he didn't.* She was dismayed. He was off her. He'd always called her Meli, never Melisande. This was the end. He no longer found her attractive. He no longer desired her. He was off her!

She told herself to persist. 'I admire you for wanting to do the right thing, darling, I really do. You have *such* a munificent heart. I am sure everything will be all right in the end. You will see Stella's body transported back to Bulgaria in one of those hermetically sealed coffins, give the daughter a couple of bucks and make sure she is safely ensconced on the plane. After that you will be a free man! The paralysing effect this whole dreadful business has had on your faculties will wear off soon enough and you will start seeing things *as they really are.*'

'Moon doesn't want to go back to Bulgaria.'

'Well, she'll have to go! She has no other option!' Anger surged through Melisande like blood bubbling up through a sharp cut in skin. 'You'd better impress it on her. You mustn't allow that little bitch to twist you round her little finger, James, you really mustn't! She's taking advantage of your good nature, don't you see? The brazen gall of it!'

'She is very young,' he said again.

'I am sorry, James, but I have very little patience where that girl is concerned. I find her tiresome beyond endurance. She was outside the house this morning.'

'Moon was outside your house? Are you sure it was her?'

'Of course it was her! She was wearing that disgusting *shinel.*'

'What was she doing?'

'Standing and staring, James. Standing and staring. Indulging her penchant for meddlesome intrusion. Spying – writing things down, in what looked like a notebook – trying to intimidate us! She's got a screw loose, that much is clear. We nearly called the police. Poor Win said it gave her the heebie-jeebies, looking at that girl, though I believe it was me Moon was after. She hates me.'

'She must have been playing at detectives. She—'

'She is a bitch, James. A manipulative bitch. She is twisting you round her little finger.' Melisande smoothed her peignoir with her hand. 'I am sorry, darling, but sometimes it is best to be brutally honest. Do you know what? I pray for you incessantly. You can move in here, if you like,' she added casually, giving his earlobe a playful tweak. 'How about it?'

'Don't do that, please.' The way he drew back, she might have announced a leprous condition. 'Thank you, but I'm afraid that – that will be quite impossible.'

'Impossible? I suppose you need more time to recover?'

'I think so. Yes. I need more time – and space. My own space.'

Melisande rose slowly to her feet. Her expression didn't change, but the turmoil inside her frightened her. It was only with great difficulty that she resisted the temptation to claw his face or strangle him with his black tie. Examining her long red fingernails, she asked him if he wanted another cup of tea.

'No, thank you.'

She sighed. 'We seem to have been overtaken by events,' she said obscurely. 'How is the investigation progressing? They haven't yet caught the killer, have they?'

'Not as far as I know. There has been nothing in the papers or on TV. I have no idea what is going on.'

'So they still don't know who did it. You don't think it's the girl?'

'What girl?'

'The daughter, James. Stella's girl. The offensive off-spring. Moon. Didn't you say the police found her hankie not far from her mother's body and that it was dripping blood?'

'The police *thought* it was her handkerchief, but they were wrong. It has the initials MM on it, but it is not her handkerchief. She's not the only one with the initials MM. It could be anybody's handkerchief.'

'Indeed it could be.' An icy calm descended upon Melisande. 'It could be my friend Lady Mariota Madrigal's – only she happens to be in Acapulco at the moment. It could also be Marcel Marceau's, the French mime artist. Or is he dead? The handkerchief could also be yours, you know.'

'I am not in the mood for jokes.'

'Your second name is Morgan. You told me your parents used to call you Morgan when you were a boy and how much you hated it.' She laughed. 'Morgan Morland – sounds a bit silly, I agree, but it matches those initials perfectly.'

'It's a woman's handkerchief.'

'Well, darling, some men get a kick out of carrying feminine articles about their person. Lipsticks and powder compacts and bottles of nail varnish. Some men wear their girlfriends' silk stockings wrapped tightly about their bodies. It's called fetish, James. One meets more fetishists than farmers, according to statistics, socially, I mean, though of course, one doesn't realize it – it isn't something one sees written on their foreheads. Soft materials can be a particular turn-on—'

'I am not in the mood for jokes,' Morland said again.

'I am absolutely, utterly, profoundly serious. What if I told you it was my handkerchief?'

'It isn't your handkerchief.'

'My unwed and unweddable sister gave me *such* a peculiar look when I announced Stella's death to her. Win didn't seem to believe that it was you who'd phoned me and told me about it. I have an idea she's been avoiding me.'

'Why should she want to do that?' Morland spoke absently. He looked at his watch.

'I believe she is afraid of me. Perhaps she's got it into her head it was I who killed Stella? Perhaps she thinks I am MM? My middle name, after all, is Mariah. Melisande Mariah.'

'Your middle name is not Mariah. You have no middle name.'

'You are right, I haven't. *But I have a good motive for Stella's murder*. Stella stole you away from me. I have been consumed by jealousy – devoured – tormented – crazed! My pride has been severely wounded. Perhaps I decided to get rid of her, so that I could have you back? Perhaps, unlike the cat in the adage, I didn't let I dare not wait upon I would?'

'What cat?'

Really, Melisande thought, he is rather stupid. He will never belong to the aristocracy of the mind, as Proust or somebody put it. And he is so fat and so pink. Heaven knows why I am so terribly keen on binding his faithless heart to mine. Of wanting to unite my destiny with his. This is quite the *wrong* kind of obsession.

'Do you think I killed Stella, James?'

'Of course I don't. I need to go now.' He stood up. 'Thanks for the tea.'

'Don't mention it. The eager way you gulped it down, it might have been the elixir of life. Goodness, you do exude clerical severity. *Must* you wear black? That rather tedious police inspector wanted to know where I was on the fatal day and I said I was at home, but I wasn't. Has it never occurred to you that good murderers are often good actors? Both species have a lot in common, haven't you noticed?'

James started walking towards the door.

'Vain, determined, egocentric – and they possess an enviable amount of sangfroid. Both species can bluff their way through the trickiest of situations. How many times have I forgotten my lines on stage and had to improvise – and no one the wiser?'

# 13

# Three Sisters?

'You would never believe this, my love,' Major Payne said, handing Antonia a gin and tonic, 'but while you've been away, I got myself embroiled in murder.'

'I have had enough of murder to last me at least a month, thank you very much. I am not starting on a new book till after Christmas.'

'I am serious.'

'So am I. No murder till after Christmas.'

'A murder took place on Tuesday. At the Villa Byzantine.'

'One thing is certain. In America they take murder mysteries *much* more seriously than they do here. Even if they call them "cozies". I wish they didn't. I believe the intention of whoever coined the phrase was to domesticate the genre, but what he, or she, succeeded in doing was to trivialize it. I strongly suspect it was a she.'

'Remember Morland? The chap we met at Kinderhook. He's asked me for assistance—'

'Nobody mixes a gin and tonic quite like you.' Antonia gave him a searching glance. 'You look thinner. You haven't been eating properly, have you? Omelettes, I suppose? Did your aunt have you over for dinner? She promised she would look after you.'

'It was Stella Markoff who was murdered. Didn't you see any English papers?'

'No, thank God.'

Payne sat down in the chair opposite Antonia. 'Stella was beheaded at the Villa Byzantine.'

'Was she? By a republican, no doubt. Or perhaps it was someone who resented being bored by lectures on the future of the Bulgarian monarchy?'

'The Villa Byzantine is in St John's Wood. It is an architectural oddity. *Faux* oriental,' Payne persisted. 'My aunt actually went and took a peek at it. She thought it perfectly gruesome – singularly suited to a beheading.'

'This is all terribly amusing, but I am not in the mood, Hugh.'

'My aunt may prove to be a valuable spy. She's quite thrilled at the prospect of doing a Mata Hari—' Payne broke off. 'Do I have the fatal knack of making everything I say sound a little preposterous?'

'You do, rather. I must admit it's part of your charm, but at the moment I happen to be tired, oh so tired. I believe I have jetlag. I can never sleep on planes. I watched a wonderful film. *The Illusionist*. I should have seen the twist at the end coming, only I didn't.'

'The Villa Byzantine belongs to a Tancred Vane who is a royal biographer. Stella showed us photos of both – at Melisande's party. Remember?'

'Melisande's agent insisted I should go on stage. Do you think I should? He said I had *something*.'

'At the moment Tancred Vane is engaged on a biography of Prince Cyril. Actually, this has nothing to do with the murder.'

'There was a Prince Leopold in the film,' Antonia said dreamily. 'He was something of a sadist where his ladies were concerned . . . I see that you have been living it up in my absence.' She had picked up a slip of paper from the little table beside her chair. 'You stayed at the Corrida Hotel in Earls Court and drank a bottle of champagne and a can of Red Bull!'

'What's that?'

'How appropriate – drinking Red Bull at the Corrida Hotel!' Antonia laughed. 'Though *not* with champagne. No gentleman of taste and discernment would do that sort of thing. *Un peu* plebeian, as you'd be the first to point out. It's a bill, Hugh. A hotel bill.'

'It's not my bill.' Payne sounded annoyed. 'No idea how it got there.'

'Are you sure you are not playing some exceedingly silly game with me?'

'I am not playing a game.'

'I refuse to believe that. It is a fact universally acknowledged that an Englishman of good breeding always plays the game whenever it offers. It is a national trait such as the rest of the world admires ... And now I must go to bed.' Antonia yawned. 'Sleep, I need sleep.' She rubbed her temples.

There was a pause.

'Why are you sitting so still? And why are you looking at me so pitifully? Stella Markoff wasn't really beheaded at the Villa Byzantine, was she?'

'She was. And I've got the newspaper cuttings to prove it.' Payne spoke in a weary voice. 'I've been putting them aside for you.'

Antonia gazed at him with slightly unfocused eyes. She tried to collect her thoughts. No, Hugh wasn't playing a game. He was not making things up. While she had been away, he had got involved in murder. Stella Markoff, the rather boring Bulgarian woman they had met at Kinderhook, had been beheaded ... Antonia remembered the curious apprehension she had felt at Melisande's party. Had she sensed something? A premonition ... Perhaps she was still on the plane, perhaps at long last she had fallen asleep and was dreaming?

She said, 'The police have no idea who the killer is?'

'At the moment Stella's daughter is their prime suspect.'

'The bloodthirsty girl?'

'The bloodthirsty girl.'

'Hasn't she got an alibi for the time of the murder?'

'No. She was arrested, but then the police released her. They don't seem to have enough evidence. I bumped into Melisande this morning and she called it an absolute

83

outrage that the girl hadn't been clapped in the cooler yet. Melisande is convinced Moon is the killer.'

'That strikes me as the most logical assumption,' said Antonia. 'Moon couldn't stand her mother. She made no attempt to conceal the fact. And didn't she go on about blood and beheadings?'

'She did. Yes. Well, maybe that's all there is to it. A sordid case of domestic violence, which has been unduly glorified by its neo-Byzantine setting.' Payne drew a thoughtful forefinger across his jaw. 'I am ashamed to admit it, but deep down, I harbour the rather illogical suspicion that the elusive Miss Hope has something to do with Stella's death.'

'Who is Miss Hope?'

'An owl-faced woman Vane was expecting on the day of the murder but who didn't turn up. Vane seemed to think that Stella and Miss Hope knew one another.'

'An owl-faced woman . . . Are you absolutely sure you are not making this whole thing up? I'll be very cross if you are,' Antonia warned. She sighed. 'You might as well tell me the whole story. You are clearly dying to.'


Some ten minutes later Antonia said, 'How utterly bizarre . . . You are right about the odd features . . . The scene of the crime in itself is rather unusual. Why at the Villa Byzantine? And why with a sword? Perhaps it was Tancred Vane who lured her to her death, wouldn't you say? He phones her and asks her to pay him a visit—'

'He claims he didn't. He wasn't at home at the time Stella was killed.'

'Have the police checked Tancred Vane's alibi?'

'They must have done. Would be scandalous if they haven't. Alibis of course can be faked. Shame I no longer know anyone at Scotland Yard. Not that I would want to, from what I hear. To think that at one time I had three Commissioners eating out of my hand.' Payne sighed. 'What would Tancred Vane's motive be?'

84

'The grandmother's letters and diaries,' Antonia said promptly. 'Didn't he covet them? I mean Stella's grandmother. I believe he tried to buy the letters and the diaries for fifty pounds?'

'Allegedly. That's what Moon said ... Royal biographers, I have no doubt, could be obsessive, cranky, ruthless and ultimately lethal. It did occur to me to ask Morland where the letters and the diaries were, yes, but he said he had no idea. In Stella's suitcase, he imagined.'

'Might be useful to know if they are still there.'

'I keep wondering about Morland. He had a guilty air that day, you know, when he came to see me. I am sure of it. Though it may have had nothing to do with Stella's death.'

'He wouldn't have come and asked you for help if he'd been guilty of Stella's death, would he? That might have been a ruse of course. D'you see Morland as a likely sword wielder?'

'No, I don't. Unless I've completely misread him.'

'Morland might turn out to be the high priest of some unspeakable suburban cult.' Antonia couldn't believe she'd said that. She was extremely tired. She couldn't think straight. She was suffering the effects of a bad jetlag.

She bit her lip but it was too late. She saw her husband nod gravely. Hugh needed *so* little encouragement.

'Why didn't I think of it? Morland's real intention was to have Stella immolated on the altar of the bloodthirsty pagan deity he happens to worship. Or rather he *and* Vane happen to worship. Stella possessed some unique characteristic that made her the perfect sacrificial victim, according to their book of magic lore. Stella had a sixth toe or an oyster-shaped birthmark on her—'

'You said Morland was determined to prove Moon's innocence, didn't you?'

'Determined is correct ... You don't want to hear about Stella's birthmark?'

'No,' Antonia said firmly. 'I don't think it's funny, Hugh.'

'You are right. It isn't. Gratuitous flippancy was something I used to disapprove of. Well, Morland keeps phoning, asking what progress I've made. He's become something of a pest. The other night he rang as the clock was chiming midnight. He just goes on and *on*. Morland seems terribly keen on doing the right thing. He's considering adopting Moon. He says he owes it to Stella. In my opinion, he's bidden adieu to good sense. I can't see any such adoption being a success, can you? He'll rue the day.'

'I agree. Moon will drive him mad.'

'Shall I mix you another g&t?'

'Yes, please. And then I *must* go to bed . . . Perhaps Moon is Morland's biological daughter, that would explain his keenness. Morland and Stella might have known each other for much longer than they made out,' Antonia mused. 'Their affair might have started years ago. He said he had been going on regular business trips to Bulgaria since 1993.'

'It seems more than likely that Moon was set up,' Payne said as he handed Antonia a glass.

'It's possible. No one drops monogrammed handkerchiefs made of fine silk beside dead bodies . . . Silly, really . . . Unless that was a double bluff,' Antonia said thoughtfully. 'Moon might have killed her mother and then planted the handkerchief, implicating herself in a deliberately absurd manner, knowing perfectly well she would be exonerated in due course. Do you think she's clever?'

'As clever as a bagful of monkeys. Is there anyone else we should consider?'

'Melisande has the best motive. Stella was her love rival. Melisande is an adroit sword wielder. She was Joan of Arc.' Antonia raised the glass to her lips. 'You noticed how expertly she handled the sword in those photos.'


As they were getting into bed, Antonia remembered something.

'Hugh, is there a *third* sister at Kinderhook? I saw a woman who looked very much like an older version of Melisande and Winifred.'

'You saw her too? So I didn't imagine her! I saw her a couple of days ago. When did you see her?'

'As we were coming back from the airport. We drove past Kinderhook. I pointed her out to you, but you didn't want to miss the cricket score on the radio. She was standing outside Kinderhook. She seemed on the point of going in. I believe she was unlocking the front door. She looked about eighty – stiff white hair – slightly stooped – long skirt – glasses?'

'Yes! Melisande was adamant that I was mistaken when I mentioned the woman. They *did* have an older sister once, but she's dead. Died a long time ago, apparently.'

'How very odd. Perhaps the third sister isn't dead . . .'

'The third sister may have escaped from some lunatic asylum and Melisande and Winifred may be hiding her. They would be reluctant to admit her existence. Like the brother in *The Cocktail Party*. I am sure you know your Eliot?'

'I don't.' Antonia yawned.

'Three of them, but they kept the third one very quiet.' Payne turned off the light. 'Wonder if it has anything to do with Stella's murder. What do you think?'

'Don't see how,' said Antonia. 'But it's very odd.'

'It's creepy. Goodnight, my love.'

'Goodnight.'

# 14

# Young and Innocent

At ten minutes to three in the morning their phone rang. With a groan, Major Payne reached out for it.

'Hello?'

'Who is that?'

He gave their phone number. What a bloody nuisance. It was probably some drunk misdialling.

'Is that you, Hugh?'

'Yes,' Payne said after a pause. 'It's Hugh Payne speaking.'

'Oh hi, Hugh. I wanted to say hi. Sorry, that's a totally dumb thing to say, but it's freezing cold here.'

'Who is it?' The next moment he knew. 'Good lord.' He raised himself on his elbow. '*Moon*?'

She sniffed. 'Yes.'

'Where are you? Not in jail, are you?'

'You wish!'

'Sorry. Where are you phoning from?'

'What does it matter where I'm phoning from? Why does everybody want to know where I am? Julia would be mad with me if she knew I was phoning you. That's James' sister. She'd be totally mad.'

'I wouldn't be in the least surprised. Do you know what time it is?'

'No. Julia is a bitch.'

'You shouldn't talk like that.'

'Julia's a bitch from hell. I don't like her. I hate her. Always asking me what I'm doing, where I'm going, why my eyes are red. She thinks I smoke pot. It doesn't occur to her I might be sad. That I might have been crying.'

'Do you smoke pot?' Really, Payne thought, I should ring off. It was some unearthly hour.

'You think I killed my mother, don't you?'

'I think you should be in bed.'

'Do you think that if a person truly defines themselves by dark actions, when their identity is actually shaped by sin, then their soul may indeed be beyond salvation?'

'I think you should be in bed,' he said again.

'It bothers me, questions like that.'

'What's the matter, Hugh?' Antonia asked, her voice muffled by the pillow.

'Sorry, darling,' Payne said.

'You called me darling!' Moon giggled. 'You are funny.'

'I wasn't talking to you. I was talking to my wife.' Payne gave an exasperated sigh and, putting his hand over the receiver, said, 'It's Moon.'

'Moon!'

'Why aren't you in bed?' Payne spoke into the receiver. 'Where are you?'

'Where am I? Outside the witches' house, if you want to know. I'm not a bit sleepy.'

'What witches?'

'The Witches of Kinderhook. I mean James' ex – Melisande – and her sister – what was her name? Winifred? Actually, she's the scarier of the two. She looks like the nice one, but she freaked me out at that party. It's the way she smiles—'

'Are you really standing outside Kinderhook?'

'Yep. I am talking to you on my mobile . . . Their house is dark . . . No. One window is very dimly lit. Whose room is that, I wonder? The witches may be casting midnight spells . . . Now I am turning round . . . Now I am looking at *your* house. I know which one it is. Your house is dark too.'

'Are you serious? Are you really in our street?'

89

'Totally. I am looking at your house at this very moment. I can't see much because your house is dark. *All* your windows are dark.'

'What's going on, Hugh?' Antonia turned on the bedside table lamp.

'You turned on the bedside light just now – or your wife did,' said Moon. 'It's an upstairs window. Doesn't that freak you out?'

Payne turned towards Antonia. 'Moon is actually in our street – looking at our house.'

'Will you give me a cup of coffee? I'm freezing,' Moon said. 'I have started walking towards your house . . . I am actually standing at your front door now . . . You've got a cool knocker. Is that a tiger's head? Or a lion's?'

'A lion's,' Payne said mechanically.

'Shall I ring or knock? I'll ring – is that OK? Now I am ringing your bell—'

Her phone went dead. The next moment they heard their front door bell ring.


As Major Payne donned his yellow dressing gown with its very vivid scarlet lining and lapels and put on his slippers, he wondered whether he would get one of those instantaneous flashes of intuitive certainty the moment he clapped eyes on her. Would he be able to say at once, *Yes, she killed her mother*? He knew it was an absurd idea, yet his heart beat fast in his chest. He turned on the lights and he started walking down the stairs. It was three in the morning, the clock on the wall told him.

He unchained the front door. Moon entered the hall and followed him into the drawing room.

'Were you asleep?' she asked.

'Well, yes. Does that surprise you? It's three in the morning.'

'Is it? I thought it was ten to midnight. Sorry. I thought you might be watching telly or reading a book or playing cards with your wife or something.' Her voice sounded hoarse and she was shivering. She sat down in one of the armchairs and crossed her legs.

Black spiky hair. They all seemed to have spiky hair nowadays. Lowish forehead, slightly oriental eyes, broad full mouth. Attractive, in a gamin kind of way. Her face was white, the dark eyes looked feverish. He couldn't see the pupils, but then his eyelids were still gummed by sleep. Had she taken some substance? Her lips were bluish. She must be frozen. She wore black mittens and the long black coat. The *shinel* with the bloodstains. Also jeans and box-fresh trainers with orange laces.

Did she look like a killer? Payne found his eyes straying to the girl's hands. What was it Morland had said? Moon had broken her wrist a couple of months ago, *ergo* she wouldn't have been able to lift a heavy samurai sword, let alone deliver a lethal blow with it.

There was something vulnerable about her – in spite of, or was it because of, her ultra-casual manner? Only sixteen – looked older, though. What a pedigree! Mother beheaded, father in jail . . .

'It's warm in here,' she said, looking round. 'Cool room.'

'Isn't that a contradiction in terms?'

'You are funny.' Suddenly she sat very still and fixed him with her dark eyes.

'I'll put the kettle on,' Payne said. 'You said coffee, right? Not tea?'

'No. I hate tea. Coffee. Black. Three sugars. I drink it mega strong – three or four spoonfuls, if it's instant.'

'Won't that be *too* strong?'

'I like it mega strong. You look sleepy.'

'I feel sleepy.'

'Did I wake you up?'

'I believe you did.'

'You've got stubble. You haven't shaved, have you?'

'*It's three in the morning.*'

As he walked towards the kitchen, Payne wondered if there was something particularly valuable in the drawing room that was small enough for her to pinch and drop into the *shinel*'s – no doubt – bottomless pockets. One of

Antonia's amber cats – the tiny but exceedingly precious Wedgwood vase – or perhaps his great uncle's silver snuff box?

Five past three. Payne didn't care for the appraising look she had given him. The girl's gaze seemed to hold a certain suggestive element . . . He was old enough to be her grandfather . . . He shouldn't have let her in . . . Most unwise. Might make all sorts of claims afterwards. Must try to get rid of her as soon as possible. Put her into a cab and despatch her back to Kensington . . . The tube closed at half past midnight . . . How long had the girl been standing in their street?

Heaven knew when he'd be able to get back to bed, if at all . . . He heard Antonia's voice coming from the drawing room. She'd come down and was talking to Moon.

Placing the three steaming cups and the tin of Fortnum & Mason's chocolate biscuits on the tray, he carried it gingerly to the drawing room.

Suddenly he was possessed by the not entirely rational conviction that Moon could not have murdered her mother, that suspecting her was a waste of time, that it was somewhere else they should be looking for the killer . . .

# 15

# Feast at Midnight

'Moon's been outside since half past two,' Antonia said brightly. She was wearing her blue dressing gown.

'Dangerous, being out so late,' Payne said, placing the tray on the low table between the sofa and Moon's chair. He stole a glance at the mantelpiece: his great uncle's snuff box was still there. 'A girl, on her own . . . London can be a dangerous place . . . How old are you exactly?'

'Fifteen and three months. D'you think I am very young?'

'I do. Morland said you were sixteen and a half.'

'Who's Morland? Do you call James Morland? That's funny! He is such a fool.' She laughed. 'He's fat. He needs to exercise. I hate fat men. He hates me. James and my mother were locked in a lewd and lascivious cohabitation . . .'

Payne glanced at the clock. 'Weren't you afraid to be out so late?'

'Nope.' Moon picked up her cup. 'God hasn't given me the spirit of fear, but of love and power and a sound mind. That's what they said at my boyfriend's church in Pennsylvania . . . My *ex*-boyfriend . . . See what I've got here.' She pushed her hand inside her *shinel* and drew out a piece of lead piping.

'An offensive weapon, eh?' Payne's eyebrow went up. 'If the police were to find it on you, you'd be in trouble.'

'It's for self-defence. It's dangerous to be out so late, you said that yourself. I'm already in trouble. The police think I killed my mother. I'm always in trouble.' Moon sighed. 'They kicked me out of my first school because they caught me bunning a zoot. Then I was kicked out of my second school.'

'Why was that?'

'That was because I used to write letters to teachers I liked. I know it makes me look like a psycho, but I'm totally normal. The police think I killed my mother. They never actually *said* it – I guess it's totally against the law to make accusations without any proof.'

'And what was your midnight vigil in aid of?' Payne sat down on the sofa beside Antonia.

'I'll tell you, but you must promise not to tell the two witches.'

'If by witches you mean Melisande and Winifred, that's not a very nice way to talk. They were very kind to you,' Antonia said.

'You drank all their Coke and ate most of their sand-wiches and cake,' Payne put in.

'You are right. I guess I'm not a very nice person. But there are things you don't know.'

'Oh? What things?' Antonia asked. She took a sip of coffee.

'Weird things. Crazy things. Things no normal person would think of doing.'

'Really? As bad as that?' Payne said. 'This sounds ter-ribly interesting.'

Moon nodded and smiled. She clearly enjoyed being the centre of attention. 'Yep. I know it is interesting. You'd never believe it if I told you what I know. Anyhow, I need to check something first. At the moment I have no real evidence, but I will get some very soon.'

Was she showing off – dramatizing herself? In all fair-ness, Payne reflected, Moon's behaviour was infinitely better than it had been at the party.

'I have a very good reason for doing what I do,' Moon went on. 'If you think I like to hang around outside

94

people's houses in the middle of the night and snoop, you are wrong. Anyway. I'll tell you about it some other time. Not now.'

Payne said, 'Is the "check" you mentioned in any way connected with your mother's death?'

'Of course it's connected. Why else should I want to put my life in danger?' Moon sniffed.

'Have a biscuit.'

'Thanks. OK. It was something my mother said. At first I didn't pay attention, my mother often talked a lot of rubbish, but then it suddenly came to me – what this was all about. It was kinda interesting – kinda weird – kinda spooky. So I decided perhaps my mother hadn't gone crazy, not completely crazy. I asked her to explain. At first she pretended she didn't want to, but then she told me the whole story. She was sucking up to me, I guess.'

'What did she say?' Payne asked.

'I see you are interested. You've done detective work, haven't you?'

'We specialize in strange cases,' Payne said, deliberately important.

'That's tope. This is a strange case, make no mistake.'

'What's tope?'

'Tope? Tope's tope. OK, cool.' She looked at Payne fixedly. 'Perhaps I could teach you American slang sometime?'

'I assume it's one of those portmanteau words one finds in Lewis Carroll. Like brillig and mimsy . . . What's tope a blend of? Dope and something else?'

'Yeah, dope's cool. I mean it means cool. The other word you want is tight, I guess, which also means cool. That's how you get tope. It sounds so dumb explaining what tope means . . . Can I have another biscuit? Thanks. I love words, actually. I mean, totally. When I haven't got anything better to do, I read the dictionary. When I'm not busy killing people.' She smiled. 'Do you know what "polymorphously perverse" means?'

'Why have you taken against Melisande and Winifred?'

'Actually I think Winifred is OK. Nothing against *her*. It's the other one that bugs me. Melisande. She keeps bothering James, you see. She keeps ringing him and stuff. He says she used to boss him around. He hates her now. Melisande is dangerous. If you only knew how dangerous.'

'In what way dangerous?'

'I guess she is crazy. I need to protect myself.' Moon produced the piece of piping once more.

'Give me that,' Payne ordered.

'If you really want it, you will have to take it from me by force. Only kidding. Here you are.' She handed him the lead piping. She was smiling. 'You can keep it, if you like.'

Antonia stirred uneasily. What were they doing, talking to a girl like this? In their house – in the small hours of the morning? It was unwise and foolish, to say the least. Moon might come up with all sorts of scurrilous allegations later on – if, for some reason, she happened to take against them. She might say she'd been abducted, held captive, enslaved, beaten, abused. The papers were full of such stories . . .

Moon took a sip of coffee, sniffed and said, 'I was planning to get into Kinderhook tonight.'

'That's called breaking and entering. It happens to be a criminal offence,' Payne pointed out.

'That handkerchief the police found,' Antonia said. 'You sure it wasn't yours?'

'You mean the hankie near my mother's body? Of course it wasn't mine. I've never used a hankie in my life.' She sounded completely truthful. 'The police are so dumb.' Moon sniffed again and her hand went up to her nose.

'Would you like a handkerchief?' Antonia offered.

'You're trying to catch me out now, aren't you?' The girl grinned. '*I've never used a handkerchief in my whole life.*'

'Hardly something you should be proud of. Here's a tissue . . . As a matter of fact, we do think something funny might be going on at Kinderhook. We believe there's a mysterious *third* sister,' Antonia said on an impulse. 'An elderly lady who looks like Melisande and Winifred. We've both seen her. But Melisande insists there are only two of them – that she has only one sister.'

A sudden rush of blood coloured the girl's cheeks. 'An old woman who looks like Melisande? So – so you've seen her? That means my mother was right! Was the old woman wearing glasses – what do you call those funny old-fashioned glasses that have no handles?'

'Pince-nez?' Payne frowned. 'The old woman did wear some kind of glasses. I wasn't near enough to see what they were . . . What do you mean, your mother was right? Right about what?' His heart had started beating fast. Something told him this was the breakthrough. 'Would you care to explain?'

# 16

# Death and the Maiden

She dreamt of Tancred that night.

Tancred was sitting on the ground beside a very turbulent river. He had been wounded. There was a nasty gash in his arm. Wild plants grew all around him and a sword that was stained red lay on the ground beside him, glistening unpleasantly in the sun.

She knelt beside him. 'Please, let me,' she said gently. 'This is the only way.' She then placed her hand over the wound in his arm. The moment she did, the blood flow was reduced to a mere trickle; a second later it stopped altogether. She didn't want to take any chances, so she kept her hand on the wound and eventually the gash closed and healed completely. There was no scar. No mark of any kind.

Tancred whispered, 'Thank you, Catherine. I knew only you could do it.'


'I am not in the least perturbed, I assure you, Inspector. Mr Vane told me that he'd given you my mobile number, so I have been expecting you to call. But I fear I can tell you very little. Very little indeed. Dear me! *Such* a terrible thing to happen! It only manages to prove the power of chaos theory. Poor Mr Vane. And that unfortunate woman!'

'We understand you met Mrs Stella Markoff at Mr Vane's house?'

'I believe I did. Yes. We exchanged a few polite words, there was no more to it than that. A pleasant woman, I thought. A little intense and nervous, but I attributed that to the fact that she didn't speak English very well. Or rather, she seemed to *think* she didn't speak English very well. Not the same thing! Astra's English was in fact excellent.'

'Miss Hope—'

'Now, I have met plenty of foreigners who *imagine* they speak good English, who have *quite* an inflated opinion of their command of the English language, without that being the case at all.'

'Miss Hope, if you don't mind—'

'No, not Astra! How silly of me!' She laughed exuberantly. 'I meant Stella. Stars, you know. She struck me as a most amiable kind of woman – if a trifle naive in her views on royalty. A bit too romantic and idealistic, perhaps? She seemed to hold the belief that royalty was needed to create an illusion of heaven on earth, of a jewel-encrusted land, of a Valhalla, no less!'

'Miss Hope, do you have any idea how long Mr Vane had known Mrs Markoff?'

'How long? Well, I only know what Tancred – that is Mr Vane – has told me. What was it – a *month*? I think he said a month, yes. What was that? Did he ever discuss Stella with me? No. Never! Mr Vane doesn't manifest the *slightest* inclination towards gossip.'

'Was Mrs Markoff's daughter ever mentioned?'

'Oh dear. She did have a little girl, didn't she?'

'Not so little.'

'That's so *tragic*. A mother dying in her prime – and such a fine, healthy-looking woman – leaving a young daughter behind – in a foreign country! No, the daughter was never mentioned.'

'Stella never referred to any problems she might have been having with her daughter?'

'Goodness me, no. We met only briefly, I told you. Like ships that pass in the night. We were destined to remain strangers, Inspector. *Were* there problems? I am sorry to hear that. Poor woman. Well, she seemed to have a gentleman friend in London, so all couldn't have been doom and gloom. She was actually planning to "tie the knot", as they say – *in the very near future*. In fact, I was given to understand that the marriage was imminent.'

'That day – the day Mrs Markoff was killed – you were expected sometime in the afternoon, only you didn't turn up? Is that correct?'

'That is correct, yes. I don't know what would have happened if I had, as you put it, "turned up". I am hopeless in extreme situations, completely futile, I fear. I tend to lose my head. Sorry – that was an unfortunate way of putting it.' Miss Hope lowered her voice. 'She *was* beheaded, wasn't she? I can't imagine myself becoming the victim of senseless slaughter, but then, who can? Can you? What kind of monster would want to do a thing like that? *Not* a Mussulman, I trust? They've been getting *such* bad press. It couldn't have been an *honour* killing, could it? As it happens, I am by no means a stranger to death—'

'What exactly do you mean by that?'

'I am eighty-four now, Inspector. Whatever opinions there may be to the contrary, I have reached the kind of age that has little to recommend it. Most of my dear friends and acquaintances have departed from this world and I am far from convinced they are in a better place. *Death is still working like a mole – and digs my grave at each remove*. The poet Herbert, you know. My second cousin, would you believe it, died earlier this year and she was *three years younger than me*. She seemed robust enough, but those, in my experience, are the very ones who go like a snap of the fingers.'

'I see what you mean . . . Well, that will be all, Miss Hope.'

'Don't you want to know why I didn't "turn up" at Mr Vane's house on the day Stella was killed? Aren't details in criminal cases considered to be *crucial*? I read somewhere that it is the details that bind *everything* together.'

'That will be all, Miss Hope—'

'This is what happened, Inspector. I was about to leave my house and was all ready to go when I got a phone call from my great niece – a dear girl, though not as predictable as I would have wished her to be – she lives in Richmond-on-Thames, did I say? Now, this is a somewhat delicate matter, Inspector, so I'd be grateful if—' .

'That's all right, Miss Hope. You don't need to tell me about your niece. That will be all,' he said in a firm voice. 'I don't suppose we'll need to bother you again, but if we do think of anything—'

'You will not hesitate to give me a ring? Yes, quite. Please do. Only too happy to assist the Law. Well, goodbye, Inspector.'

'Goodbye— Wait a minute.'

She laughed. 'You've already thought of something?'

'How did you know that Mrs Markoff had a gentleman friend in England?'

'How did I know? Goodness. Didn't I say?'

'No.'

'I am sure I did.'

'You didn't.'

'Well, it was like this. Stella seemed really excited that day – the day she came to Mr Vane's house – when the two of us met. She kept glancing at her hand, twiddling her fingers. She was wearing an engagement ring, I noticed at once. My eyesight, I am glad to report, remains excellent. I was presumptuous enough to comment on the ring's delicate beauty and elegance. That's when she told me. She blushed like a girl and said that she was engaged to be married and that her fiancé was in fact *English*.'

'I see.'

'I gave her my sincerest congratulations – which, when you come to think of it, in the light of what took place, makes the whole thing *so terribly tragic*.'


For a couple of moments she remained very still, looking down at the mobile phone in her hand. That had been a close shave. Never underestimate the police. A very little thing of course, a minor slip-up, but Inspector Davidson was clearly someone who paid attention to seemingly irrelevant details. What would have happened if she had failed to think fast, 'on her feet', as they said? Well, she could have pretended to be muddled. Miss Hope was an old lady and one expected old ladies to get muddled. She didn't think he would have started harbouring any serious suspicions about her, would he?

No. An old lady of eighty-four, brandishing a sword?

She laughed at the idea.

Of course it would be a different matter altogether if, for some reason, he got it into his head that she was *not* an old lady. She didn't think the inspector would go back to Tancred and start asking him questions – whether Tancred happened to overhear Miss Hope's conversation with Stella concerning Stella's engagement ring, forthcoming nuptials, husband-to-be, and so on.

Well, no such conversation had ever taken place.

She had made it up.

I don't exist, she thought. I am the phantom lady.

(She hadn't overdone the twittering, had she?)

# 17

# Devices and Desires

*I did not kill my mother,* Moon wrote, tears streaming down her face. *Nobody seems to believe me, but I didn't kill her. I didn't like her, but I didn't kill her. I guess I used to love her when I was a kid, when I was nine or ten and we lived in Bulgaria, but it all feels like a dream now. I remember her taking me mushroom-picking in the Vitosha mountain once. We saw a roe deer, which stood very still and stared back at us. My mother held me by the hand and whispered, 'She's going back to her child. Her child is waiting for her.' I know it's dumb, but thinking about the roe deer and her child and my hand in my mother's hand makes me want to cry.*

Tancred Vane sat in front of his computer, working on the historical background of the Prince Cyril biography.

*The Bulgarian monarchy was a casualty of the rival totalitarianisms of Hitler and Stalin in the 1940s. The independent Bulgarian kingdom was a product of the balance-of-power diplomacy that characterized the period preceding World War I. The practice of despatching dashing German princes to fashion modern kingdoms out of backward Balkan lands was fanciful, arrogant, even absurd; the motivation was a typically nineteenth-century blend of faith, greed and intrigue.*

He heard the front door bell ring. Miss Hope. Couldn't be anyone else. He glanced at his watch. On time, as

always. The feeling of vague unease returned. He remembered his dream. Stella Markoff trying to warn him –
pointing to her wired lips—

Nonsense!

The front door bell rang again. He clicked on Save and
rose.

The lodge, he reminded himself. He would have to
tackle the matter of the lodge.


'You, my dear boy, are devoted to your art to the exclusion
of everything else. That can be quite dangerous,' Miss
Hope said. She was watching Tancred Vane as he wrote
down something she had said earlier on. As usual they
were sitting in his study, she in the window seat, he beside
his desk.

'Dangerous?' Vane looked up with an abstracted smile.
'Surely not? In what way dangerous?'

'Well, you allow this biography to claim every ounce of
your attention, not to mention your energy. In consequence, I fear, you may be missing out on some of the
things that *really matter in life*.'

'You don't think the Prince Cyril biography matters?'

'No. To be perfectly honest, I don't. Why are you looking so very shocked? It's in the Bible. *Do not put your trust
in princes.* Ah, Tancredi, my Tancredi, perhaps one day I
will write a story about you!'

'What kind of story?'

'It will be the kind of story that moves like a series of
tapestries as it enacts the consequences of an artist's strange
encounter with his own being. It will be an extended meta-
phor for the separation, even estrangement, between the
artist and the conventional world, and the artist's sense of
an inner glory and necessity, which can be shirked *only* at
the expense of his true relationship to himself.'

'What do you mean? Sorry – all this is a bit above my
head.'

'Do you think you know yourself? Tell me truthfully!'
Her eyes were fixed on him.

'Do I know myself? Well, I think so, yes. Don't most people?'

'No! Of course they don't.'

'In that case perhaps I don't . . . I don't really know.'

'I was once told that I had no idea what I was really like, that I hid my feelings even from myself. It was even suggested that there was a great wild forest within me, of which I was not aware.'

'A forest?' Miss Hope, Vane decided, was in a decidedly fanciful mood today. He was not in the least interested in the wild forest inside her, honestly, though of course he wouldn't dream of saying so. It wouldn't do to hurt the old girl's feelings.

'*As the river flows to the ocean, my soul shall flow to thine,*' she murmured. 'For some reason I am haunted by these lines.'

'Shall we continue? You started telling me about the fancy dress party at the lodge?'

'Oh dear!' Miss Hope threw up her hands in a gesture of mock despair. 'From the sublime to the ridiculous! Very well, Tancred. You shall have your fancy dress party if that's what you want. I remember it was crazy weather for January. A sudden balmy spell had swept a froth of showers and the fresh breezes of April into Sofia in the dead of winter . . . The fancy dress party was Cyril's idea.'

'Was Prince Cyril a good host?'

'He was a terrible host. He liked to say tactless and embarrassing things to people. But there were *always* a lot of guests at the lodge. Some people don't mind being insulted and discomfited, I suppose, so long as it is a prince of the blood who does the insulting.'

'What was the lodge like?' Tancred asked. He had a particular reason to want to know about the lodge.

'It was made of creamy-coloured limestone and had a shiny, rather intricate, steel-trimmed art nouveau canopy. A most enchanting building . . . You look as though you want to ask something?'

'N-no – nothing.' He couldn't bring himself to say it.

105

'Are you sure? You have a secretive mouth, you know. Cyril's fancy dress party was not of the ordinary kind. Everybody had to impersonate a character from fiction and had to behave consistently all the time, and at the end of the party a specially selected jury had to decide who or what one's character was. The person who was voted to have acted his or her character with the greatest conviction got a prize.'

'What kind of a prize?'

'A box of cigars for the men, a box of the finest chocolate creams for the ladies. I don't need to tell you that there existed among Prince Cyril's entourage a *tendresse* for all things Teutonic. So, unsurprisingly, we had several Brünnhildes and Nibelungen and half a dozen Siegfrieds.'

'What character did *you* dress up as?'

Miss Hope's lips hovered on the edge of a smile. It was as if she knew some strange secret, which she would almost, but never wholly, divulge. 'Nannies don't dress up, Tancred. But you might be amused to know I was made to recite a funny English poem! On account of my extreme youth, no doubt. So I recited "The Young Lady of Clare". Do you know it? No?' Miss Hope clasped her hands on her lap and cleared her throat.

*'There was a Young Lady of Clare, Who was sadly pursued by a bear; When she found she was tired, she abruptly—'*

She looked at him. 'Can you guess what it was the Lady of Clare did?'

'Retired?' Tancred suggested. 'Perspired?'

'*Expired*, Tancred. She expired! That unfortunate Lady of Clare! Edward Lear, I think. Well, it was at that very same party that Cyril decided to make me his confidante. Till then he'd treated me with amiable indifference. Oh, he was so unpredictable!'

'What was it he confided in you?'

'Well, he started by telling me that he preferred bad weather to good weather. If he woke up in the morning and saw it was grey and drizzly outside, he felt reassured that life would go on for ever. Sunny days, on the other hand, made him want to hide under the covers and think of dying.'

'Think of dying! How very strange.'

'He was a very strange character. Prince Cyril had an "innate" dislike of wrapping paper. He called it "my peculiar animus". He was sick at the mere sight of it! An "inexplicable" feeling surfaced within him, he said. For that reason he found Christmas particularly trying.'

'I assume presents were given to him unwrapped?'

'They were. It eliminated the element of surprise completely. Oh, his oddities were endless! In his study he kept different seals to suit his different moods. I remember one particular occasion when the Montenegrin chargé d'affaires and various other dignitaries stood round, waiting for him to seal a document. "Has anyone seen my mellow seal?" Cyril asked. But the mellow seal seemed to have vanished into thin air.'

'What happened?'

'Cyril went on smiling – he was in a mellow mood, you see – but then he became furious – which was fortunate since he decided to use his "furious" seal instead, after which he calmed down. There was a collective sigh of relief, I remember, like a gust of wind.'

'I wonder if he was a manic-depressive – bipolar?'

'He used to say things like, "My pain is crushing when I suffer, but my joy, when I'm happy, is also inexpressible." He said it in German, of course. Well, that night – the night of the fancy dress party – he told me how much he enjoyed racing up and down the streets of Sofia in his Lagonda Rapier and the high price he had paid for his pursuit of speed records when his beloved dog Fritzie was catapulted out of the car and killed!'

Tancred Vane looked up slowly. 'I thought you said before his beloved dog's name was Sascha?'

'Sascha was Prince Cyril's *second* beloved dog, Tancred. He had *two* dogs.' Miss Hope's eyes remained steady. 'Prince Cyril then spoke to me about international affairs and the possibility of war, which he gave every impression of relishing. He seemed convinced of a German victory! I must say his abstractions and absolutes had an unmistakably Teutonic stiffness about them.' She adjusted her pincenez. 'What happened next took me completely by surprise, it was so terribly sudden.'

'What happened?'

'He started whispering in my ear that he felt the irresistible urge to make love to me. He said fresh young girls were his passion, that my smooth cheeks drove him to distraction, words to that effect. Again he spoke in German. I misunderstood him completely – oh dear! I was so naive, so innocent!' Miss Hope gave a girlish laugh.

'You mean – Prince Cyril made a pass at you?'

'Well, yes, since you choose to put it like that.'

'What did you do?'

'I said – oh, what was it? No, I can't remember. I am so sorry, Tancred . . . I must look up my diary notes . . . Call me a muddle-headed old ass, but I can't remember a thing! Don't look so disappointed, it's not the end of the world.' Her hands continued to be clasped on her lap, but now she was looking out of the window. There was a pause. 'Tell me, Tancred, how would you feel if this project of yours were to be snatched away from you?'

'What do you mean, snatched away?'

'If you were to learn that, for some reason, you couldn't go on writing this silly biography? Would you be upset?'

'Would I be upset if—?' He broke off. Had he misheard? Had she said 'this silly biography'? 'Of course I would be upset! Terribly upset!'

She did look odd today and no mistake! The way she sat, something taut about her, like a spring. Her pince-nez kept catching the sun and flashing its reflection back at him.

'You haven't heard of someone making trouble, have you? Of someone trying to prevent the biography from being published?' Tancred said in an anxious voice. 'Cyril's nephew – King Simeon – or some of the other living Coburgs? I haven't heard anything from the Fleur-de-Lis Press. I am sure they would have informed me if there'd been a problem.'

She smiled indulgently. 'Of course they would have. The estimable Fleur-de-Lis Press would have been the first to know, should anyone have started muddying the waters. Their legal department would have got in touch with you without fail. No, nothing of the sort. Nothing as literal as that.'

'Thank God . . . What do you mean "nothing as literal"?'

'I have been trying to understand you better, Tancred, to see what kind of person you are . . . What your priorities are . . . *Life is so short* . . . I care an awful lot about you, you know.'

'I care about you too,' he said after a pause.

'Do you, Tancred? Do you really? My dear boy.' She rose slowly from her seat. Her shoulders, he noticed, were less hunched than before. 'That is what I always thought, but it's good to hear the actual words spoken out. I knew it from the very start of our association. I knew we were *meant* to be together, work together, exist together, the very moment I saw your photograph, the very moment I heard your name!'

'Really? What photograph?'

'Oh Tancred, you have moved the flowers from left to *right*.' She pointed with her forefinger.

'Have I?'

'Yes!'

Her face had gone pink. He didn't see what the fuss was about, but she seemed absolutely delighted by this discovery. She meant the little bronze vase with the petunias she had brought him during her previous visit – pale mauve with deep red complicated veins that made them look like a medical diagram of human lungs.

He didn't know why he chose that particular moment to tell her about the lodge.

# 18

# Light Thickens

'I saw something on the internet last night. You know I've been looking for information on the internet as well? I told you, didn't I?'

'No, you didn't. Information – you mean information about Prince Cyril?' She resumed her seat beside the window.

'Yes. I told you sources were scarce. King Simeon's office sent a very stiff letter saying he was reluctant to discuss his late uncle with anyone. Anyhow. I've been looking for information on the internet and last night I found something.'

'What did you find?' She didn't sound particularly interested.

'It was an architectural enthusiast's website. Some Italian – lives in Siena – who seems to be a nut about royal residences. He displays pictures, photos, plans, drawings of European royal palaces, past and present, and so on. There was a picture and a plan of the royal palace in Sofia. A very detailed plan.'

'I have little patience with detailed plans,' she said.

'This Italian had got hold of the original plan somehow, that goes back to the time the palace was first built in the 1880s – after Bulgaria's liberation from Turkish rule in 1878. The palace was built for Bulgaria's first German prince, Alexander Battenberg.'

'I am perfectly familiar with the historical facts, Tancred.' Miss Hope was looking out of the window, shading her eyes.

'The palace is very small. I mean, as royal palaces go.'

'Bulgaria is a very small country, Tancred. Once, centuries ago, it was the largest kingdom in the Balkans, but then it became the smallest. It has had a turbulent history. The Berlin treaty was particularly unfair to it.'

'The royal palace in Sofia is no larger than a Viennese *rentier*'s residence, someone wrote.'

'That is quite true. Here we go again, exchanging bits of not very interesting information, instead of which we could have been talking about things that really matter!' She was looking at him with great intensity. 'That's *exactly* the point I wanted to make earlier on, Tancred. We could be talking about things that *matter*.'

'The plan shows the main building and the gardens around it – but it shows no lodge.'

Miss Hope bowed her head slightly. 'What do you mean, no lodge?'

'There are stables and a pavilion or two and a pagoda and what looks like a small ornamental lake, but there is no sign of a lodge.'

'*Where thou lodgest, I will lodge,*' she murmured.

I've started slipping up, she thought calmly.

It was inevitable that sooner or later she'd make a mistake. She had always known that, so she was not particularly surprised. Inspector Davidson had caught her out first – then she had given the dog a different name – and now this ridiculous absence of a lodge. Keep your head, she told herself and felt the irresistible urge to laugh out loud. *Keep your head*. Had Stella ever been given the same advice?

'Let me show you the plan.' She saw Tancred, silly boy, pick up a sheet from his desk and half rise from his chair.

She put up her hand. 'No need. I believe you. I believe you unconditionally. I know you are incapable of telling a lie. Your noble nature would never allow it. Well, what can I say?' She gave a contemptuous shrug. 'It is no doubt some busybody's awkward drawing. I am sure this so-called "plan" you have in your possession will be conspicuous for the absence of a lodge . . . And what does the absence of a lodge signify to you?'

'What does it signify? Why – don't you see? The lodge has played such an important part in your narrative. That is where Prince Cyril and Victoria lived – that's where Victoria went when she was upset by Giovanna – the party you just described took place at the lodge – it was at the lodge where Prince Cyril made a pass at you!'

'Of course I see. My dear boy! I see *perfectly*. The question now is, *who* do you believe? Me – or some espresso-sipping Sienese?'

'It strikes me as extremely odd that—'

'I hope, Tancred, you are not suggesting that I make things up? That all this time I have been perpetrating some infernal swindle?' Miss Hope seemed greatly amused by the idea. She gazed out of the window. The next moment her expression changed. She gave a little gasp and pulled the blind down.

'What's the matter?'

'Tancred, there is a man outside!'

'What man?'

'He's coming up the steps . . . He is about to ring the front door bell.' Her voice quavered slightly. She took off her pince-nez and placed it on the little table beside the window seat. 'Now listen very carefully, Tancred. I wouldn't open the door if I were you. *Please, don't open the door*. Or if you do, on no account allow this man into the house. Something terrible is going to happen if you let him inside the house.'

# 19

# Mrs Henderson

'You have been exceedingly kind, Miss Darcy.'

'Not at all. I didn't wake you up when I phoned this morning, did I?'

'You didn't. Don't worry. I do tend to wake up awfully early. To tell you the truth I was not aware that she wasn't in her room. I had no idea that she'd sneaked out last night either. Moon can be terribly argumentative, so I try not to appear prying or spying. Sometimes I find myself within an ace of giving her a clip on the ear, but of course that would never do.' Julia Henderson shook her head. 'She'd probably try to knock me down.'

'Do you really think she would? Is she violent?'

'I think she can be. Yes. She's certainly thrown things at her late mother – and at poor James. Do help yourself to some coffee.'

'Well, I intended to take a look at Brompton Oratory,' Antonia elaborated untruthfully. The real reason for her visit was to try to learn more about Stella and the events of the fatal day. 'I then suddenly realized I was standing in your road. So I decided to pay you a visit. Hope you don't mind.'

'Not at all. It's a pleasure to have you,' said Julia Henderson graciously and she urged Antonia to have a slice of Madeira cake.

Antonia glanced round the room. It was light, unclut-
tered and pleasantly furnished in a minimalist way. Julia
Henderson looked a very pleasant kind of woman too – late
forties, early fifties, unobtrusively smart in pastel-coloured
cashmere, open weather-beaten face, short brown hair, next
to no make-up, forthright, sensible, no-nonsense manner.

Did she play golf? Antonia had seen an array of golf
clubs in the hall. They might have belonged to Julia's late
or former husband – Antonia was assuming Julia was
either widowed or divorced. No, the clubs all looked as
though they were in regular use.

Strong sunburnt wrist, Antonia thought as she watched
her hostess pick up the coffee pot. Likes to spend time in
the open. Julia's handshake had been extremely firm. Yes,
without doubt her hostess was the golfer.

Julia had been in the process of writing a cheque. She
sighed, waving her gold-topped pen. 'Bills! They expect
me to subtract a thousand pounds from my little capital at
a moment's notice.'

'I know the feeling,' Antonia said with a smile.

'I am sure you don't. I am ready to bet you are
much more prudent and disciplined than I shall ever be. I
live at the top of my income, you see. I hate economizing.
I am in constant dread of ruin. I keep borrowing money
from poor James—' Suddenly realizing she was talking to
a perfect stranger, she broke off and apologized for being
a bore.

She had mentioned a committee meeting she needed to
attend, but that wasn't till five in the afternoon, so Miss
Darcy needn't worry. She seemed a well-balanced, easy-
going woman, with only the slightest hint that she might
be formidable if she chose. Moon had suggested Julia was
a prying dragon. She had called her a 'bitch from hell'.
Teenage angst, Antonia thought. Probably more than mere
angst. Moon, she imagined, took drugs. Drugs made you
paranoid.

Julia Henderson asked if Antonia's interest in Brompton
Oratory was purely aesthetic. The implied question was

whether Antonia might not have been seeking some form of spiritual solace.

'It's a lovely place . . . Actually, I needed to make some notes for a book. I am thinking of setting a scene in a Catholic church.'

'Murder in the cathedral? *Of course*. Murder mysteries. Moon said you were a writer. I didn't *quite* believe it at first. She is a terrible liar, you know, but James confirmed it. I intend to order your books from the library. I never have any time for reading, I'm afraid – always too much to do – but I promise I will read your books. It always makes such a difference when one knows the author!'

'Do you think so?' Antonia wondered why knowing the author should make such a difference to one's reading habits, but that seemed to be the generally held view. It was frequently suggested that readers felt inspired to buy a book or take it out of the library if they 'knew' the author. Something in that. Her publisher wouldn't be so keen on her going on signing tours if they didn't believe more copies would be shifted off the shelves that way . . .

'It is a great relief to know that Moon was in safe hands,' Julia was saying. 'Otherwise, I'd have been wondering what she might have got up to. Who she'd been with and so on. So would poor James. Well, she is the kind of girl who could have been *anywhere*.'

Antonia smiled. 'Wouldn't you have believed her if she told you she had been with us?'

'No, not really. She keeps doing things she shouldn't. While her mother was alive, there was always some kind of trouble – including an attempt at joyriding in James' car! James caught her moments after she had managed to pick the car door lock and he frog-marched her back to the flat. She hated him for that. She said some awful things to him. I believe she kicked him.'

Antonia asked if Moon could drive.

'She says she can. It was her American boyfriend who taught her to drive, so heaven help us. No licence of course. She's not old enough for a licence. Actually, I saw the *A–Z* in her room, so she might have gone to

Hampstead last night in James' *old* car,' Julia said thoughtfully. 'The "uncool" one. The one he intends to sell.'

'She told us she hitched a lift from someone . . . We put her in a taxi this morning.'

'That was extremely kind of you.'

'You'd better check – or perhaps your brother – otherwise you may get a call from the police if the car is found abandoned somewhere.'

'Yes. We will check.' Julia took a sip of coffee. 'I must say things aren't as bad as they were. Not so long ago Moon was either openly hostile to poor James – or she made a big show of ignoring him. Rolling up her eyes each time he said something she deemed "dumb" and so on. He was clearly on the "enemy" side, you see – bracketed with her mother whom Moon seemed to regard as the ultimate foe!'

'But the situation's changed since her mother died?'

'Oh, yes. There's been a marked improvement. I believe in being fair. Moon's become more manageable – more sociable – no question about it. A little more subdued, if that were possible – or should I say less exuberant? She's started talking to James – mainly complaining about me.'

'Where is she now?'

'James took her to the zoo. Not *my* idea of a fun afternoon.'

'You would rather be on the links, playing a round of golf, I suppose?'

'Well, yes. How did you—? Oh, it's the golf clubs in the hall – of course! I keep forgetting you are something of a detective. I suppose you've got to be observant to be able to write detective stories? I enjoy playing golf every now and then, but I am not what you'd call a lethal golfer. I must admit I am not terribly good at it . . . I thought Moon would sneer when James suggested the zoo, but she seemed quite excited. She said the zoo would be "crunk" – heaven knows what that means. She employs the most abstruse argot sometimes.'

One of Hugh's portmanteau words, Antonia thought, and she ventured a guess. 'Crazy and drunk?'

'Sorry?'

116

'Crunk – a blend of crazy and drunk. That's what I imagine it is. I may be wrong of course.' Must ask Hugh, Antonia thought.

'It made James laugh. It was good to see them like that. They looked happy together, like father and daughter.' Something about the way Julia Henderson said this made Antonia wonder whether she had really relished the sight. 'They were laughing and joking – she was teasing him and he seemed to like it.'

'Is she his daughter, do you think? I mean his real daughter? I hope you don't mind my asking.'

'Well, the idea did occur to me. I even persuaded myself there was a resemblance between them. Do you think there's a resemblance? I imagined Moon's nose was the same shape as James'.'

'Does your brother have his own children?'

'James has a son and a daughter. But they haven't been in touch for the last few years. Some argument over money. James has a lot of money, you see—' She broke off.

Her expression changed.

Julia depended on her brother financially, that much was clear to Antonia. A second marriage – the marriage to Stella – might have absorbed a fair amount of James Morland's capital. Stella might have insisted on donating money to the Bulgarian Monarchist Party or the Bulgarian Poets' Association or some other worthy cause. There wouldn't have been much left for Julia . . .

Stella's death must have come as a relief . . .

Julia—?

(Should one really suspect *everybody*?)

# 20

# Sorry, Wrong Number

'What did you make of Stella?' Antonia asked. 'Did you like her?'

'No, not particularly, if I have to be perfectly honest. I found her irritating – intrusive. She came over to talk to me each time something went wrong between her and Moon. She didn't seem to realize that I could be busy. She was entirely wrapped up in herself. She tended *not* to listen when I talked, but she expected me to give up whatever I was doing and pay very close attention to her jeremiads.'

'She complained about Moon?'

'Yes. She frequently felt hurt by her daughter. Moon couldn't talk to her save with a gibe and sneer. Moon kept calling her the most offensive names – "lardy lump" – "brainless *baba*" – clearly terrible insults for a woman who regarded herself as the most marriageable of belles! Moon had jeered at her for "picking up" James. She had suggested her mother was "gagging for it". She had referred to her poetry as "shit". And so on and so forth. Terrible bore.'

'How did Stella meet your brother?' Antonia asked.

'It was Moon who brought them together. That, at any rate, was Stella's version of the event. James had lost his way in Sofia where he was on a business trip. He bumped into Moon and asked for directions and she took him to the cafe where her mother had been waiting for her. Some such rigmarole.' Julia waved a dismissive hand. 'You'd met Stella, hadn't you?'

'Yes. At Melisande's party.'

'Stella confided her most intimate fears in me. Things I didn't really want to hear.' Julia grimaced. 'She seemed to find poor James *terriblement anglais* and it bothered her. No, she didn't quite put it like that. A little too reserved, a little too "English", was what she said. She moved into his flat at his suggestion, but nothing much actually *happened* between them, she said. No "real intimacy". She seemed to have mixed feelings about it. She seemed to find James' restraint at once flattering and frustrating.'

'Is that how she put it?'

'Not quite. That was my interpretation. Stella talked a lot about "respect" and "consideration" and how "gentlemanly" James was, but at the same time she made it clear she'd rather things were a little bit more – you know. She was maddeningly prudish. She went on about the importance of "personal warmth" and "affection" and "passion" in one's life. She was particularly emphatic about "passion". Passion was "essential" for her poetry.'

'I expect she was looking forward to the wedding?'

'She was. She was excited about it, but she was also worried that James might change his mind and abandon her at the altar. She didn't believe she could survive the humiliation and the pain, she said. She feared that her daughter might do something that would blight her chances of conjugal bliss for ever. There were other things as well.' Julia frowned. 'Stella seemed to have developed some peculiar phobia concerning Melisande – but she never explained exactly what it was all about.'

'She didn't drop any hints?'

'No. She was probably afraid I might spill the beans to Melisande . . . Morbid undercurrents seemed to be part of Stella's nature. She went on moody, listless rambles in Kensington Gardens. She seemed prone to tormenting anxieties of all sorts. On one occasion she actually said, "Oh, how good I am at finding things to worry about!" She seemed to believe she had cancer.'

'Oh yes. She suspected she had a tumour on the brain. She said she was afraid of having a scan.'

'Once or twice she told me it would be so much better for everybody if she ended her life. Her exact words, if I remember correctly, were, "Sometimes death comes not as an enemy but as a friend."'

'Do you think she might have been contemplating suicide?' Antonia wondered if that could be a possible answer. *The assisted suicide solution.* Stella might have been unable to bring herself to do the deed and got someone else to help her – *paid* them – people did do that sort of thing. Would the person have used a sword though? It was a very bizarre idea. And why do it at the Villa Byzantine?

'I didn't really believe she would kill herself. I thought it was nothing worse than flirting with self-destruction.'

'Did you by any chance see her the day she died?'

'No. But she'd talked to me the day *before*. She floated in, wearing swirling white crepe, high-necked, with scattered crystal new moons and stars. It was beyond ghastly. Try to imagine an inflated Titania. I tried not to look shocked. It was going to be her wedding dress, she said. She expected me to admire it – which I did.'

'So she was in a good mood?'

'Yes! She'd thought of a way of making her peace with Moon, she said. She and Moon had had their first decent conversation in ages and that had made her very happy. She told me she had a plan.'

'What kind of a plan?'

Julia shook her head and said she had no idea. Stella had been terribly mysterious about it. 'I am afraid I was not paying much attention. I was in a hurry. I was about to go out. I got the impression that the plan involved Stella doing something Moon was extremely keen on. She didn't say what it was, but I think she hinted that there was risk involved.'

'Risk?'

'Yes. Some irregularity.' Julia waved her hand. 'Oh, it was all terribly garbled.'

Suddenly Antonia had a very clear idea in her head as to what Stella had been planning to do. Her heart beat fast. She felt certain she was right.

'Did Stella talk about her visits to the Villa Byzantine?'

'About her sessions with the royal biographer fellow? She did. I must admit I was never particularly interested. I believe something happened there, at the Villa Byzantine, which unsettled her – some woman she had met at Vane's house, who wasn't who she claimed.'

Soon after, Antonia rose to her feet.

'No, no, it's been no trouble at all, Miss Darcy. I enjoyed our chat. You must come again. I will tell Moon that you called, or would you rather I didn't?'

'That's all right. Give her my regards.'

They walked out into the hall.

'I will. You aren't driving, are you?'

'No. I came by tube. I'd like to go for a walk in Kensington Gardens . . . Such a pleasant day, isn't it?'

The telephone rang and Julia picked it up. She grimaced apologetically at Antonia.

'Julia Henderson speaking. No, this is not the Corrida Hotel— Oh, *you* are the Corrida Hotel! Sorry!' She laughed. 'Yes? Problem over a credit card? Whose card? What are you talking about? Sorry, you must have got the wrong number. I have never stayed at the Corrida Hotel in my life—'

Antonia stood gazing idly at a framed photograph that was on the little round table beside the telephone.

'Oh, that's my brother! James Morland is my brother. Sorry. His phone number is the same as mine but for the last digit. Zero instead of nine. Yes. My number ends in nine, his in zero.' She rolled her eyes at Antonia. 'My brother lives next door. He is out at the moment. I will tell him to get in touch with you the moment he comes back.' She put down the receiver. 'So sorry. This happens all the time. I get phone calls from people who want to speak to James. Same number but for the last digit. Well, he's moving out next month, so I hope there won't be many more calls.'

121

'Moving out?'

'Yes. He's bought a place in Chelsea. A small Regency house. He's intent on playing father to Moon.' Julia Henderson sighed. 'He told me he wanted to devote himself to Moon's upbringing and education. He talks about hiring private tutors and so on. Apparently she is terribly clever. Did you find her clever?'

'As clever as a bag of ferrets. That's how my husband put it ... That's you in the photograph, isn't it?' Antonia pointed. 'I am always fascinated by people who take golf seriously. Especially women.'

'Oh dear. My Surrey past is catching up with me. Don't I look ridiculous in that little cap? Actually I don't take golf at all seriously. I don't know why I keep that silly photo there. I've been meaning to put it away.'

The photograph showed a somewhat younger Julia Henderson wearing a golfing outfit, holding a golf club aloft and beaming triumphantly at the camera.

Underneath her name in careful script was written: *Ladies County Golf Champion 1999.*

# 21

# Up at the Villa

Major Payne was immediately struck by how isolated the Villa Byzantine was, how secluded the lane along which he was walking. Its high banks, crowned by massive over-hanging trees and ferns, made it a dark tunnel by night and, he had no doubt, a sylvan unfrequented corridor by day.

He swung his rolled-up umbrella as he strode purpose-fully in the direction of the house. Around him autumn leaves were being whipped up, swirled and scattered by the wind—

*Skirling and whirling, the leaves are alive!*
*Driven by Death in a devilish dance!*

He wished he weren't so well crammed with English literature! He had parked his car outside the tunnel. When the strange house loomed before him he whistled. He'd never seen anything like it before.

He stopped and stared.

He was put in mind of a fantastic growth – he might have been standing in front of some giant poison mushroom!

Horizontal orange-red and yellow stripes – heavy use of stucco – arched windows – a domed roof. He was put in mind of Edward James and his surreal piles Monkton House and Las Pozas. It was that kind of house. Surreal. Bizarre. The Villa Byzantine.

He thought of Sir Christopher Wren's epitaph – *Si monumentum requiris, circumspice*. If you wish to recall me, look around you. Did the Villa Byzantine reveal anything about Tancred Vane?

A well-to-do bachelor of irreproachable if somewhat florid taste, leading a life of blameless bookishness. A collector of rare objects. The kind of chap who notices at once if his silver has become tarnished or his precious leather-bound volumes and rosewood tables too exposed to the glare of daylight.

Or would he turn out to be something more sinister? A connoisseur of the recherché, an aficionado of the fantastic? Like one of those bachelors in L. P. Hartley's short stories . . .

As he walked towards the front door, Payne happened to glance up at one of the first-floor windows. He saw a white hand pull down a parchment-coloured blind with what he imagined to be a frantic gesture. A ring flashed in the sun—

Payne rang the front door bell. A couple of moments later he rang again. The utter silence that met his ear had the quality of an animal's freezing in its burrow. He was aware of great tension – or was the tension inside him? Eventually he heard cautious footsteps coming down the stairs, which creaked a little.

The door opened tentatively and a face appeared. A youngish man's face – well-bred, if indeterminate, features – receding chin – flushed – indecisive. What was that the chap was wearing? *Not* a bow-tie? Major Payne had an aversion to bow-ties. Instinctively distrusted bow-tie wearers.

'Mr Vane?'

'Yes?'

'My name is Payne.' Silly that their names should rhyme.

'Yes?'

'We haven't met, but I was wondering whether I could have a word with you?'

'What about?' Tancred Vane spoke in an abrupt manner, which, Major Payne felt at once, did not come naturally to him.

Tancred Vane's eyes travelled over the intruder's immaculately knotted regimental tie, his double-breasted blazer with its silver buttons, his sharply creased trousers, and came to rest on his perfectly polished brogues—

Payne saw his expression change – soften. It was almost as though the royal biographer had expected somebody else – somebody who looked as though they needed to be scared off—

Major Payne said, 'We have what is sometimes called an "acquaintance in common". A foreign lady. *Had.* She is, alas, no longer with us.'

'What foreign lady?'

'A Bulgarian lady.'

'You don't mean you knew—?'

'The tragic Stella Markoff. *Yes.*'

The door opened a crack wider and now Payne could see the royal biographer's left as well as his right hand. He wasn't wearing any rings. The hand which had pulled down the blind hadn't been his.

Vane was not alone. Could *she* be with him?

Vane's face had turned a deeper shade of pink. The next moment he shot a glance over his shoulder.

'What – what's this about?'

Vane's *sotto voce* clearly indicated he didn't want the person inside the house to hear what he was saying.

'I'd better put my cards on the table, Mr Vane. I believe it will make things simpler.' Payne lowered his voice. 'I am a private investigator.'

'You are a detective?' The biographer drew back a little.

'Yes. I would be grateful if you treated this as the most confidential of communications. A day or two before she was killed, Stella Markoff sought my professional advice,' Payne improvised. 'Mrs Markoff was extremely worried about a certain matter.'

'What matter?'

'It seems she met someone at your house—'

A sound came from inside the Villa Byzantine – a floorboard had creaked.

'—an elderly lady who introduced herself as Miss Hope.'

'Miss Hope?'

'Yes. Is Miss Hope a friend of yours?'

'Why do you want to know?'

'Is she here, by any chance? She is here, isn't she?'

After a moment's reflection, Vane nodded, then put his forefinger across his lips, indicating that on no account should Payne go on. The royal biographer's face was now the colour of beetroot.

'*I see.*' Payne's upper lip was so stiff, it might have been injected with Novocaine.

He found himself reconstructing the scene that had taken place moments before he had rung the front door bell.

She had been looking out of the window. She had seen his approach. She had recognized him. She had panicked. She had pulled down the blind. She feared he would recognize *her*. She had begged Vane not to let him inside the house. She might have said Payne was dangerous – that he was a criminal or a lunatic. That would account for Vane's initial hostility.

Major Payne decided to take the bull by the horns.

'I don't suppose you are familiar with the actress Melisande Chevret?'

# 22

# Phantom Lady

'I scribbled my phone number on a piece of paper and slipped it to him,' he told his aunt some forty-five minutes later as she was buttering a second crumpet for him.

'Most enterprising of you. You think he'll ring you?'

'I believe so, yes.' Payne glanced at his watch. 'As soon as he gets rid of her. The moment I said "Melisande Chevret", his eyes rounded – became as big as saucers. The name seemed to strike a chord at once. He gave several nods when I put an imaginary phone to my ear and mimed dialling a number.'

'How perfectly extraordinary. What d'you think has been going on, Hughie?'

Payne looked up at the ceiling. *'Weird things. Crazy things. Things no normal person would do.* That is how Stella's daughter put it.'

'Surely, Hughie, you can't take anything that gel says seriously? From what you've told me, she's not to be trusted one little bit.'

'In this particular instance,' Payne said thoughtfully, 'I am prepared to give Moon a chance.'

'You don't think the gel chopped her mother's head off?'

'She might have done, but, as it happens, I don't think she did.'

'You suspect Miss Hope?'

127

'I suspect Miss Hope, though of course no such person as "Miss Hope" exists. I believe that Miss Hope is in fact the actress Melisande Chevret.'

'Heaven knows I am no expert, but I bet you'll find in the end that the gel did do it after all.'

'Well, you may be right, darling. It may be her, as you say. I am doing my best to keep an open mind. As a matter of fact, I haven't counted anybody out yet. Not even Tancred Vane. Or James Morland.'

'*The garden of live flowers*. I find I have started saying the first thing that pops into my head. Is that a sign of dotage?' Lady Grylls poured herself more tea. 'Are you comfortable in that chair? You don't think this room is too narrow?'

'No, not at all. It's comfortable. It's cosy.'

'I must admit I feel a little cramped up here, Hughie. I know I wanted a house in St John's Wood more than anything in the world, but now that I've got it, I find myself regretting my decision. Last night I dreamt I went to Chalfont again.'

'You aren't serious. After everything you said!'

'I find this place too small and stuffy, Hughie.'

'You used to find Chalfont too big and draughty.'

'Do you think it's perverse of me?'

'As a matter of fact I do, darling. Terribly perverse.'

'You don't think I could change my mind and buy Chalfont back?'

'No. Too late. The Russians won't have it. They'll laugh at you – or shoot you. Given how hard you bargained and how you bullied them and how you drove them mad and everything. You got *exactly* the price you wanted.'

'They can have their filthy money back, down to the last rouble.'

'That would be a ridiculously large amount of roubles. Actually, they paid you in pounds. What garden of live flowers? Is that Genet? No, I'm thinking of *Our Lady of the Flowers*.'

'It's in *Alice*, actually. To find the Red Queen, Alice had to go *in the most unlikely direction*. It all happens in the garden of live flowers,' Lady Grylls explained, 'and that's how detectives in detective stories try to find the killer, I believe? I expect Antonia's making pots of money out of her books?'

'No, not pots.'

'What's *Our Lady of the Flowers* about?'

'Male prison romances. Not for your tender eyes.'

'Must make a note to ask Provost to get it out of the library for me. Now then, back to *l'affaire* Stella. Let me see whether I've got this right.' Lady Grylls pushed her glasses up her nose. 'The dead woman's daughter told you that her mother was convinced that the old nanny she met at the Villa Byzantine was no other than Melisande Chevret in disguise?'

'That is correct.' Payne bit into a crumpet.

'Stella believed that Melisande took James Morland's desertion jolly badly, that she tipped over the edge. Stella feared she might be in danger. Stella imagined that Melisande might steal one of Tancred Vane's treasured possessions – or even kill Tancred Vane – and make it look as though Stella had done it?'

'Yes. Or that she herself might be killed.'

Lady Grylls observed that the late Stella appeared to have been rather a paranoid sort of person.

'Maybe not so paranoid, darling. Stella did die a spectacular and rather gruesome death after all, don't forget.'

Idly Payne picked up a pen and started drawing something on one of the napkins. That handkerchief, he thought. How did the handkerchief fit into the new set-up? Did it fit in at all?

'How did Melisande manage to lure Stella to the Villa Byzantine?' Lady Grylls asked. 'Have you any ideas?'

'Um. She asks someone to phone Stella and pretend to be Vane. Some trusted friend from the acting fraternity – an old flame – or her ghastly agent Arthur ... Stella is asked to go to the Villa Byzantine. Melisande – as Miss Hope – has already ascertained that Vane would be out that morning. Melisande has already stolen one of his front door keys. She gets into the house, unhooks the sword and then waits for Stella?'

129

'Are you going to involve the police? Or are you and Antonia playing a lone hand?'

'The good old days of the solitary sleuth are over, alas. The police are already involved in any case.' Payne took a sip of tea. 'I've been trying to imagine the kind of guff Melisande – as Miss Hope – has been feeding Vane.'

'Tales of Balkan imbroglios, princely picnics and duels at dawn? D'you think she made *everything* up?'

'Well, she must have done. Perhaps not everything. She probably did research and got some of her facts from various royal biographies – but I expect her imagination has been central to the enterprise.'

'She must be frightfully convincing. Or else this Tancred Vane is a complete sap. *Is* he a complete sap?'

'Something of the well-bred naïf about him. A pleasant enough chap, but not a terribly forceful personality. All right, a bit of a sap, perhaps . . . When I first met Melisande Chevret, I decided she couldn't be a very good actress, mainly on account of her manner being so affectedly actressy, but clearly I was wrong. She must be terribly good after all.'

'Something's not right, Hughie. I don't know exactly what I mean, but— Very well, let's assume it was Melisande Chevret who killed Stella. Her aim was to eliminate Stella, and that she managed to achieve, correct?'

'Correct.'

'Why then, in the name of sanity, did she continue visiting the Vane fellow? What was the *point*? You said she was in his house today. We are now – what? Five days after the murder? She's achieved her aim. She's got rid of her love rival and so on. So why doesn't "Miss Hope" simply disappear?'

Major Payne scrunched up his face. 'One possible explanation is that she has gone completely mad and she has actually persuaded herself she is "Miss Hope" now. Is that too feeble? Or she might have started playing some other, more sinister, game. She might be intent on ruining Tancred Vane's reputation as a royal biographer. She might have taken against him, for some reason.'

'She's got a sister, did you say? What's the sister like? Equally cuckoo?'

'Not at all. Winifred is the soul of well-bred reserve. A paragon of discretion and good sense. Nothing like Melisande. Well, something must be done about Melisande Chevret – before it is too late.'

'You think she might run amok or something?'

'She might. Morland told me she'd been trying desperately to win his affections back. He got me on the phone this morning. He said he was unable – as well as reluctant – to go back to Melisande. He said that whatever he'd felt for her once was no more. But apparently she keeps ringing him. He has now stopped answering her calls. He believes she is unhinged.'

'You look worried.'

'I am worried about Vane. Why hasn't he phoned? I hope he's all right.' Major Payne looked at his watch. 'If she gets it into her head that he suspects her of not being who she says—'

The next moment Major Payne's mobile phone rang – but it wasn't Tancred Vane.

## 23

# Into the Mouth of Madness

One thing I am absolutely determined to do – the next time I go to the Villa Byzantine I will go *as myself*.

The time for masquerade and mimicry is over. The comedy must end. The truth shall set me free and keep my soul from going astray. It was idiotic of me to present myself as an octogenarian in the first place. Whatever possessed me? Couldn't I think of something *simpler*? Well, I wanted to get instant access to Tancred and that was the *best* I could think of. I seem to be cursed with the kind of mind that has been described as tortuous.

I need to wash the lines off my face. I must stop walking with a stoop. I need to take off this ridiculous wig. Perhaps I could burn it? The action will symbolize my newly found freedom.

Serenity and peace are starting to sweep over me in great tidal waves, unleashed, I suspect, by the relief that Hugh Payne's visit was nothing worse than 'merely routine'.

What a charming pathway this is! Clumps of azalea and rhododendron planted to the right of it, with a few late-flowering roses. It looks as though the shrubs have perspired in the air. I stoop down and pick up a fallen petal. I crush it between my fingers, and I have there, in the hollow of my hand, the essence of a thousand scents, unbearable and sweet. My love appears to have enhanced my appreciation of Nature. What is it they say? A feeling for Nature is the privilege of cultivated minds not entirely absorbed in the material necessities of life.

Was Hugh Payne's visit 'merely routine', though? Those were his words, as Tancred reported them to me, but he is frightfully brainy – that handsome Major with his *faux buffo* manner! Why were they whispering? I couldn't hear a word of what they said. No, Tancred would never lie to me. I mustn't be suspicious.

I must control my emotions or, like a firework, I may explode and be pulverized into a thousand sparks!

But what of the superficial, nay, pointless princely life on which Tancred has been expending so much time and energy? The so-called 'biography', with the writing of which I have been 'assisting' him?

An image floats into my head. The Communists making Prince Cyril dig his own grave, shooting him in the back of the head, then pushing him in. Something similarly drastic needs to be done about the book. That so-called biography. I couldn't possibly allow poor Tancred to be discredited and become the laughing stock of the literary elite!

I was desperate for his attention, for his love, that's the reason I did it. I acted irresponsibly, but what I have done, I shall undo.

I am sure Tancred will understand. I don't suppose he will get cross with me. One doesn't get cross with those one cares for.

Tancred cares for me as much as I care for him. He said so himself with his own lips. Tancred loves me. Tancred would never lie to me. Never. *Never.*

Tancred. Tancred. Tancred.


'Why are you out of breath?' Winifred said. 'Where have you been?'

She stood looking at Melisande. Her sister's face was pale and her hair was uncharacteristically dishevelled, wild, almost. Winifred had seen her sister with hair like that only once before, at the final curtain of a play that had been booed by the audience – some feeble forgotten French farce. Melisande had ripped off her wig even before she had reached her dressing room and burst into tears.

'*In paradise*. Isn't that what Irene tells Soames on her return from her tryst with Bosinney?'

They were standing outside their house, under a pale sky bruised with garish clouds.

'You look – different,' Winifred said.

Melisande explained that she had felt a little odd, so she had gone for a therapeutic ramble. She had wanted to get some fresh air. 'I did some light shopping.'

'Shall we go inside?'

'I am afraid of going inside. It's an unlucky house. That's where I met Stella. The face of the grandfather clock reminds me of Papa Willard at his most censorious. My bed with that scarlet canopy might have been a catafalque, it is so creepily portentous. The window curtains keep moving even when all is still. And there is a *smell*.'

'What kind of smell?'

'Can't say exactly. Not of rare and subtle flowers, to be sure. I believe it's a metaphysical kind of smell. *Horror and corruption stalk in the shadows*. Where's that from?'

'*The Duchess of Malfi*?'

'Arthur phoned to say he might get me a part in a new play that focuses on the dynamics between four women who reside in a brothel in the jungle, but I said no . . . I should never have become an actress. I could have been an air hostess – an MP's secretary – or a magician's assistant. I'd have been so much happier. Perhaps tonight I will sleep outside – in the garden! In one of those sinister sleeping bags we got for Christmas? They look like *body bags*. High time someone used them.'

Winifred pointed to her sister's shopping bag and said brightly, 'What did you buy?'

'Oh, the usual organic rubbish. Watercress. Tofu. A vegetarian steak. Eggs that couldn't have cost more if they'd been made of gold. Preposterous. What's the point of a healthy diet? I do *not* intend to live to be a hundred. Life after thirty-eight is one long compromise.'

'One of your buttons is missing.'

'I wish I could be as balanced and splendid about my sorrows and disappointments as you have been about yours. I should have learnt to worship at the shrine of established routine. Plumping cushions and so on. I was wrong to think of myself as transcending mundane human laws.'

'Let's go inside and I will make you a cup of tea.'

'What am I going to do with the rest of my life? I loathe looking at pictures. Books bore me, really. I can't cook. Going to the theatre is out of the question. I only *pretend* to like gardening. What am I going to *do*?' Melisande suddenly clutched at her sister's hand. 'Please, help me, Win.'

'This is all to do with James, isn't it?'

Melisande's eyes started filling with tears. 'He turned off his mobile. I was in the middle of telling him something extremely important. I heard the roar of animals in the background and somebody laughing like a hyena. Then he turned off his mobile, just like that. I think he was at the zoo – with that girl, Stella's daughter – who I suspect – I very strongly suspect – is *his daughter*. The whole thing is incredibly sordid. That girl chopped off her mother's head.'

'You can't be sure—'

'I can be. I have every intention of calling the police and telling them what I know. The things she said at my party. They should arrest the little bitch and put her in jail at once. No one but the daughter could have killed Stella. Who else *is* there?'

Winifred noticed that Melisande was wearing the jacket from her Chanel Boutique suit with domed buttons and gold studs, but the skirt came from some other suit, Winifred couldn't tell which one. This sort of thing had never happened before. Her sister had always been so particular about what she wore.

'Perhaps it was James who did it?' Melisande said in a thoughtful voice. 'Perhaps he and Stella were playing some game and it all went horribly wrong?'

'What game?'

This is awful, Winifred thought. My sister has gone mad. What am I going to do? Who did one phone? Should I perhaps contact Antonia and Hugh? But how could they help?

'Couples play games when they start experiencing difficulties. Neither of them could be described as being in their prime. Swords are notorious phallic symbols.'

'Let's go inside, shall we?' Winifred held her sister gently by the arm. 'I will make you a cup of tea and then you can have a lie-down.'

'James is a pig. They should keep him in a pigsty, put a piggy ring through his piggy nose and feed him pigswill!' Melisande broke into paroxysms of sobbing laughter. '*Grunt-grunt*. People will go to the zoo to look at him. *Grunt-grunt*. What a fat, pink and stupid pig, they will say. Hello, James. Isn't it time you were converted into sausages?'

'Come on, Meli—'

'*He turned off his mobile phone*. He is the most pig-headed and pig-like of pigs. So degrading, expecting a pig to love you. He is actually a lousy lover. I now count my married days with Chevret as the happiest in my life. I should never have divorced Chevret. Never.'

'Chevret was cruel to you.'

'Chevret possessed the perfect diffidence and unobtrusive reserve which mark a person of high birth and breeding.'

'He had awful habits. And he made futile little jokes that drove you mad. That's what you always said.'

'I do believe you were secretly in love with Chevret, that's why you talk like that. We should sit in the garden and dine alfresco. Incidentally, the pince-nez has disappeared.'

'What pince-nez?'

'The Miss Prism pince-nez. The pince-nez was my lucky charm. It was on my dressing table and now it isn't. In fact I haven't seen the pince-nez for some time. It was my lucky charm. Someone's taken my lucky charm—'

Covering her face with her hands, Melisande burst into tears. Winifred put her arm round her sister's shoulders and led her into the house. She was aware of tense currents vibrating through Melisande's body. It felt as though her sister were full of wires that vibrated with electricity.

This is the kind of complication I could have done without, Winifred thought.

Later she noticed that Melisande's bag contained no shopping.

# 24

# The Case of the Lethal Golfer

'You seem disappointed it's me. Who did you want it to be?' Antonia asked.

'Tancred Vane, actually. I've been expecting him to ring.'

'You saw him? You talked to him?'

'I did. Melisande was with him.'

'At the Villa Byzantine? So Melisande *is* Miss Hope.'

'Yes.'

'Does she know you know?'

'She probably suspects,' Major Payne said. 'She saw me through the window. I'll give you the details later. Vane said he'd call, but hasn't so far . . .'

'You don't think he's in danger, do you?'

'I don't know. Why doesn't he ring? I wonder whether to call the police—'

'Where are you?'

'At Aunt Nellie's.'

'Give her my love, won't you?'

'I shall. She is convinced you make pots of money from your books. Did you know that by 1939 Enid Blyton was earning more than the then Chancellor of the Exchequer?'

'I wouldn't mind earning more than the Chancellor of the Exchequer. Though the current one would be a hard act to follow. The Osborne wallpaper fortune has been estimated at – was it four million pounds?'

'Where *are* you? What's that chirruping sound?'

'Birdsong. I am in Kensington Gardens. I'm sitting on a bench beside Peter Pan.'

'You sound as though you are about to embark on some awfully big adventure.'

'Perhaps I am. Perhaps I already have. I had coffee with Julia Henderson earlier on. Julia Henderson is James Morland's sister.'

'You seem to be imbuing the name "Julia Henderson" with extra special significance.'

'Julia said something very interesting. Stella talked to her the day before she was killed. Stella was keen on making her peace with her daughter. She had a plan. She was about to do something. She hinted there was an irregularity involved.'

'What kind of irregularity?'

'I believe she intended to commit a crime.'

'Are you serious? Would you care to specify the nature of the crime?'

'*Steal Tancred Vane's sword.* My theory,' Antonia went on, 'is that Stella meant it as a peace offering. That was the reason why she went to the Villa Byzantine on the morning she was killed. She had already stolen one of Vane's front door keys during her previous visit. Tancred Vane had told her he would be at the British Library that morning.'

'Did she go to the Villa Byzantine alone?'

'No. I have an idea – it is only an idea, mind – that Julia Henderson went with her. I believe Julia might have driven Stella in her car.'

'You think it was Julia who beheaded her?'

'You may think I am sacrificing probability to wild speculation, but, you see, Julia does fit the bill. She had a good motive for wishing Stella dead. Julia depended on her brother financially. I got a palpable sense that she hadn't wanted her brother to marry Stella. Stella considered Julia her friend and confided in her. Julia is a champion golfer, yet she was eager to conceal the fact. *She has very strong wrists.*'

'This is all most ingenious, but it doesn't quite tally with the Melisande-as-Miss-Hope theory, does it?'

Antonia admitted it didn't – though did it have to?


After she'd rung off, she went on sitting on the bench under the statue of Peter Pan, thinking.

Stella was dead, but her daughter was still very much alive. James Morland was a rich man. If he were to act on his decision and adopt Moon, she would share in his fortune. He had bought a Regency house in Chelsea, which he intended to share with Moon. He had talked about hiring private tutors for her.

Julia Henderson couldn't be happy about any of this. Of course not. Could Moon be in danger? Moon was still living at Julia's flat. Was that why Morland had bought a house? To get Moon away from his sister? Was Morland concerned about Moon's safety? Did Morland suspect that his sister might be behind Stella's death and that she might try to kill Stella's daughter as well?

Antonia heard Julia's voice once more. *My Surrey past is catching up with me.* Julia had pulled a droll face. What else had she said? Something about . . . bull-fighting? Not exactly—

*I have never stayed at the Corrida Hotel.*

The Corrida Hotel. Antonia frowned. She hadn't imagined it, had she? Bull-fighting. Bulls? Bulls were important somehow. One particular bull?

Something began to stir at the back of her mind . . .

# 25

# The Tremor of Forgery

'I don't think anything's happened to him. He is a big boy, isn't he? Or are you saying that royal biographers can't defend themselves? Do have another crumpet,' Lady Grylls urged her nephew.

'No, thank you, darling.'

'What a shame. You aren't eating the Patum Peperium sandwiches either. Provost made them specially for you. I read somewhere that second murders were "vulgar". In detective stories, that is. Do you think they are vulgar?'

'No, not really.'

'I am so glad. I like second murders. Prevents boredom from setting in. I have a feeling practically everybody wants to write detective stories nowadays. Goodness, Hughie, you do look worried. Wouldn't you care for a game of snap? I always find it takes my mind off things.'

'No, thank you, darling.'

'Only the other day Constantia was saying – remember Constantia?'

'Big crumbling house in Norfolk, breeds borzois, unflaggingly jolly?'

'That's the one. Constantia was saying she had a clever idea for a detective story. She was wondering if Antonia would be interested in using it. Pay attention now. A character is addressed by other characters, alternately, as Lady Flora and Lady Beaufort – it's the same character, you see. Those readers who know about such things assume that the author is simply ignorant about the aristocracy, as practically everybody is these days, and is confusing baronets' wives with earls' daughters, but, as a matter of fact, that seeming confusion is a vital clue to the killer's identity.'

Major Payne observed that the tangles of nomenclature in the peerage were so tricky, they could trip up even the initiated.

'Constantia's plot hinges on the premise that a knight's widow is impersonating a peer's daughter and she commits a series of murders to prevent being found out – a great fortune is at stake – what d'you think, Hughie?'

'Mind-blowingly ingenious,' Payne said absently.

The next moment his mobile phone rang.

'Hello? Hello?' He hadn't recognized the number but then Vane hadn't given him his phone number.

'Hi, Hugh. That puzzle you set us at the party. The party at Kinderhook. Do you remember?'

'Good lord, it's you!'

'Were you expecting someone else?' Moon's voice said. 'Don't you remember the puzzle? You set us a puzzle. *The music stopped. She died. Explain.*'

'Sounds incredibly silly. Who gave you my number?' Payne passed his hand across his face.

'I got your number off James' mobile. He doesn't know about it. He'd be very cross if he knew, so don't tell him, please.'

'Look here, Moon, I'm terribly busy at the moment. I'm expecting an important call. What the hell is that racket?'

'We are at the zoo. Don't ring off, please! Can you hear the monkeys? I love animals, which means I am a good person. James has gone to get me an ice-cream.'

'I don't think I set you any puzzles at the party.'

'You did. There could be more than one solution, you said. Do you want to hear *my* solution?'

'I am expecting an urgent call—'

'Your solution was that *she* was a blindfolded tightrope walker. The music was her cue to step off. One day, the

142

machine playing the music broke down. *She* stepped off too early and fell to her death. Right?'

'I am going to ring off now—'

'This is my solution now. Pay close attention,' Moon said. '*She* was a blind swimmer, who swam out from her boat every day. She played a radio in her boat, so she knew where to swim back to – are you following? The transmission suddenly cut out because damp had got into the radio, so she could no longer find her boat and drowned. Cool, eh?'

Payne agreed it was cool and eventually the conversation was brought to an end.

His mobile rang again.

This time it was Tancred Vane. So he was alive and well.

Payne heaved a sigh of relief.


Tancred Vane sat slumped in his chair, a glass of whisky in his hand, a look of extreme dejection on his face.

'That's the exact question Stella asked me. *Do you know the actress Melisande Chevret?* I said no. Then the name slipped out of my mind completely, but of course it came back to me the moment you mentioned it.'

'Well, it confirms the story Stella's daughter told me. It proves that Moon did *not* lie.' Payne leant back in his chair. 'Did Stella say anything else about Melisande?'

'No, she didn't. She might have done if I'd shown any interest, but I didn't encourage digressions. I wanted her to get on with her story about her grandmother and life at the royal palace in Sofia.'

They were sitting in Tancred Vane's drawing room. The biographer had suggested the study or the library, but Major Payne had been eager to see the scene of the crime.

It was a warm room of soft textures and deep rich colours, with amber and maroon striking the predominant note. There seemed to be no hard surfaces, only silk melting into velvet and velvet into brocade. The room basked in the soft glow of indirect lighting and the shimmer of gold leaf. There were several art nouveau lamps in the shape of mermaids, an ottoman and a mahogany baby grand, on which stood a signed black-and-white photograph of Princess Anna of Montenegro wearing a slouch hat. A magnificent volume bound in blue leather embossed with the heraldic fleur-de-lis of Bourbon France lay open on a round malachite table.

Producing a magnifying glass, Payne sprawled on the floor, Sherlock Holmes-fashion, but not even the slightest patch of discoloration was discernible. The blood had gone. Tancred Vane explained that he had had a cleaning crew at the house early that morning; they had spent three hours rubbing and scrubbing away. The window curtains had already been changed. The police had said he could. Where had the sword hung? Vane pointed. The nail was still there, a particularly monstrous nail with a head nearly as big as a ping-pong ball.

'Stella said her daughter would like the sword. It was the kind of thing her daughter was interested in. She asked how much a sword like that would cost and seemed profoundly shocked when I told her the price I'd paid for it.' Tancred Vane paused. 'Is the daughter still under suspicion?'

'I believe she is, but the police don't seem to have enough evidence for an arrest. That bloodstained handkerchief now – did they show it to you?'

'They did. It had the initials MM. I told them I'd never seen it before.'

'Did you never doubt Miss Hope was the genuine article, Vane?'

'I must confess I didn't. Not even after she began to make mistakes – getting names and dates wrong and so on. Not even when she described a non-existent lodge!' The royal biographer sighed. 'She kept apologizing for being such a "muddle-headed old ass". She said she had never been a particular devotee of the French cult of *lucidité*. She did say droll things. She made me laugh.'

'You didn't get any pinpricks of doubt every now and then?'

'I did – but I dismissed them. I went on believing her. I thought it was her age. Elderly ladies do get confused. I never for a moment imagined she was much younger than that.'

'Melisande Chevret can't be any more than fifty-five or six . . . She made herself look a quarter of a century older because she needed to fit into her historical narrative,' Payne said thoughtfully. 'Miss Hope was a girl of fifteen when she became nanny to Prince Cyril's son – and that was in 1941, you said?'

'Yes . . . I suppose it *had* to be 1941. A year earlier would have made her too young to have been employed at the palace and it couldn't have been a year later either since in 1942 Bulgaria had already abandoned its neutrality and joined the war as an ally of Germany. The idea of an English girl working for a pro-Nazi German prince would have raised eyebrows. She kept it all on the edge of credibility, I can see that now.'

'She seems to have thought the whole thing through very carefully. I never thought Melisande was particularly clever,' said Payne. 'It seems I was wrong . . . Miss Hope was a good raconteuse, I take it?'

The royal biographer said that that would have been putting it mildly. There had been something mesmeric about Miss Hope's tales of life at the palace. She had come up with the most fascinating details, with all kinds of absurdities and amusing trivialities.

Tancred Vane frowned. 'There were things that didn't quite add up, things that were somewhat out of kilter – but I never really suspected—'

'What things? Give me an example.'

'Um. All right. Would a royal prince in the 1940s have his mistress and illegitimate child living in the palace grounds? *Would* he have paraded them at royal events? But I never questioned any of it seriously. Miss Hope always managed to end on a cliff-hanger of sorts. It made me *long* for our next session.'

'Ah. The Scheherazade effect.' Payne nodded. 'She set out to get you hooked and succeeded.'

145

'I can't believe that all along she was after that poor woman. I simply can't. Makes me sick, thinking about it. And why did she continue coming after Stella's death?'

'My aunt asked the very same question.' Major Payne admitted that the precise reason for the continued visits still eluded him.

'She is mad – must be,' Tancred Vane murmured. 'I have been in thrall to a mad woman.'

'What exactly did she say when she saw me through the window?'

'She said something terrible would happen if I let you in. She begged me not to open the front door. Later – after you left – she said she'd made a mistake. She'd taken you for somebody else. She apologized profusely for alarming me. She said she was an old fool. She had problems with her eyes. She said she needed new glasses.'

'Do you think she managed to eavesdrop on our conversation? I believe I heard the creaking of a floorboard.'

'No idea. I found her exactly where I'd left her in my study, sitting by the window. Well, her face was very flushed and I thought she looked a little tense. She did ask who you were, what you wanted and so on . . . I told her *part* of the truth – that you'd been asked by James Morland – Stella's fiancé – to "look into the matter" since he didn't trust the police.'

'She left soon after?'

'Yes. She complained of feeling a little under the weather. Old age catching up with her at long last, she feared. She seemed nearly her old roguish self again – though, come to think of it, she didn't give me her usual peck.'

'Did she usually give you a peck?'

'Yes . . . on the cheek.' Tancred Vane blushed. 'No, I can't believe she killed Stella . . . Not with the samurai sword . . . The whole thing is ridiculous – grotesque! And yet it *must* be her! Stella looked really frightened the day she met her – she kept staring at her – she then blurted out all those questions! How old was Miss Hope? Where did she live? She then asked me if I knew the actress Melisande Chevret. It all fits in, doesn't it?'

'It does, old boy. I'm afraid it does.'

'Why *did* she continue coming after she killed Stella? I keep puzzling over it. It makes no sense. What was her purpose?'

'I am sure the answer will present itself to me in due course. It always does. A near-miracle almost invariably comes my way and it clears and illuminates the path I must follow . . .'

There was a pause, then Tancred Vane said, 'How did Melisande Chevret get into the house that day?'

'I believe she stole one of your keys.'

'If she was already inside the house, she would have had to go and open the front door when Stella rang the bell, wouldn't she? They would have come face to face. Would Stella have entered – if she'd been confronted with the one person she feared most? Wouldn't she have run away?'

'She would have.' Payne nodded. 'But perhaps there was no confrontation? Maybe Melisande left the front door ajar.'

'Ajar?'

'Endeavour to visualize the scene. Stella rings the front door bell. There is no response. She then sees the door is actually ajar. She pushes it – tentatively steps into the hall – calls out. *Hello? Mr Vane?* A muffled voice comes from the drawing room. *Come this way! I am here.* Melisande has a deep throaty voice that can easily be taken for a man's.'

'Miss Hope didn't have a deep throaty voice.'

'No, of course not. She put on a different voice for you. *She is an actress.* You don't expect Mother Courage to speak in the same way as Lady Bracknell, do you, or Ophelia like Mrs Danvers, or a Hounslow hairdresser like Hedda Gabler – yet they could all be played by the same actress.'

'I wonder if she was in love with me,' Tancred Vane suddenly blurted out.

# 26

# Love from a Stranger

Major Payne cocked an eyebrow. 'In love with you? Did she give any indication that she might have been in love with you?'

'Nothing direct or overt. It was the way she looked at me and some of the things she said. It was also the *way* she said them. Today, for example. It was quite extraordinary. She started speaking about what matters most in life. She talked about priorities – about knowing oneself. She looked at once solemn and sad. Her eyes were very bright. She – she kept staring at me.'

'You know how the mad come into a room, too boldly, their eyes exploding on the air like roses.'

'I hope you don't think I have been imagining things?'

'No, not at all, old boy. I don't think you are the fanciful kind. Do go on.'

'Well, the idea that she might be in love with me kept occurring to me, but each time I dismissed it as absurd. *Not at her age.* Now you have told me that she – Melisande Chevret – is in fact in her mid-fifties, the whole thing doesn't seem so terribly absurd. So it's possible, I suppose? It's possible, isn't it?'

'Yes. An amorous obsession is perfectly possible. That would certainly explain why she persisted with her visits ... But if Melisande Chevret did kill Stella,' Major Payne reasoned, 'it was because she regarded Stella as her rival – as the interloper who stole Morland from her. She cut off her head because she was hoping to win Morland back. She was in love with Morland. One can't quite reconcile any of it with a simultaneous obsession with a younger man.'

'Wrong psychology?'

'Wrong psychology. On the other hand, it's not the kind of thing one can explain in rational terms, so one mustn't always look for logic. People fall in and out of love all the time. There are no rules. In the course of her visits Melisande Chevret may have developed a crush on you.'

'You mean I may have ousted James Morland and taken his place in her affections?'

'Precisely.'

'I must admit I became very fond of her. Though not, perhaps, in the way she might have wanted me to,' Tancred Vane said. 'I came to regard her as the aunt I never had.'

'But if she is in love with you – why does she go on pestering Morland? She keeps phoning him. He told me about it. Can she love *both* of you with equal passion?'

'I wouldn't have thought it possible . . . I must admit I found some of her behaviour bewildering. She – she seemed delighted out of all proportion when she saw I'd moved the flowers she'd given me from the left to the right on my desk. She saw that as some very special sign. Wasn't there a name for that kind of obsession? I seem to remember reading about it somewhere. About the woman who fell in love with George V?'

Payne looked at him. 'Good lord. Yes. You are absolutely right. It's a famous enough case. The woman was French, and she got a bee in her bonnet that she and George V were soulmates, destined to be united for eternity. The fact that George V was already married to Queen Mary didn't seem to bother her one little bit. She started hanging around outside the gates of Buckingham Palace, watching out for "signals" from the King. She actually imagined the King was sending her messages by leaving a window open or shut – by drawing the curtains across the windows – or *not* drawing them.'

'I think there is a medical term for it?'

'Indeed there is. *Les psychoses passionnelles*. It was a Frenchman, de Clérambault, who coined the phrase. *Les psychoses passionnelles* usually involve a woman who develops the intense belief that a man is in love with her.'

'How – how do you know so much about it?'

'Oh, I know all sorts of pointless things.' Payne waved a self-deprecating hand. 'The "patient" or "subject" may have had little or no contact with the object of her delusion, but what she experiences is the absolute conviction that he is as much in love with her as she is with him. It's a pathological condition . . . What's that on the table?' Payne pointed. 'Not her glasses, are they?'

'It's her pince-nez. Yes. She left it behind.'

Payne leant over. He held the pince-nez in front of his eyes. 'Plain glass. This is nothing more than a theatrical prop. May I keep it? Or should I say "them"? Is pince-nez plural? I must admit I find Miss Hope's divided passions a little difficult to swallow, but perhaps all will be clear after I have talked to her. I think I will pay her a visit tonight.'

'You are going to call on Melisande Chevret? Do you think you will be safe?'

'I am not sure,' said Payne gravely, 'so I intend to take my wife with me.'

# 27

# The Double Clue

Antonia didn't get home until seven in the evening. She found her husband in the sitting room, whisky and soda in hand and pipe in mouth, staring out of the open window into the gathering darkness.

'Such a warm night,' he said.

'You haven't eaten, have you?'

'I had a sandwich. And an apple.' Payne pointed to the sky with the stem of his pipe. 'A notable nimbus of nebulous moonshine. D'you remember the full moon the night Corinne Coreille died?'

'I do . . . Not many stars tonight.'

'Would you like a drink?'

'No, thank you. You poor thing, you must be starving. I am a bad wife. I don't take sufficient care of you.' Antonia sighed. 'There is never any proper food in the house and all we do is sit around having drinks and talking.'

'Nothing wrong with that.'

'We keep trying to solve mysteries.'

Payne shrugged. 'We can't help it if things happen to us.'

'Do you know any other couples who try to solve mysteries?'

'Not a single one. We not only try, we actually *solve* mysteries,' he corrected her. 'Don't make us sound futile and eccentric, please.'

'We have an unorthodox lifestyle, by any standards. You must see that. We are different from most other couples.'

'We are rather exceptional, I agree.'

'Perhaps we should try to go out and meet other couples more. We keep getting dinner invitations, which we turn down. I think it's all my fault. If your mother had been alive, she'd have regarded me with disapproval and contempt.'

'Nothing of the sort. She wouldn't have.'

'Mothers-in-law don't like to have daughters-in-law who rush about, being adventurous.'

'My mother would have adored you. She was adventurous herself. I've told you!'

'Yes, you have.' Antonia paused. 'Bletchley Park, 1944. The Enigma Code.'

'Old Churchill thought extremely highly of my mother.' Payne held up an imaginary cigar. '*Not only our youngest and cleverest but our prettiest decoder. Old Churchill gave her a DCB. Old Churchill had a thing about Mama. She covered the family name with glory.'

'Belinda de Broke, Dame Commander of the Bath. It is an unusual, rather striking sort of name.'

'It suited her. She was an unusual, rather striking sort of woman. Pity you never met her. She broke her neck driving in the Andes. She was with my second stepfather. Chap called Talleyrand-Vassal. He was twenty years younger than her.'

'Did he survive?'

'No. He broke his neck too. I was glad about that. Talleyrand-Vassal was a rotter.' Payne rose. 'Have we got any crushed ice? I want to get you a drink.'

'Nobody mixes a martini like you.' Antonia sat down on the sofa.

'I mix martinis like a god.'

'Do you know what I did today after we spoke on the phone? You'll never guess. I went to Earls Court.'

'Why Earls Court?'

'There was something I had to do.'

'Another brainwave?'

'It was Julia Henderson who provided me with the clue. It's the longest of shots. I'll tell you all about it when I am sure.'

'How about going on a neighbourly visit tonight?' Payne consulted at his watch. 'Or are you too tired?'

'What neighbourly visit? You don't mean Melisande, do you?'

'I do mean Melisande.' He told her about his conversation with Tancred Vane.

'Delusional love . . . You don't think she will open her heart to us, do you?' Antonia glanced down at the open book Payne had left on the sofa. '*Sexual Obsession and Stalking.*'

'Got it at the library. On my way back from the Villa Byzantine.'

She looked down at the open pages and at the bullet-shaped pencil that lay between them. 'You have been underlining. You can't do that in a library book, you know. They could fine you for defacing. *Maladie d'amour,*' she murmured, turning a page.

'Also known as *mélancolie érotique*. Why do these things sound so much better in French? Look further down. The condition is also known as "old maid's psychosis".'

'Melisande is not an old maid.'

'Clearly there are variations . . . Enigma Variations . . . Shall we have some Elgar, to set the tone?'

'No, not music. Not now. Can't concentrate if there's music. So . . . The sufferer believes that the subject of their delusion secretly communicates their love by subtle methods, such as body posture, arrangement of household objects and other seemingly innocuous acts.'

'Vane said she kept staring at him. She patted his cheek on a regular basis. She insisted on giving him pecks. She brought him some flowers that looked like human lungs. When he moved them to the right of his desk, she looked enraptured. She turned very pink. She was convinced he was sending her a signal. She took it for a declaration of his love for her.'

'Love via lungs . . .'

153

'Did you know that, if stretched out, our lungs would cover an area the size of a tennis court?'

'De Clérambault's Syndrome . . .'

'That's another name for the same condition. Gaetan de Clérambault was head of an institution for the criminally insane. He was attached to the Préfecture de Police in Paris and couldn't have been entirely *compos* himself. He shot himself in 1934.'

'Did he?' Antonia looked up. 'Really?'

'Yes. Makes one wonder. Are loony doctors attracted to their profession because they are aware of some mental kink in their psychological make-up, or does a daily dose of the criminally insane prove fatal in the end?' Payne glanced at his watch. 'Would you like another drink before we go?'

'No, not another drink. I intend to be as clear-headed as possible.'

'And I intend to take my old army revolver with me.'

'You aren't thinking of effecting a citizen's arrest, are you?'

'Not quite, but we must be ready for a reaction. I rather doubt our probing questions will be welcome. She may become agitated. She may try something. There is a full moon, that's when awful things tend to happen.' He waved towards the open window. 'If it *was* Melisande who killed Stella, she is probably very strong. She must have been able to lift the sword and swing it.'

'She can't really be in love with both Vane and Morland, can she?'

'I would have said no . . . Oh well, perhaps we'll know soon enough . . . Has it ever occurred to you, my love, that you and I lead about as extraordinary a life as any two people who didn't found a religion or didn't personally lead an invasion of a foreign empire? Let's push along.'

As they were crossing the hall, the telephone rang. Major Payne picked it up.

It was his aunt.

'Hughie!'

'Actually, darling, we happen to be on our way out,' Payne said. 'We are off on an important and potentially dangerous mission—'

'I won't keep you long. Have you managed to have that woman arrested? I mean *la fausse* Miss Hope.'

'No, not yet. As a matter of fact, we are on our way to her place at this very moment. I don't know about having her arrested, but we are certainly going to try to persuade her to confess.'

'How perfectly thrilling,' said Lady Grylls. 'You must tell me all about it when you come back.'

'We most certainly shall.'

'One more thing. What's the meaning of the cryptic message you left behind?'

Payne looked at his watch. 'What cryptic message, darling?'

'WW. You wrote that on one of my napkins.'

'I never—' He broke off. 'Oh. I did. Sorry. I did doodle on the napkin. I had the handkerchief on my mind. The handkerchief the police found at the scene of the crime. It was made of very fine silk. I do apologize, darling. I'd been mulling over those initials. No – not WW but MM. I wrote MM. The initials are Stella's daughter's, though the blasted girl swears she's never used a handkerchief in her life. It's the one clue that doesn't quite fit in with the rest of the puzzle.'

'MM, did you say? Oh yes.' Lady Grylls laughed. 'I must be looking at it upside down. What did you say? Speak up, will you? You are mumbling.'

'Upside down . . . *Not* MM but WW . . . Good lord.'

'What's the matter?'

'Of course. *Of course.*'

'Of course what?'

'Aunt Nellie, you'll never believe this, but you've just solved the mystery of the killer's identity for us.'

'What do you mean, Hughie? I thought you knew that all along. It's the actress. Melisande Chevret? Isn't it?'

There was a pause.

'No,' Major Payne said. 'It is not the actress.'

155

# 28

# Enigma Variations

They were back in their sitting room, reviewing the case in the light of the latest discovery.

'Funny that no one saw it earlier,' said Payne. 'The police didn't. We didn't see it either. We should have, but we didn't. Well, it did occur to me that Melisande didn't quite match the Miss Hope profile. She couldn't have been in love with two men at the same time. Of course she couldn't. "Miss Hope" loved Vane and Vane alone. We were actually there when it happened! We were witnesses!'

Antonia nodded. 'Yes. She saw his photo and heard church bells ... Her gaze became remote ... Her eyes seemed to fix themselves on some distant and perhaps glorious horizon. Suddenly – suddenly she looked years younger, almost girl-like ... I noticed the change, yet I convinced myself I'd imagined it ...'

'She became obsessed with Vane from the word go. Perhaps it had been waiting to happen, that sort of thing. That would explain why she went on visiting him after Stella's death. The condition is known as "old maid's psychosis". Winifred *is* an old maid. It all fits in. I want to kick myself!'

'We have been looking at the case the wrong end up. Literally. *Not* MM for Moon Markoff, but WW for Winifred Willard. *Winifred is Miss Hope.*'

'Stella only met the two sisters once, at that ghastly party at Kinderhook. When she bumped into "Miss Hope" at the

Villa Byzantine, she thought that it was Melisande she was seeing. The reason for her mistake is obvious,' Payne went on reflectively. 'There is a resemblance between the two sisters. Melisande is the actress. One expects women who are actresses to dress up. Melisande's sitting room was full of framed photos showing her in various theatrical parts. It was a natural enough mistake to make in the circumstances.'

'There was a photo hanging on the loo wall at Kinderhook,' Antonia said. 'Did you see it? Of Melisande as Miss Prism or some such preposterous pedagogue-like figure in pince-nez.'

'Of course! Stella probably saw it too!'

'It might have been that very same photo that gave Winifred the idea for her disguise in the first place.'

'There is of course a strong psychological factor that is central to the confusion,' said Payne. 'Stella had been feeling guilty. She knew Melisande was distraught when Morland jilted her. She was nervous of Melisande – afraid of her.'

'It never occurred to her she might have made a mistake?'

'No. Why should she think it was Winifred who'd dressed up as Miss Hope? It made little sense. After she moved in with Morland, Stella became paranoid. She believed Melisande was out to get her in some way. Well, she did die a violent death – but it was the wrong sister who delivered the blow.'

'What reason would Winifred have had for wanting to kill Stella?'

'Winifred starts her delusional romance with Vane. She has succeeded in passing herself off as "Miss Hope", former royal nanny to Prince Cyril's bastard baby. Everything seems to be going well – till the day Stella turns up at the Villa Byzantine. Winifred and Stella exchange a couple of words. *Stella gives every indication of having recognized her.* Stella stares at her, then asks Vane questions about Miss Hope's age and so on. Vane mentions the fact to Winifred – you see?'

'Winifred fears the game is up?'

'Yes! She has no idea Stella has taken her for Melisande. Winifred believes that sooner or later Stella will tell Vane who she really is. She knows that a revelation like that will put paid to her "romance". Something needs to be done about it. She needs to act fast. Stella has to be silenced. What's the matter?'

'The sword, Hugh. The samurai sword. Call me unimaginative, but I can't see Winifred brandishing a sword. And why kill her in Tancred Vane's drawing room? Tancred Vane is the love of Winifred's life! To be with him is her dearest wish. She wouldn't dream of causing him any upset. The very last thing she would want to do is desecrate his drawing room. You said his drawing room was a work of art. Think about it!'

There was a pause.

'Perhaps that particular killing method was chosen with good reason . . . Perhaps the murder is not as irrational and grotesque as it looks, rather it was a mixture of planning and impulse, brutal, yet clever and ingenious.' Payne drew a thoughtful forefinger across his jaw. 'Winifred intended to throw suspicion on Stella's daughter. A sword is the kind of weapon Moon *would* employ. Winifred had heard Moon eulogize the bloody delights of an electronic game called Hammers of Hell. Maybe that's what gave her the idea?'

'Maybe it was.'

'You don't seem too convinced. Incidentally, why did you undertake that trip to Earls Court today?'

'I will tell you *only* if there is a follow-up. I expect a follow-up—'

'Won't you at least give me a hint what it's about?'

'That bill from the Corrida Hotel. For champagne and so on. You said it wasn't yours. Well, I deduced it was James Morland's. He must have dropped it when he visited you here.'

Payne stared. 'You're right. Good lord – *yes*. He did drop some papers the day he came – he wanted to show me the opera tickets. Hello – what's up? No, don't tell me. First things first. Let's go to Kinderhook and talk to Miss Hope.'

# 29

# The Rise and Fall of the British Nanny

It was only a short walk under the full moon – that patron of lovers and plotters, Major Payne murmured.

Kinderhook had the dignified and somewhat forbidding air of a cathedral. There was a patriarchal solemnity about it.

'Will Winifred unwind all the wiles she wound?'

'Don't you ever get tired of spouting *bons mots*?'

'I find it helps release the tension . . . This is actually a paraphrase of something Francis Thompson wrote in "The Mistress of Vision".'

'Are you tense?'

'I believe I am.' He patted his pocket, making Antonia wonder whether he had taken his old army revolver with him after all.

'You don't think she will try to hold us hostage or anything like that, do you?'

Winifred Willard's part of the house was dark. They saw light only in Melisande's windows. Perhaps the two sisters were together? That would complicate matters. Payne thought he had no other option but to ring Melisande's front door bell.

The door opened almost at once and Winifred Willard stood on the threshold. She might have been waiting for them. The hall light was on and her ash-blonde chignon gleamed. She looked radiant, happy, years younger. Her cheeks were a little flushed. Her eyes were bright.

She was clad in a high-collared silk dress in dove grey that reached below her knees, four strings of pearls, each row separated by diamond buckles on either side of her neck, and pearl earrings. Her shoes were red, shiny, with silver buckles, the only vaguely eccentric touch about her get-up – it put Antonia incongruously in mind of Dorothy. Innocence and witchery? Perhaps not that incongruous after all.

'Hugh! Antonia! What a lovely surprise!' Winifred clapped her hands. 'Would you like to come in?' She opened the door wide.

Whatever Antonia had anticipated, it wasn't such a spontaneous display of hospitality. Payne too was puzzled. Divided psyche, he thought. Or could it be a trap?

They went in.

'Poor Melisande is laid low. That's why I am here, playing the nurse. Melisande appears to have had a nervous breakdown of sorts.'

'Oh, I am so sorry,' Antonia said.

'She will be fine. She's had nervous breakdowns before. I must say it completely ruined my plans for the evening. My sister never seems to tire of imposing her temperamental vagaries and physical needs on me – even when she is prostrate and unconscious!' Winifred laughed. 'I am not as callous as I sound! Dr Olwyn gave her an injection. She is asleep at the moment, so you can't see her.'

'As a matter of fact we wanted to see you,' Payne said.

'Did you? How perfectly splendid. I was just having coffee. I am experimenting with a new blend. Would you like to join me? I'd be terribly interested in your opinion. I must say this is a most welcome diversion. I'd resigned myself to a solitary vigil. I am reading the latest Anita Brookner. Another masterly study of well-bred desolation,' Winifred prattled on. 'Isn't it odd how some authors never vary? She must be getting on. Her outlook has remained remarkably unchanged—'

She led them into the shadowed half-light of the drawing room.

Three low-voltage table lamps. A thin wood fire crackling in the grate. Leaping shadows over the chintz furniture. The air was filled with wood smoke that was subtly tinged with an essence of tuberose and regale lilies.

A silver tray with a single coffee cup stood on the low coffee table beside a silver pot and a cream jug. Winifred asked them to sit down. 'Coffee, yes? I could do with another cup. Won't be a jiffy.' She picked up the pot and walked jauntily out of the room.

'I can't think how she could possibly have anything to do with the murder,' Antonia whispered.

'She is driven by unconscious forces,' Payne said calmly. 'She doesn't know who she is.'

When Winifred reappeared with the fresh pot of coffee and two more cups, he remarked in conversational tones, 'How do you find the Villa Byzantine? Not too – florid?'

Antonia froze, her eyes fixing on the steaming pot in Winifred's hand. Shock tactics. Hugh had decided on shock tactics. Would Winifred drop the pot and let it explode like a bomb on the floor? Or might she try to blind Hugh by splashing scalding coffee into his face?

Winifred did neither. She placed the pot carefully on the tray, then pushed the latter towards the centre of the table. Her hands were thin, with long sensitive fingers, and she wore a delicate diamond ring on her fourth finger. How could these hands—?

'It's an extraordinary place, isn't it? Tancred inherited it from an elderly cousin of his who went to live in Morocco and died there.' A little line appeared on her smooth forehead. 'I suppose it *is* florid. Yes. You are quite right. The *mot juste*. Something of a white elephant too. I have been trying to persuade Tancred to sell it and buy a house somewhere around here. When we are married. I saw just the right place the other day – a Queen Anne house – not far from Keats House. Do you like Keats? *A hundred swords will storm my heart, Love's fev'rous citadel.* This always makes me shiver. Some think Keats morbid. I can see why.'

'A hundred swords,' Antonia echoed.

'Sugar? Cream, Hugh? If I remember correctly you have an unquenchable passion for cream,' Winifred said with unexpected archness. She laughed her tinkling girlish laugh once more.

Bonkers, Payne thought. 'You must be thinking of somebody else,' he said pleasantly. 'I drink coffee black. No sugar.'

Antonia looked at the book on the coffee table. It was not the Anita Brookner Winifred had told them she had been reading, but *The Rise and Fall of the British Nanny* by Jonathan Gathorne-Hardy. Was that where she had been getting her ideas for Miss Hope?

'Black and unsweetened. That's how real men drink their coffee, apparently. Brutes like it bitter. Sweet is for sissies. That's what my poor sister says,' Winifred prattled. 'Melisande claims she knows everything about men, but, *entre nous*, she often talks nonsense.'

'Thank you,' Payne said, taking his cup from her hand. He took a tentative sip.

'Antonia? Cream? No? No sugar? How about a drop of cognac, Hugh? No?'

Antonia wondered whether Winifred had put something in the coffee. Poison – or an overdose of some strong soporific substance. Though what *would* Winifred do with their bodies? Well, she could phone the police and say they had both collapsed shortly after they had arrived, so the poison would be something that simulated botulism symptoms. Winifred would have to go to their house first and prepare fish-paste sandwiches or whatever. How would she find contaminated fish-paste though? Not terribly practical. But then so was cutting somebody's head off with a sword.

Antonia watched her closely for a flicker of sly malevolence or some other giveaway sign, but Winifred's expression remained serene. Eerily serene. That's what breaking bread with the Borgias must have felt like. I mustn't imagine things, Antonia told herself firmly. But it was difficult – the situation was far from normal.

162

She tried to catch her husband's eye. He gave a slight nod as though to say, the coffee's OK. How could he be sure? Certain drugs had no taste at all.

'Tancred adores cream, so do I. We are very naughty about it. But we must be careful. Not healthy, really. My sister wouldn't approve. Melisande believes in "choreographing" one's digestion.' Winifred giggled. 'The coffee is not too strong, I hope?'

'No. It is fine. First-rate coffee.' Payne cleared his throat. 'I understand Vane is writing a biography of Prince Cyril of Saxe-Coburg-Gotha? Am I right in thinking the Coburgs used to provide studs for most of the royal houses of Europe? I find royal lives fascinating. The parallel existence, the exclusivity, the utter strangeness of it all – a life without the bother of British Gas, Thames Water, the Halifax or, for that matter, the Taxman!'

Winifred smiled appreciatively. 'There was a time when people believed that royal families were needed to create an illusion of heaven on earth, of a jewel-encrusted land, of a Valhalla. A monarch was hailed as a representative of the majesty of history – a link in a chain that leads back to the Middle Ages that in turn connects to antiquity and beyond – to the beginning of recorded time when – when—'

'When the first hero slew the dragon of disorder and established the rule of law?' Payne suggested.

'I couldn't have put it better.' Winifred shot her visitor an admiring glance.

'There's of course the distinctly unheroic view. Remember Huckleberry Finn? *All kings is mostly rapscallions.*'

As Winifred laughed exuberantly, Antonia suddenly realized what their hostess had said several moments earlier. 'Did you say you were going to be married?'

'Oh yes. We are. Sometime next spring. I would hate to be married in winter. Isn't it funny that I should always have thought of myself as "not yet married"? I knew it would happen sooner or later. I didn't mind waiting for Mr Right. You know what they say? Marry in haste, repent at leisure. Next April would be perfect.'

163

'A week after Easter, perhaps?'

'Yes!' Winifred brought the palms of her hands together. 'Tancred and I haven't yet had a serious discussion about it, but we are going to, sometime this week. Tancred is so terribly busy at the moment, poor darling.'

Payne said, 'I understand Prince Cyril is taking up all his time and energy.'

'Don't I know it! Talk of the limitations of human effort! I've been trying to impress it on him, but he wouldn't listen.' Winifred shook her head in an exasperated manner. 'Things keep going wrong with that biography. If it's not one thing, it's another. It seems to be jinxed. Poor Tancred hasn't collected as much information as he would have wished – *and some of what he's already got is not entirely reliable.*'

'In what way "not entirely reliable"?'

Winifred took another sip of coffee, cast a glance round the room as though to make sure no one was lurking in the shadows. 'One of Tancred's so-called "sources" may not be who she says she is. I have the strongest suspicions. I have had them for some time. A Miss Hope. Rather, a woman who calls herself Miss Hope. You mustn't breathe a word!'

'We wouldn't dream of it,' Payne promised.

'Poor Tancred hasn't got an inkling. He is too decent, too trusting, the most ethical person I have ever known – though I wish he didn't assume everybody was like him! Tancred doesn't seem to have a safety valve. I fear it will come as a terrible blow to him when all is revealed. As it happens, I am investigating the matter at the moment.'

'You are?'

'*Yes.* It is quite serious. Deception on a grand scale. Impersonation. Misrepresentation. Misinformation. You seem surprised! It's as bad as that, yes.' She gave a mirthless laugh. 'I am determined to get to the very bottom of it. In fact, I have come to regard it as my duty.'

'Have you made any interesting discoveries?'

'I have. I believe I know now what this woman does. I also know *how* she does it. She – the *soi-disante* Miss Hope – has rented a room in a house in St John's Wood. She arrives, carrying her disguise in a bag. She is a woman in her mid to late fifties. She emerges as elderly Miss Hope and totters her way to the Villa Byzantine. Her landlord is under the impression that she is an eccentric actress who is practising for a part! She tells Tancred all manner of preposterous stories. The mind boggles, really. For example, she has suggested that Prince Cyril and *not* Hitler might have been responsible for King Boris' death! She has been hinting at fratricide!'

'Golly.'

'She is completely irresponsible. Once her visit is over, she returns to her rented room, removes her disguise and takes the tube back to wherever she lives. Somewhere around here, I believe. She spends her evenings poring over books which she's got from the library – royal biographies and so on. But she has started slipping up. *On one or two occasions she's even omitted to remove her disguise.*'

'That's how you knew, I imagine?' The third sister, Antonia thought. She exchanged looks with Hugh.

Their hostess inclined her head. 'Yes.'

'Poor show,' Payne harrumphed. 'Jinxed, did you say? Something in that! Didn't Vane's other source get herself killed? The Bulgarian woman we met here last month, as a matter of fact? What was her name? Astra?'

'Stella. She was James' friend. That was awful, wasn't it? *She was beheaded.* Poor Tancred's drawing room might have been some sort of sacrificial ground! Incidentally, there was something about the inquest in today's *Times*.'

'Was there?' Payne wondered whether Winifred could be trusted about anything she said. Winifred appeared highly suspicious of Miss Hope and was hoping to have her unmasked, but Winifred *was* Miss Hope. Was that what psychologists called disassociation? 'What does *The Times* say about the inquest?'

'Oh, nothing much. Only that it was going to take place on such-and-such a date. You are interested in murder, aren't you? I suppose that's why you went to the Villa Byzantine?'

'Well, yes. Morland asked me to look into the matter . . . So Vane told you about my visit?'

'Every little detail. We were on the phone for *hours*. Tancred tends to tell me *everything*. I am sure all that will change once we get married! Does your husband tell you *everything*?' Winifred turned towards Antonia with an amused smile.

'I don't know. You'd better ask him.'

'Hugh?'

'Practically everything,' said Payne solemnly. 'I have no secrets from Antonia.'

'How did you and Tancred meet?' Antonia asked.

There was a crack as a log on the fire collapsed and went up in a gush of pale flame.

# 30

# Spellbound

'It's one of the most remarkable stories you are ever likely to hear. I'd hesitate to describe it as a romance, though it's that all right. I must admit I was exceedingly romantic as a girl.' Winifred Willard gave a self-deprecating laugh. ' I used to identify with Juliet – with Héloïse – with Isolde! Too embarrassing for words!'

'I bet you know Tatiana's letter to Onegin by heart?'

'Why, yes – Hugh, how did you—? Goodness, I do believe you have a sixth sense!' She lowered her eyes. 'It all started with a photo. That woman – Stella – had taken a photo of Tancred with her mobile phone camera. She wanted a memento, apparently. She showed us the photo of Tancred – it was the day James brought her here – you remember?'

'Oh yes. Melisande's birthday party.'

'It is extremely difficult to explain what I felt, it was such an intensely personal experience, it was also so very extraordinary, but, as a writer, Antonia, I am sure you will understand. I hope Hugh won't say it's the craziest thing he's ever heard in his life?'

'I wouldn't dream of it.'

'No. Of course not. It wouldn't be your style. You see, till I met Tancred, I'd been leading a narrow, solitary sort of life, devoid of any significant human contacts. I kept reading books. I felt intellectually superior but I don't think

I was ever happy. I tended to indulge in melancholy introspection. The river of my existence was, as they say, sluggish. I yearned for the torrent of life, and yet I'd convinced myself that – that I'd found – how can I put it?'

'That you'd found contentment in deprivation?'

'Yes, Hugh! You seem to understand me so well. But then – then I saw Tancred – his photograph – his face – his smile – his *eyes*. That's when – it happened. It was quite incredible. I experienced a quickening in my spirit. I felt an immense burden lift from my heart. Suddenly – suddenly I felt free. My spirit *leapt* out of its confines!' Winifred threw her hands up and opened them, as though she were releasing a dove.

'Remarkable,' Payne said.

'I felt as light as the proverbial feather. I wouldn't have been at all surprised if I had started levitating. And then – then there was the jubilant ringing of bells! I knew in that instant that, whatever happened, I could never go back to my old constraints and restrictions. You heard the bells, didn't you? Well, I must say that's the closest I have ever come to a religious conversion. I hope you won't think it terribly peculiar of me?'

'Not at all, dear lady. Not at all.'

'Do you remember in *Death in Venice*, when Aschenbach begins to see Tadzio as a bearer of death? Well, I saw Tancred as a bearer of life. No! *As life itself*. You do understand, Antonia, don't you? I am sure you do.'

'I believe I do,' Antonia said gravely. She did her best to keep her face expressionless. (Why did they always have to meet oddballs?)

'I managed to engage Stella in a conversation about Tancred Vane. I believe you'd gone by then? I did it most casually,' Winifred went on. 'I asked how she had established contact with him and so on. She showed me the advertisement. She took it out of her bag. It was a newspaper cutting from the *International Herald Tribune* – royal biographer Tancred Vane seeking information about Prince Cyril of Saxe-Coburg-Gotha and the Bulgarian royal family – words to that effect. Well, I knew exactly what my next action should be.'

'You phoned him?'

'No. I feared that might be a little too forward. I have had a very strict upbringing, you see. My father used to make me write thank-you notes to him each time he punished me! I have remained, in many ways, an old-fashioned kind of girl.'

'You wrote to him?'

'I sat down and wrote Tancred a letter, yes. Like Tatiana! It was a very formal missive. Stiff and uninspired.' Winifred gave a self-deprecating smile. 'I addressed him as "Dear Mr Vane". Tancred wrote back by return of post. He declared himself delighted by my letter. He said he was *longing* to meet me. He invited me to visit him at the Villa Byzantine. He said he would be counting the hours—'

Of all the elliptic accounts, thought Antonia. What Winifred was omitting was the highly significant fact that she had written to Vane as 'Miss Hope', former nanny to Prince Cyril's son, and that she had offered to share her 'reminiscences' with him. That of course was the only reason why he had written back by return of post and asked her to visit him at the Villa Byzantine.

'Needless to say, Tancred and I "clicked" at once. Our very first meeting felt as though it had been pre-ordained. It was exactly as I had imagined it would be. We sat facing each other and we talked and talked! We couldn't keep the smiles off our faces. It felt as though he and I had known each other *all our lives*.'

There was a pause. Payne remembered something de Clérambault had written. That patients with this particular delusional disorder frequently cast a quasi-religious veil over their feelings. Patients were unlikely to seek help since they did not regard themselves as ill.

He cleared his throat. 'Going back to what we were saying earlier on, do you think it at all possible that it was Miss Hope who killed Stella?'

Winifred remained thoughtful for a moment or two, then said quietly, 'What would her motive have been?'

169

'Perhaps Stella tumbled to her secret? Discovered she was an impostor?'

'Yes . . . That is possible.' Something like a shadow passed across Winifred Willard's face and her expression changed a little. Her smile faded. She looked confused.

'Did you know that a bloodstained handkerchief bearing the initials WW was found by Stella's dead body?'

'No. How extraordinary. I had no idea.'

'Do you think it might be yours?'

Oh dear, Antonia thought.

'I don't think so.' Winifred slowly rose from her seat. 'I believe my sister is calling me. I am sorry. I will need to go upstairs. Would you mind frightfully if I said au revoir?'

Antonia and Payne stood up. Their visit was at an end. They hadn't heard anyone call.

# 31

# Divided We Stand

It was a bland golden morning, but oh so deceitful! At around eight o'clock the sky was as bright as a jewel and she stood in the back garden, holding up her hands to the sun, but then suddenly and without any warning a mist descended between her and the brilliant young red willow and chilled her to the bone. Quarter of an hour later the electric coffee pot gave her an electric shock, which for a minute or two staggered her considerably. Such an *alarming* kind of pain, she thought – a kind of *abstract* snakebite.

She heard Melisande moan in her room – what was she saying? *Watch over her in the Labyrinth . . . Protect her from the Voices . . . Protect her from the Visions.* Were those lines from a play or a prayer? For whose protection was her sister pleading? Had Melisande got it into her head that Winifred might be in danger? Had Melisande lost her mind completely?

The night before, Winifred had started putting her plan into action.

She had phoned Tancred and arranged to meet him at the British Library. He had sounded taken aback, poor boy, but he had agreed to it. She had pretended to be the Other – that ridiculous Miss Hope! She said she had something of vital importance to impart to him. A matter of life and death, no less. It was a melodramatic way of putting it and she had spoken breathlessly. It was not Miss Hope's usual style, but then old ladies were notoriously unpredictable.

Oh, how she hated Miss Hope! How she *despised* her. Well, today was going to be Miss Hope's last outing. Yes.

Winifred Willard laughed happily. It wouldn't be so very odd for a woman in her early eighties to disappear suddenly and without a trace, would it? Miss Hope might stumble into some black hole – the kind of place where bogus nannies vanished, perhaps? The Hole of Lost Hope?

Two hours later, still laughing, she walked out of the front door of Kinderhook.

*The world is remorseless, vast, inexorable in its operations – and Tancred needs protection from it.*

Her lips moved as she walked briskly down the street and hailed a taxi with her umbrella. He needs me, she whispered. He needs me. He needs me.

The thought gave her wings.

She was on her way to correct her mistake. Her one folly. It was imperative that she remove the one obstacle to their happiness. What she had done, she would undo.

'St John's Wood,' she told the taxi driver. 'Place called the Villa Byzantine. I'd be happy to direct you. Or perhaps you know it? It is the most striking house. Like something out of a fairy tale.'

At the conclusion of their last meeting, Tancred had told her that his editor had contacted a Professor Goldsworthy – an authority on European royalty in exile who apparently knew everything there was to know about the Bulgarian royal family and life at the palace in Sofia between the wars – and asked him to take a look at what Tancred had written so far. Tancred had said he would send all his notes to Professor Goldsworthy by the end of the week – electronically – as an attachment.

The news had come to Winifred as a shock. She realized that Goldsworthy would see at once that Miss Hope's 'reminiscences' were nothing but brazen fabrications. Goldsworthy was sure to say that, to the best of his knowledge, no such person as 'Miss Hope' had ever existed. Poor Tancred would be made to look an incompetent fool. Even though it was all Miss Hope's fault, some blame would invariably attach to him. His publishers – the immeasurably insignificant Fleur-de-Lis Press – might start questioning Tancred Vane's integrity, the trustworthiness of his previous royal biographies. They might decide they didn't want to commission any more books from him. Poor Tancred would be distraught, devastated. Royal biographies were his life!

No. She couldn't allow any of that to happen. She needed to undo the damage. She would certainly make a clean breast of what she'd done – nothing but a full confession would do! She would explain to Tancred — humbly and apologetically – the *exact* reason she had acted the way she had – but she would do it in her own time. Not under duress. Not as a result of 'exposure'. She would confess to Tancred after they had been married a month or two, perhaps. *Yes.* She was sure Tancred would understand. Of course he would understand. To love was to forgive.

Tancred loved her.

But the book – that so-called biography – had to disappear first.

She intended to make it look like an accident. One of those unaccountable calamities. Writing was known to disappear from computers without a trace. She had heard the most incredible stories. Viruses were often blamed for it. The Trojan Horse. The Bayley Bitch. She laughed. Such outlandish names!

She also intended to take the notebook in which Tancred had recorded everything she told him – all those preposterous stories she had made up! The notebook would also disappear without a trace. She would burn it, then scatter the ashes.

Winifred had no qualms about what she was going to do.

'I think someone's interested in you,' the taxi driver said, his eyes on the mirror.

'You are absolutely right. Someone *is* interested in me. I regard myself as an extremely fortunate woman,' Winifred said happily. She didn't quite hear what the driver said next – something about a car tailing them?

That was an odd little episode last night, she thought. She had to admit she didn't quite know what to make of it. Hugh and Antonia were a highly civilized couple of the kind she and Tancred would be very soon. Hugh and Antonia seemed to suspect Miss Hope of beheading Stella. It was Hugh who had voiced the suspicion. Although Antonia had said nothing, it was clear her mind was working along the same lines.

One had only to look at them and one immediately knew how close they were, how alike. *Two minds with but a single thought*. Like her and Tancred. One didn't often come across couples that moved in such perfect harmony. Perhaps when she and Tancred had been *imparadised in one another's arms*, as Milton so aptly put it, they would become best friends with the Paynes? They had so much in common! They could visit the theatre together, then dine at Le Caprice or the Ivy. They would have the most interesting and stimulating conversations about literature and the arts and the crowned heads of Europe.

Hugh had such a straight nose and such steady blue eyes. She had noticed at once not only his fine features, but also the lineaments of intellectual power, even of nobility. She also liked the way he parted his hair. It was of course Hugh's intelligence that had impressed her most. Hugh simply bristled with ideas. Not a common feature of military men, she reflected, certainly not of *majors*. The only thing that bristled in the majors she had once known was their moustaches! Winifred laughed and pretended to cough when she saw the driver glance at her curiously.

Hugh was very much the gentleman scholar type. She could see his finely boned head bent over an outsize edition of the OED, a magnifying glass in his hand, though he would look equally good on the moor. On the moor he would be clad in a Victorian shooting jacket in heavy blue and grey tweed, belted and with four patch pockets with the flaps buttoned down, a light blue shirt, red tie (the only vaguely rakish element in his attire), dark grey corduroy trousers and black gloves. Hugh would be surrounded by adoring dogs and of course he would be smoking his pipe.

Well, if she had not already been *spoken for*, she might have *fallen for* Hugh. Winifred smiled. Clichés had a comic charm of their own!

Would Tancred be jealous if he suspected her of falling for another man? Tancred seemed always so terribly pre-occupied with his literary efforts, forever in a world of his own, but Winifred felt certain he would become jealous if she were to give him cause to be – not that she ever would!

She remembered how, on entering the Villa Byzantine for the very first time, she had stood inside the hall that smelled so sweetly of beeswax, rose petals and lavender, how she had spread out her arms and thought, *I have arrived.*

As a matter of fact, Hugh and Antonia were right to sus-pect Miss Hope of having killed Stella. Winifred nodded to herself. She wouldn't put *anything* past that faded spinster with her phoney pince-nez and her Ivy Compton-Burnett hairnet.

Miss Hope was already guilty of deception on a grand scale. Miss Hope's accounts of life at the royal palace in Sofia were nothing but a figment of her warped imagina-tion. A farrago of lies. Miss Hope had blended fact and fiction – like the story of Prince Cyril's affair with a cabaret singer. Well, Cyril *had* had an affair with a cabaret singer called Victoria – one of many – but he had never actually had her living in a lodge in the grounds of his brother's palace.

There had been no lodge, as Tancred had so cleverly dis-covered. And of course Prince Cyril had never had a son called Clement – or Clemmie, as Miss Hope insisted on referring to him. Prince Cyril had never played with a samurai sword, nor had he been an Edgar Wallace aficion-ado. Miss Hope had made all that up. Miss Hope was nothing but a delirious fabulist, a serial liar.

Winifred had given the matter very careful consideration and reached the conclusion that it wouldn't be inappropri-ate if it was Miss Hope herself who undid the damage she had done. The architect who constructs a poor edifice should do the demolition job herself. Why should Winifred do somebody else's dirty work?

Besides, Miss Hope needed to be punished. *Yes*. Miss Hope had become too big for her boots. Miss Hope was turning into a proper nuisance. Miss Hope seemed to have got it into her head that Tancred was in love with her. Call me Catherine, indeed!

Winifred looked into the mirror. Miss Hope's carefully arranged white hair was as stiff as a wig, her hairnet was in place, the lines on either side of her mouth were deeper than ever before, which suggested that not only age but her sins as well had finally caught up with her, only this time she was wearing her gold-rimmed half-moon glasses, not the pince-nez with the black ribbon.

Winifred was going to make sure that Miss Hope did the right thing. She would watch over her like the proverbial hawk. Miss Hope was tricky. There were indications that Miss Hope didn't like the idea of reaping what she had sown. That must be the reason for her looking so down in the mouth. Miss Hope was feeling humiliated and she resented it. Oh, how she resented it!

Miss Hope might be tempted to cause greater destruction than she needed, out of sheer spite. Smash Tancred's computer with her umbrella – reduce Tancred's Chinamen to smithereens – splash ink all over Tancred's gold-and-green study – rip his curtains apart, even! It would be the final flick of the serpent's tail.

Desecrating Tancred's den, the lovely Pupil Room, would be an act of wanton malevolence, but Winifred wouldn't put *anything* past Miss Hope. No, I mustn't take any chances with her, Winifred thought. She didn't care for the malicious glint in Miss Hope's eye. There was also something sly and calculating about Miss Hope's expression. Did the old witch believe she could outwit her?

Did Miss Hope kill the preposterous Stella and then plant Winifred's handkerchief beside the body? That was a definite possibility. Miss Hope must hate Winifred as much as *she* hated Miss Hope. That hadn't always been the case, though. Winifred frowned. She had a vague notion that a link of some kind existed between them . . .

Winifred found herself thinking of the day Stella died. It had been a Tuesday. She couldn't say what she had done that day. Her memory was a complete blank. The only thing she remembered was returning all the manuscripts her publishers had asked her to read and evaluate with a note saying she was too busy, dealing with an important private matter.

(*Could* she have been at the Villa Byzantine that day?)

'Where did you say the house was, madam?' Winifred heard the taxi driver's voice. 'What number?'

'Further down the road ... I don't think there is a number ... Yes, that's it. You can stop here. It's only a short distance.'

'Is that a tunnel? Blimey. Wouldn't you like me to drive you to the house?'

'No, thank you, my good man. There's nothing I enjoy better than a bracing walk,' she said crisply. 'It's such fine weather.'

'Looks like rain,' he muttered.

'I have my trusty old umbrella with me.'

'There may be a storm.'

'So kind of you to care, but I am not in the least afraid of storms.'

She paid him and got out. What an impudent fellow! She glanced up with narrowed eyes. The skies glared down at her like the polished interior of an angry oyster shell. 'The many-splendoured weather of an English day,' she heard Miss Hope murmur.

Winifred remained silent. She hadn't liked the way the driver had been looking at her. She feared he might decide to linger and spy on her ... Follow her even ... No – he was gone ... Thank God!

She entered the tunnel. Above her, sinister yews spread their sombre branches like the roof-span of a crypt. She thought, *I must be very careful now. I am dealing with a woman who is as unpredictable as she is unbalanced.*

Halfway down the tunnel of trees she heard what sounded like the slamming of a car door somewhere.

# 32

# The Exterminating Angel

A lugubrious El Greco horizon suffused with inky rain – a sudden flash of lightning darting across the sky, then a second one. The driver had mentioned a storm. It's the kind of setting that lends itself to melodrama, she thought.

Under the low-hanging clouds the Villa Byzantine loomed, gloom-shrouded and desolate. More yews – thick and black and forbidding. Why did she keep noticing yews? Yews were said to be symbols of death.

An earlier splash of rain had soaked the fallen leaves into a paste of dark slush under her feet. Miss Hope exclaimed, 'Oh dear, look at me. Up to my eyes in mud. People will think I have been playing catch-as-catch-can with pigs!'

Winifred Willard didn't say a word. She stood by the front door, opened her handbag and took out the key. She had managed to have a replica made of one of Tancred's keys – she'd never told him, but she didn't think he would mind. No, of course he wouldn't.

She unlocked the door and went in. She stood in the hall and breathed in the sweet smell of lavender, beeswax and pot-pourri. She smiled again, remembering those fifties American films. *Honey, I'm home!* It was always the husband who said it, the wife was invariably in the kitchen, baking a cake.

There was a clap of thunder. All the window panes rattled. Although it was only morning, the hall was dark.

She didn't really like this house. It had a certain – atmosphere. She wouldn't have called it a happy house. No. The sooner Tancred got rid of it, the better.

'Now this is what I want you to do. Please listen very carefully. I would be extremely grateful if you didn't interrupt.'

Winifred had spoken with strange incisiveness. Happening to glance into the tall silver-framed mirror on the wall, she noted that Miss Hope's face was now quite expressionless.

'Would you stop for a moment, please?'

But Miss Hope didn't stop. She pretended she hadn't heard. It was clear that Miss Hope resented being told what to do. She was stubborn as a mule. They started going up the stairs.

The front door opened noiselessly and was shut at once.

(If she had glanced back over her shoulder Winifred would have seen the killer, but she didn't.)

The killer stood in the shadow of the grandfather clock and listened as Winifred Willard proceeded to give instructions to Miss Hope.

'Everything must disappear. Some of it is bona fide, which is a shame. I am sure you know that Tancred *did* have other sources of information, you were not the only one. I am talking about *reliable* sources, but it is all mixed up with your lies – so it is no good.'

(Talking to herself, the killer thought.)

'Tancred will be *so* upset,' Miss Hope bleated. 'Can't we keep *some* of it?'

'I am afraid we can't. There is no way round it,' Winifred said. 'Allow one rotten apple in – and the whole barrel is contaminated.'

'Tancred will be devastated.'

'Tancred will understand. It will be a shock at first, but he will understand. I will explain everything to him. What good are bogus biographies to anybody?'

'Some people would read *anything*. Books with titles like *Reheated Cabbage* and *Pregnant Widows*.'

179

'Should such people be encouraged?' I don't know why I am talking to her, Winifred thought.

'Tancred will have a nervous breakdown.'

'He won't. Tancred is a young man. He is strong and resilient.'

The door to Pupil Room was open. The owl doorstop was in place, preventing the door from shutting. The doorstop was in the shape of an owl whose solemn bespectacled face, it suddenly struck Winifred, looked uncannily like that of Miss Hope.

Pupil Room was sunk in gloom. The curtains were half-drawn across the windows. The moment she entered, a flash of lightning lit the study with searchlight brilliance and while it lingered, dimming and brightening, for a split second too bright to look at, the inevitable thunder rolled and cracked.

Winifred crossed to the desk and switched on a brass-base table lamp. She glanced at the book that lay on the desk. *Waiting for Princess Margaret*. An *anti*-memoir, Tancred had called it. Flawed but fascinating. Winifred's eyes strayed to the petunias in the small vase – they were quite dead now. Tancred's 'domestic help' was far from efficient. Winifred pursed her lips. When they were married, she'd give the slouch the sack.

Her eyes passed over a sepia photograph showing Hitler shaking King Boris' hand. Tancred believed the photograph had been taken in 1943, at the start of the fatal visit. Boris had died soon after his return from Germany. There had been rumour and endless speculation that Hitler had had something to do with the death . . .

Winifred turned on the computer. As she waited for the icons to come up, another clap of thunder shook the windows and the next moment the rain came, a battering kind of sound, like a hail of bullets . . . It was a firing squad that had executed Prince Cyril . . . There seemed to be reminders of death everywhere today . . . There had been a dead mole in the garden that morning . . . Winifred had put on her gardening gloves, picked it up, wrapped it in an old copy of the *Telegraph* and dropped it in the bin. She was not the least bit squeamish.

Documents. Exactly what she wanted. There it was. For a second she hesitated. No – never slack your hand in the day of battle!

Prince Cyril biography. *Delete.*

She stooped a little, her eyes above the half-moon glasses fixed on the computer screen. Her hand became busy.

Click – click – click – and *click.*

There it was. So easy. The work of a moment!

All gone. The so-called 'biography' was no more. Thank God.

She could imagine Professor Goldsworthy waiting in vain for the Vane papers . . .

It was all over! The relief of it! The damage had been undone. She felt the knot in her stomach start loosening. She had been envisaging problems. She had imagined Miss Hope might put up a fight!

'Well done,' she told Miss Hope. 'Now take Tancred's black leather notebook – there it is – and put it in your bag. We'll deal with that later. How about a bonfire tonight?'

Winifred thought she heard the stairs creak, then the sound of footfalls across the landing. Suddenly she remembered the slamming of the car door she had heard earlier on. Had she imagined it? Could Tancred have returned? Her hand went up to her mouth. What if Tancred were suddenly to come into Pupil Room? What would he do when he realized she had destroyed the Prince Cyril biography? Well, it would be a shock – he might fly off the handle – he might get into a blind rage, pick up the owl doorstop and—

She told herself that such wild fantasies were unworthy of her. Tancred would never hurt her. Besides, she couldn't imagine Tancred in a blind rage – going berserk – no, of course not – why, he was the gentlest of men – apart from being a gentleman.

She heard a scraping sound – *exactly* as though the owl had been removed from the space between the door and the floor.

'You must get out of here, quick,' Miss Hope whispered urgently in her ear. 'Don't stand and stare. Turn round. Look behind you!'

Winifred's hand went up to her forehead. 'I have the strangest feeling there are *two* people inside me.'

The next moment the blow fell.

Without a sound she slumped to the floor.

# 33

# Murder in Pupil Room

It was some time after lunch.

Major Payne pointed with the stem of his pipe. 'Look at the rain!'

'It's horrible. Enough to break the windows. It's been now – what? Three hours?' Antonia sighed. 'England's got so little to recommend it, really. It's on days like these that I dream of emigrating to Italy. What was it you said about Morland? You thought he looked guilty when he came to you asking for help – he had a haunted air about him?'

'He seemed guilty, yes. I don't think I imagined it. But Morland has no motive as such. Why should he want to kill the woman he was about to marry, the woman for whom he had ditched Melisande Chevret? He loved her, didn't he?'

'Actually, Hugh, I don't think he did.'

Payne's left eyebrow went up. 'What's this? Don't tell me it's anything to do with the . . . Corrida Hotel?'

'Well, it is . . . I have a theory,' said Antonia a little apologetically.

The next moment Payne's mobile phone rang and he took it out of his pocket.

'Sorry . . . What slaves we are to these things . . . Hello?'

'Major Payne? Oh, Major Payne! Thank God!'

'That you, Vane? Whatever's happened?'

'Something dreadful – she's been killed – the body is in my study – lots of blood—'

'Slow down a bit . . . Who's been killed?'

'Miss Hope!'

'There's no such person as Miss Hope.'

'I mean Melisande! *Melisande Chevret*. The actress!' The biographer's voice rose on a hysterical note.

'*Melisande?*' The next moment Payne remembered that Vane was a bit behind with his facts. But explanations could wait. 'Are you sure she is dead?'

'Yes. Her head has been bashed in. It's terrible. She is in Pupil Room – my study – there's blood everywhere!'

'Have you called the police?'

'I haven't! I thought I would call you first.' Vane's voice quavered. 'I am frightened, Major Payne. It's happened twice! *Two murders in my house*. The police will say it's me! They are bound to!'

'Don't jump to conclusions, Vane. And don't touch anything. We are coming.' He turned to Antonia. '*Allons-y*.'


They drove through the pelting rain. The windscreen wipers writhed like living things as they struggled to keep the flood in check.

'What if it *is* Melisande who has turned up dead?' Antonia murmured. 'For some reason, Melisande might have gone to the Villa Byzantine dressed up as Miss Hope . . .'

'That, my love, would be one of those logic-defying twists which are relished by genre addicts and condemned by the unhooked as nothing better than annoying childish tricks.'

'Don't you think you are driving too fast?'

'Melisande might have gone to the Villa Byzantine dressed up *as her sister* dressed up as Miss Hope. Sorry. I forgot you disapproved of double bluffs.'

'What I disapprove of is speeding in a deluge. Please,

184

Hugh, don't look at me – keep your eyes on the road! We'll have an accident!'

The Villa Byzantine was fully illuminated and looked incongruously festive. It brought to mind the Royal Albert Hall at the start of the Proms. Tancred Vane seemed to have walked about turning on all the lights.

'Leaving his fingerprints everywhere, silly fellow,' Payne said.

'Well, his fingerprints are already everywhere,' Antonia pointed out. 'He needn't account for them. It's his house.'

Tancred Vane ushered them in. He was deadly pale. His bow-tie was askew. He didn't say a word. He was shaking. Payne patted his arm. The royal biographer led the way up the Carrollian staircase and into the study.

Major Payne's eye had become practised in taking in swiftly every detail of what a murder scene had to offer. The body lay face downwards beside the mahogany desk. He knelt beside it and, overcoming his extreme revulsion, gently tipped the head to one side so that he could get a good view of it.

Eyes open and glazed. Theatrical make-up. Vertical lines painted in, from nose down to each side of mouth. Somewhat smudged. White wig. Tight curls. Helmet-like coiffure of the 'indestructible' kind. No, not indestructible – it hadn't succeeded in cushioning the blow – the blows – she had been hit several times. It hadn't prevented her skull from being smashed.

So she had come to the Villa Byzantine as before, dressed up as Miss Hope . . . What could have been going on in her mind?

'It's Winifred all right,' said Payne. He rose to his feet.

The royal biographer stared. '*Winifred?*'

'Yes, Vane. Her name is Winifred Willard.'

'I thought her name was Melisande Chevret.'

'This is Melisande's sister. It was she who was in love with you. Winifred was Miss Hope. We thought it was Melisande but then we had a sudden revelation. Thanks to my aunt, actually. It happened last night.'

'Thanks to your aunt?'

'You would be perfectly justified in imagining that all reason had disintegrated and the universe had turned into a brainless harlequinade, but I assure you—'

'She's been killed with the owl,' Tancred Vane said wildly. He pointed to the blood-bespattered doorstop that lay halfway between the body and the study door. 'Somebody picked up the owl and hit her with it.'

'That indeed was the way it was done,' agreed Payne.

'She phoned me last night – at some unearthly hour. She said she wanted to meet me urgently this morning – *not* here – at the British Library. At midday, she said. She said she wanted to speak to me. It was a matter of life and death. I tried to call you – but I couldn't get an answer. I left a message.'

'Did you?'

'Yes! I left a voice message. Just before I set off.'

There was a pause as Payne produced his mobile phone. 'So you did, old boy. At . . . five to eleven . . . This may be important.'

'You think that I'll have to prove I have an alibi?'

'It's possible. The police may want to make sure. How long did you stay at the British Library?'

'An hour or so . . . I browsed in the bookshop, then had a cup of tea . . . I thought that Miss Hope might say something important – that she might confess to the murder! That's why I went. Lord. I keep calling her Miss Hope . . . She didn't turn up of course . . . She never intended to go to the British Library, did she?'

'No. Winifred Willard intended to come to the Villa Byzantine. She wanted you out of the way,' said Payne. 'Why? I think my wife may have the answer. At least she looks as though she does.'

'I believe this is yours, Mr Vane.' Antonia had wrapped her handkerchief round her hand and was holding up a black notebook. 'Your initials are on the flyleaf.'

'Yes. It's mine. These are my notes for the blasted biography. Where was it?'

'Inside Winifred's bag.' She pointed.

186

'She took my notebook?' Vane blinked. 'But – why? Why?'

'Maybe because it contained lies? All the stories she made up for you . . . I imagine she meant to destroy it,' Antonia went on slowly, 'so that you should not be put to shame. Perhaps she realized that she had acted irresponsibly and that you would become the laughing stock of the literary world? I believe she did it out of consideration for your reputation as a biographer – since she loved you so much – she was very much in love with you, you know.'

'Was she really in love with me?'

'She was mad about you,' said Payne. 'She was contemplating a spring wedding.'

'Was there a deadline for what you had written?' Antonia asked. 'Were you expected to send any of it to your publisher?'

'No . . . Actually, yes . . . Yes!' Tancred Vane's hand went up to his forehead. 'Professor Goldsworthy was going to read my notes. Professor Goldsworthy is a historian – an expert on East European monarchies – knows his Bulgarian royal family inside out, or so I've been told . . . He was to act as a consultant . . . He had agreed to look at what I'd written . . . My editor had made arrangements—'

'Did Winifred know about Goldsworthy?'

'I – I told Miss Hope I was going to send him the biography by the end of the week. Via email. As an attachment. She knew, yes.'

'That explains it. That's most probably the reason why she came here.'

'I've got it all saved on my computer—' Vane broke off. 'You don't think she—? She couldn't have—?'

'You'd better check,' Major Payne said.

The royal biographer staggered towards the desk and turned on the computer. 'She called it "that silly biography". I thought she was in an odd mood that day.' He gazed at the screen and his hands became busy. 'It's not here. It's gone. *All gone*. The whole file. You are right. She's deleted the Prince Cyril file! She's destroyed it! She's even emptied the Recycle Bin! I have no back-up!'

Payne regarded him sympathetically. 'It wouldn't have been any good to you, would it, given that it was all untrue . . . Shall we go downstairs? We'll need to call the police. It would look jolly peculiar if we delayed any further.'

'The police . . . My God . . . I don't think I'll be able to explain all this . . . About Miss Hope . . . They won't believe me . . . They'll think I'm mad . . . They'll say I did it . . . They'll take me away . . . Would you – would you stay with me?'

'Of course we will, old boy.'

'Should I call my solicitor?'

'No, not yet. It would be wrong to put the cart before the horse, you know. Don't let's rush things. *Festina lente* and all that rot. Perhaps I could use the phone in the hall?'

They walked down the staircase in silence. Major Payne picked up the phone. Antonia and Tancred Vane went into the drawing room. Vane produced two globular cut-crystal glasses and silently poured out brandy.

He spoke. 'Who killed her? Why did they kill her? What reason could anyone have had for wanting Melisande Chevret's sister dead?'

Scared out of his wits, Antonia thought. She watched him gulp down his brandy. He choked and started coughing.

'Would you like some water?' Antonia asked.

'No. I'm fine . . . What's going on? Who killed her? Do you know?'

'Well—'

Antonia wondered about him. Could he have left the British Library early, come back and surprised Winifred in his study? What if he had caught her red-handed? He might have got so distraught, so angry at the destruction of his brain-child, that he flipped. He might have picked up the owl and—

'Do you believe it's the same person who killed Stella Markoff?' Tancred Vane asked.

'It's got to be the same person,' said Antonia. 'It would be an incredible coincidence if Winifred's murder turned out to be unconnected to Stella's. I don't think we are dealing with two different killers.'

'Could her sister have done it?'

'Melisande? That's an interesting idea. Well, she certainly had an excellent motive for killing Stella. Melisande was jealous of Stella. She is still intent on getting her fiancé back . . . Yes . . . But why should Melisande want to kill her sister?'

'Perhaps Miss Hope – Winifred – knew something about Stella's murder – what if she had proof that Melisande had done it?' Tancred Vane suggested. 'What's Melisande like? No, don't tell me. I don't want to know. Not now.' He took a sip of brandy. 'Did you say she was an actress? I used to have a thing about actresses—' He broke off.

There was a pause.

Major Payne came into the drawing room. 'The police will be here in about twenty minutes. They remembered at once that they had been to the Villa Byzantine once before.'

'Of course they'd remember. It was only last week,' Antonia said. 'It's an unusual enough name.'

Tancred Vane put down his glass. 'They will think it's me. I know they will. They'll put me in handcuffs.'

'They won't. Don't be an ass. They wanted to know who I was, what I was doing at the Villa Byzantine and so on. They were rather tedious about it . . . Brandy, eh? I could do with some brandy. May I? Thank you . . . I say, old boy, there's something I've been meaning to ask you – what happened to those letters and diaries? The ones that had belonged to Stella's grandmother.' Payne spoke conversationally. 'You didn't manage to persuade her to sell them to you, did you?'

For a moment Tancred Vane looked blank. He didn't seem to know what Payne was talking about. 'Oh God, no. No.'

'Did you really offer her fifty pounds for them?'

Vane wetted his lips. His eyes shifted their gaze from Payne to Antonia. 'As a matter of fact Stella suggested an exchange – the diaries for the sword, but I said no – wouldn't have been an equal exchange – the samurai

189

sword is *much* more valuable than the diaries. Besides, I wasn't entirely convinced of their authenticity—'

'I know who the killer is,' Antonia said suddenly.

'You do?' Payne raised the brandy glass to his lips.

'There is only one person who could have killed Stella *and* Winifred.'

Payne cast a glance at their host. Tancred Vane had given a little gasp. His forehead glistened with sweat.

'I have an idea Stella's murder wasn't premeditated – was it?' Payne said quietly.

'I don't think it was. Something precipitated it. I believe an event took place,' Antonia went on slowly, 'either in the car or soon after they arrived at the Villa Byzantine. I may be wrong, but I believe that Stella made a discovery. I think she tumbled to a certain shocking secret—'

There was a scraping noise. Tancred Vane had risen to his feet and pushed back the elegant velvet-upholstered spoon-shaped chair with carved arms and legs, in which he had been sitting. He was holding his hand to his mouth. 'I'm afraid I'm going to be sick—'

He made for the door. He was walking so fast, he slithered on the polished parquet floor and nearly fell. Major Payne looked as though he was going to follow him but thought better of it.

He glanced back at Antonia. 'What shocking secret?'

She told him.


Antonia told the police as well. She had been contemplating testing out her theory, but decided this was not the time for games.

She was unsure of the inspector's reaction, but she needn't have worried. Inspector Davidson listened to her carefully, making notes. He then asked her what she did and his expression did not change when she told him she wrote detective stories. He was certainly interested in her 'theory'. He asked her to explain her reasons. He agreed it was something of a long shot. There was hardly any 'concrete evidence'.

'He might give himself away when he realizes I am aware of what has been going on,' Antonia said.

There was a pause, then the inspector said, 'Very well, Miss Darcy. We won't do anything till you hear from him. *If* you hear from him. You still believe he will contact you?'

'I think he will. He'd want to know what my next move would be . . .'

'Is there anything you'd like us to do?'

'You can make inquiries at the Corrida Hotel in Earls Court . . . Then there's the car,' Antonia said thoughtfully. 'You'd better check the car. There is a *second* car, are you aware? I think that's the one that's been used . . . There may be blood – DNA—'

34

# Les Liaisons Dangereuses

So the cat's out of the bag. Antonia Darcy *knows*, Julia Henderson thought. She pulled her sable coat round her for she suddenly found she was shivering.

Walking out of the Corrida Hotel in Earls Court, she got into her car and started the engine.

No. Antonia Darcy couldn't possibly *know*, not for sure. Antonia Darcy *suspected*. Was it possible that she had seen them in a compromising situation – holding hands, cuddling, kissing? Had they ever been that careless?

Julia knew exactly what must have happened. Antonia Darcy had heard her speaking on the phone when she came to her flat – she'd come to snoop of course, Julia saw that now. Antonia Darcy had noted down the mention of the Corrida Hotel—

There was something else Antonia Darcy knew, Julia couldn't say exactly what, but she felt sure it must link up with the Corrida Hotel in some way. *Yes.* Antonia Darcy had laid a trap and was now biding her time. Antonia clearly believed there would be a – well, a reaction.

Clever woman. Knew how to use her brains. Had nerve. Julia admired people who had nerve. She had to admit she had rather liked Antonia Darcy. Her sort of woman. She'd enjoyed talking to her. Having a gossip about Stella. But perhaps she had told her more than she should have . . .

Antonia Darcy was a detective story writer, so she was probably more interested in the intricacies and perversities of human behaviour than in seeing justice done. She might also be keen on verifying whether traps worked in real life . . .

Would Antonia Darcy turn out to be one of those public-spirited bores? Julia couldn't stand public-spirited bores. She herself had no moral scruples. She thought of the couple of occasions on which she had done things that counted as criminal offences – such as forging her brother's signature on his cheques. James had never got wise to it.

It had been easy. Child's play. All Julia had to do was get hold of one of his cheque books, then practise signing James' name on a sheet of paper. That had been fun. Well, poor old James never so much as glanced at his bank statements and he seemed to trust her implicitly. She would do it again, if she had to! Julia nodded to herself. She needed money. She always needed money, alas.

Julia had already managed to pinch Stella's letters and diaries – the grandmother's letters and diaries – she'd found them tucked away at the bottom of Stella's suitcase. She intended to try and strike some sort of bargain with Tancred Vane. It might be tricky. Oh well, that could wait.

Julia's thoughts turned back to her brother. Antonia Darcy would never be able to prove a thing – unless poor old James got flustered, lost his nerve and gave himself away . . .

Must talk to him, warn him. Would it be any good? Was it too late? Why didn't he answer his mobile phone?

Where *was* he?


'It's the biographer guy and your sister.'

'What do you mean?'

'They did it. They are the killers. They are in it together.'

'What are you talking about?'

'At first I thought it was one of the witches. Melisande or Winifred. Everything was pointing first to one, then to the other witch, but soon I started putting two and two together. Suddenly I *knew*.'

'Knew what?'

'That they were in it together of course, James. Your sister and the biographer guy.'

Moon blew a giant bubble with her chewing gum. The television set was on, but she had muted it – they were showing *Lethal Weapon 4*, a film she quite liked, though she had already seen it four times and knew it by heart, so she was not interested.

'I saw the *pattern*. I deduced that it had been them all along. I didn't immediately know *why* they had to kill my mother. I worked that out later on. I am smarter than Mrs Fletcher, I keep telling you. Actually, I'm not at all surprised your sister Julia is the killer.'

'You aren't serious, are you?'

'I am serious. *Julia, dear Julia is peculiar*. You don't know your sister at all well, do you, James? You think you do, but you are wrong. You don't. You are too busy making money. You know the stock market, but you don't know your sister.'

'You should go to school. School is better than tutors. I'll get you into a good school. The very best,' he went on, though he found it very difficult at the moment to conjure up a picture of a future that made sense, let alone one that was happy.

'I don't want to go to school. I don't *need* to go to school. I know everything I need to know.'

Morland had missed most of what Moon had told him earlier on. He had been too preoccupied with his own thoughts to pay close attention.

'Julia is the biographer guy's secret girlfriend,' she went on. 'I guess Julia contacted him as soon as Mother started going to that weird place with the weird name. Pizza-at-nine.'

'You mean the Villa Byzantine?'

She laughed. 'Mother kept saying how rich the biographer guy was, how educated, how cultured, how delicate, all that shit.'

'Language, Moon,' he said absently.

'She chattered about him all the time and about his house and how strange and *baroque* everything was. The biographer guy has a collection of Chinamen and an *owl* doorstop in his study, can you imagine? All extremely baroque and cultured. Mother showed Julia the pictures she'd taken on her mobile. Of Sacred Crane and his baroque house.'

'His name is Tancred Vane.'

'No, it's Sacred Crane,' she said firmly. 'Julia's curiosity was, as they say in books, piqued. She said to herself, I must have this man. You look as though you don't believe me.' Moon heaved a sigh. 'You need to trust me more, James.'

'I trust you.'

'You need to trust me *more*.'

I shouldn't have smoked that awful thing, Morland thought. His head was spinning. He was finding it hard to focus. He was feeling a little sick. It didn't seem to have any effect on *her*. She said she smoked spliffs quite often. She liked the feeling it gave her. The feeling of power – she felt she could do – *anything*.

'Now listen very carefully. This is important. Julia decides on a plan of action. She contacts the Sacred guy. She tells him some incredible tale and gets him interested.'

'What incredible tale?'

'How the fuck d'you expect me to know? I wasn't sitting inside her head taking notes, was I? Something about those diaries and letters. All that shit. Perhaps she said she could make him photocopies of the diaries and give them to him for free.'

Moon was becoming impatient. She no longer enjoyed making every little detail fit in. She was getting bored. She yawned.

'Sacred got interested all right. Maybe Julia's voice reminded him of his late mother's voice? Guys like Sacred are all twisted inside. Most English guys are twisted inside. Sacred agrees to a meeting. They meet and they talk and then – then they become lovers.'

'You are making this up, aren't you?'

'Julia is strong and domineering. Sacred Crane is weak and perhaps he likes to be whipped, or tied up, so it was a perfect match. Julia then asked him to help her. She told him she wanted Stella Markoff dead – eliminated.' Moon made a slashing gesture across her throat with her right hand.

'Why should Julia want Stella dead?'

Morland really didn't know what to do. Should he tell Moon about Antonia Darcy? About what Antonia Darcy had done? Moon might be very young but she was intelligent, what she called a 'smart cookie'; she was faster and cleverer than him, so she might – she just might think of a way out. He knew he was clutching at straws.

'Julia knew that once you were married to Mother, she would have to say goodbye to all the money you've got in the bank. Julia planned *everything*. I was going to be the patsy. That's why she used the sword, to throw suspicion on me – because I am maladjusted and mad about swords and beheadings and blood and stuff. I am the most obvious suspect, see?'

A lot of silly nonsense, Morland thought, though of course he didn't dare say so. The next moment he frowned. What was it Moon had said earlier on? Something which had sent an inexplicable shiver down his spine—

'Julia drove Mother to the Villa Byzantine in her car. Sacred was there of course, but it was Julia who killed her. Julia took the sword off the wall and – *swoosh*.' Moon yawned. 'I hate this hotel – I really hate it – couldn't we go some other place? I liked the Corrida Hotel better. Why don't we go there any more?'

Her voice rose plaintively. She sounded like a child now. They were sitting on the double bed. Outside it was a grey afternoon. The rain had stopped. It was very quiet.

'When are we moving into your new house, James? I like the new house. I think it's the coolest house ever.'

'I am glad you like it.'

Should he tell her? What a mess he had got himself into. What have I done? Morland thought in sudden panic.

196

'One thing I must make clear, James. When we get married, I am *not* taking on your name. No way. Moon Morland sounds the dumbest name ever! What's the matter with you? I don't like it when you look sad. Come here,' she said softly. *'Come here.'*

At the touch of her hand he shut his eyes. His physical reaction was so sharp, so powerful, so overwhelming, it blotted out all rational thought. Not that there'd been much rational thought in the first place.

Each time it felt like that very first time—

Holding her, smelling her, *tasting* her. He had feared he might faint with the ecstasy of it. He had broken down and wept. Never before had lovemaking been such an uplifting experience – so glorious, so infinitely rewarding!

He made a sound at the back of his throat, a kind of whimper.

She drew his head towards hers and kissed him on the lips.

## 35

# The Cry of an Owl

It was the following morning. Antonia had made herself a cup of coffee when the telephone rang.

'Miss Darcy? James Morland speaking.'

'Oh, hello.'

There it was. She had been right. It hadn't taken him too long. She looked at the clock: ten minutes past ten.

'Would it be possible for me to have a word with you?'

'Of course. I've been expecting you to call,' Antonia said conversationally. Let him see he was not mistaken. Let him realize that his worst fears had been confirmed. Don't let there be the slightest doubt in his mind that she *knew*. 'Would you like to come to us? You've been to our house before, haven't you?'

'Would your husband be there?'

'Would you rather he weren't?'

'I suppose he knows?'

'He knows, yes.'

'Do the—?' Morland broke off. Clearly he was going to ask whether the police knew too, since in the end that was what really mattered. He was probably clinging to the hope that he might be able to strike some kind of a bargain with Antonia. 'I will be with you in about an hour,' he said tonelessly.

Despite herself, Antonia felt sorry for him. She believed

that girl had led him on. Still, he was the adult. He should have known better. A fifteen-year-old girl.

There was such a thing as self-control.

She hadn't seen him since the evening of Melisande's birthday party at Kinderhook and she wondered whether she would have recognized him if she bumped into him in the street. Probably not – not unless he reminded her where they'd met and who he was.

At the party he had looked florid and festive in his Paisley-patterned tie. He hadn't said anything remotely interesting, certainly nothing memorable. Blissfully uncomplicated, Hugh had said. Devoid of hidden depths. He was a recognizable type. One saw chaps like James Morland at superior gentlemen's clubs – dozing at board meetings – taking their time over the wine list at expensive restaurants, usually in the company of a horsey lady – watching a cricket match at Lord's, Pimm's in hand, a white panama on their head, their face the colour of ripe tomato.

He looked different now.

He had lost weight and his expensive tweed jacket hung loosely on him. A candy-striped silk handkerchief stuck out of his breast pocket. His face was extremely pale and haggard as though with lack of sleep. Gone was the ruddy hue. He didn't seem to have had a haircut recently. He hadn't shaved either. In a funny kind of way he looked younger, raffish, somewhat dissolute. His eyes were bright, feverish.

'Would you like some tea or coffee?'

'No, thank you.'

'Won't you sit down?'

He sat on the sofa, making it creak. He was still a heavy man. She glanced at his hands. Big, well-tended hands—

'Why did you pay my bill at the hotel?' Morland spoke without preamble. He was staring at the floor. Keeping custody of his eyes like a nun, Antonia thought incongruously. 'What business was it of yours?' He sounded a little breathless.

199

'It was none of my business, you are right.' She remained standing, giving herself, she reflected, an advantage of sorts.

'You had no right to meddle in my affairs. No right at all.' His voice rose slightly. 'My private life is my own.'

Antonia walked slowly away from the sofa and stood beside the window. She hoped he wouldn't make a scene. Hugh would be down any moment now. Not that she feared Morland would try to assault her. Still, she would feel safer with Hugh in the room.

'I wouldn't have gone to the Corrida Hotel,' she said, 'if it hadn't been for Stella's murder.'

'You think – the two are connected? The hotel and the murder?'

'I believe they are . . . Not the hotel as such—' Antonia broke off. 'There has been a second murder.'

This time he looked at her. 'What second murder?'

'Winifred Willard was killed yesterday at the Villa Byzantine.'

'Winifred? Melisande's sister? Are you serious?'

'We saw the body.'

'I don't believe you.' He shook his head. 'Melisande would have told me about it. She would have telephoned me. You are lying.'

'Melisande has been admitted to hospital. She's had a nervous breakdown. Didn't you know?'

'I don't believe you. You are lying,' he said again. 'What gave you the idea I'd stayed at the Corrida Hotel?'

'You dropped a receipt the first time you came here. It was headed "The Corrida Hotel, Earls Court". You had paid for a room, a bottle of champagne and a can of Red Bull. I thought it an unusual combination. I didn't think you were the kind of man who would drink champagne with Red Bull. Actually, you didn't seem to know what Red Bull was when it was mentioned – don't you remember? At Melisande's birthday party?'

'I don't know what you are talking about.'

'I am sure you do. For some reason the combination of a *corrida* and a bull stuck in my mind. Then – then I suddenly remembered that at that same party Stella's daughter went into a sulk because there was no Red Bull among the drinks on offer.'

'What's that got to do with anything?'

'Red Bull again, see? The champagne was for you, the Red Bull for Moon, correct? A bit later several other things clicked into place—'

Antonia paused as her husband, looking extremely smart in a dark blue blazer and very dark grey trousers, sauntered into the room. She felt herself relaxing. She had no doubt that Hugh would be equal to knocking Morland out should the latter decide to turn nasty at some point in the proceedings.

Major Payne gave an amiable nod in the direction of their visitor and mimed to Antonia, as though to say, Carry on, carry on, don't mind me, it's your pigeon. He then stood beside the cocktail cabinet in a posture that brought to mind a fielder in a cricket match alert for the ball. She saw him glance at Morland's hands. Was Hugh considering the possibility of their visitor launching a sudden attack?

'When I was at your sister's – you were at the zoo at the time – Julia received a phone call. The call came from the Corrida Hotel. Apparently,' Antonia said, 'there was something wrong with your card. A sum that needed to be paid. The Corrida Hotel again, you see? And then Julia mentioned the fact that you were moving out – that you had bought a Regency house in Chelsea. You'd told her you and Moon were going to live together?'

'These are private matters. Julia had no business to talk about it to you,' Morland said stiffly.

'You had hinted that you intended to adopt Moon. Julia thought Moon might be your biological daughter. I suspect you encouraged the notion. It made any apparent closeness acceptable. What more natural than a father and daughter sharing a house together after the mother's tragic death?' Antonia paused, but he remained silent. 'Julia said something else, which also fitted in with the theory that had started forming in my mind. She told me that Stella had commented on the fact that – that—'

Payne cleared his throat. 'Care for a drink, Morland? Or is it too early?'

'No, nothing.' Morland glared at Antonia. 'What had Stella been commenting on?'

'She—' Antonia bit her lip. She didn't quite know how to put it. Why was sex always such a ticklish subject? Why was she such a prude? But there was no way round it. Sex after all was at the very heart of this affair.

'Stella was a bit concerned about your lack of ardour. She found your attitude towards her a little too "decent", a little too "gentlemanly".' How idiotic this sounded! 'She feared she might be abandoned at the altar. I found myself wondering about the true nature of your relationship with her. You left Melisande for Stella. You asked Stella and her daughter to move in with you. You were planning to marry Stella. You were at great pains to convey the impression that you were smitten with her—'

'I *was* smitten with her.'

'I am inclined to doubt that,' said Antonia. 'So, I asked myself, why would you want to play the impetuous lover if you didn't really care about Stella? Why were you so keen on marrying her? I puzzled about the urgency in particular. The only explanation that presented itself was that it wasn't Stella you were after, but her daughter.' Antonia's eyes were once more on Morland's hands. 'You were mad about Stella's daughter.'

'You are a raving lunatic,' said Morland.

'Her fifteen-year-old daughter.'

'You told me she was sixteen and a half, Morland. With hindsight, I believe you felt uncomfortable revealing her real age to me,' said Major Payne. 'That can be interpreted as guilty conscience, you know.'

'You wanted to marry the mother, so that you could have permanent easy access to the underage daughter,' Antonia went on relentlessly. 'A difficult, troubled, somewhat delinquent girl. You had already started an affair with her – while making everybody believe that you disliked each other ... I assume your trysts were held at various hotels?'

'You had no business to pry into my affairs. It's scandalous that you should have eavesdropped on Julia's telephone conversations. It's an absolute outrage. I have a good mind to report you to the police.'

Antonia shrugged. 'There was only one telephone conversation and I didn't eavesdrop. I just happened to be there when Julia answered the call.'

'You – you actually set a trap for me. Who do you think you are? Haven't you got anything better to do? You went to the Corrida Hotel and paid my bill. They told me it was my sister, but it was your name – *Antonia Darcy* – that was on their computer. You introduced yourself as my sister! You had the gall to impersonate my sister. Don't you know that that's a criminal offence punishable by law?'

'I expected a reaction from you, which I have now got.'

'You don't have a scrap of evidence,' said Morland. 'It's all a theory. Nothing but a wild hypothesis. Parlour games. Red Bull and champagne!' Morland laughed but it wasn't a particularly convincing performance. 'Complete and utter bull!'

'I spoke to a chambermaid at the Corrida Hotel. She told me you arrived with a dark-haired girl wearing a long black coat that didn't look too clean. You booked a room—'

'Those foreign girls would do anything for money! They'd say exactly what you want them to say! How much did you give her? I am sure you bribed her. Lies, all lies! Moon was not—' He broke off.

'She wasn't wearing the *chinel*?' Antonia gave a little smile.

'Watch out, Morland. You keep giving yourself away, you know,' Major Payne said.

'As a matter of fact, you were captured on camera. *You and Moon*. There are security cameras in the hotel lounge. The manager let me see the recordings,' Antonia went on bluffing boldly. 'The police saw them too.'

'The police? You mean you've contrived to get the police involved in this nonsense? You don't honestly expect me to believe the hotel manager allowed you any access to their security cameras? I think you are the greatest liar who ever lived. D'you often play games with people's lives?' His hand went up to his chest. Antonia hoped he wouldn't have a heart attack and die in their drawing room. 'Even if it is as you say and we were caught on camera, what proof is there that any "impropriety" ever took place? It's not as though we've been caught in flagrante, is it?'

He was no fool, Antonia thought. There was another pause.

'I am planning to adopt Moon,' Morland said in a thoughtful voice. He sounded almost calm now. 'Poor girl, she's got no one in the world. I was very much in love with Stella. I adored Stella. I was devastated when she died. I propose to take good care of Moon. I feel it's my duty.'

So that was going to be his line. A good lawyer, if it ever came to that, would be able to get him off without any particular difficulty, Antonia reflected.

'I needed to talk to her in private. She can be difficult, she doesn't really like me, so I thought a change of location might be conducive to a constructive discussion about the future, hence the hotel,' Morland went on. 'Moon's never been anywhere near the Villa Byzantine. That handkerchief was not hers. She has nothing to do with any of this lunacy . . . I don't know what I'm doing here. I really don't. Wasting my time. I'm going. I've had enough.' Somewhat shakily Morland rose to his feet.

Antonia said, 'Stella's death was a direct consequence of your affair with Moon.'

'There are very strict libel laws in this country, Miss Darcy, as I'm sure you are aware,' he said with a ghastly smile.

'Stella died minutes after she tumbled to the fact that you and her daughter were having an affair. There were letters. Stella found them. She read them.'

Morland had started walking towards the door. He halted and turned round. 'What letters?' There was a harsh, even ragged, edge to his voice.

'Highly compromising letters written by Moon to you. Letters that made it obvious to Stella that her daughter and you were lovers. The letters were in the car.'

This was an audacious guess, but Antonia couldn't resist it. She remembered Moon telling them how she'd got in trouble at school for writing letters to teachers she 'liked'. Something did happen in the car, Antonia was certain of it. She didn't believe Moon had simply chosen that particular time to regale her mother with details of her affair with James Morland.

'What car are you talking about?'

'Your car. Your *second* car.'

'The *un*cool one,' Major Payne put in. 'The one you keep in the garage. Moon's been driving it, hasn't she?'

'I believe you are both mad. You are a danger to civilized society. You shouldn't be at large. You need psychiatric help,' Morland said, but the bluster had gone.

His expression had changed at the mention of the letters. He was making a visible effort to pull himself together.

'How did Winifred die?' Morland asked after a pause. 'Was she beheaded too?'

'No. Her head was bashed in. It was a ferocious attack.' Payne produced his pipe. 'Somebody took a crack at her skull. Three cracks, to be precise. The blows were dealt with the doorstop from Tancred Vane's study. A genuine Victorian article in the shape of an owl.'

'You certainly had a good motive for wanting to be rid of Stella,' began Antonia. 'However—'

'You are wrong if you think you can pin either murder on me,' Morland said. 'I killed no one. I am not a killer.'

'We know you are not,' said Payne. He started filling his pipe with tobacco from the tobacco jar. 'On the morning Stella's murder took place you were attending a board meeting. The police checked. You have an unbreakable alibi. And we don't think it was you who followed Winifred to the Villa Byzantine either. Yours was not the hand that picked up the owl.'

Morland gazed glassily at him. He looked puzzled and oddly disturbed by Payne's last words. 'The owl?'

It was at that point that his mobile rang.


Once more Antonia bit her lip. One could always trust a mobile to add drama and suspense to an already fraught situation!

Morland took his mobile out of his pocket with a mechanical gesture.

'Yes? Yes, it's me—' He swallowed. He didn't make any effort to disguise his feelings. His expression changed.

Extreme tenderness mingled with fear.

It was Stella's daughter, Antonia knew at once.

'Where are you? What – what's that noise?' Morland glanced from Payne to Antonia. He looked like a trapped animal. 'What do you mean, *after you*? Who is after you?'

The police, Antonia thought. The police were after her.

'You aren't driving, are you?' Morland groaned.

She was driving his car – the *second* car. Antonia went on filling in the gaps. The police were after her. It was all over. It should have happened sooner. Poor lovelorn Winifred needn't have died.

'I love you too – please stop the car – you may have an accident – you have nothing to fear!' Morland cried, throwing all caution to the winds.

'Actually, she has everything to fear,' Payne said in a loud voice. 'The game is up, Morland.'

Antonia wished Hugh didn't use such melodramatic phrases.

'Hello? Moon? Hello? *Hello*?' Morland slumped down heavily on the sofa. He gazed wildly at Payne. 'An owl? Did you say an owl?' Some kind of realization seemed to have dawned on him. His face was grey, ashen. 'But—'


It was the owl that had sent shivers down his spine the day before. He had remembered.

Moon had told him her mother had mentioned the owl

to her, but Stella couldn't have known about it! Vane had bought the owl the day Stella was killed. *After* she was killed. Vane had shown him the owl while they were sitting in the library at the Villa Byzantine.

Morland remembered the exact sequence of events. Vane had poured out two drinks, then gone up to the round table in the middle of the room and reached for one of the packages he had brought with him earlier on. The owl had been in a red cardboard box with golden stripes. There had been a blue star in the middle of the lid.

'Bought it this morning. For Pupil Room. That's what I call my study. Clever birds, owls. Symbolize the wisdom of the author—'

Vane had babbled on. He had been a little hysterical.

No, Stella couldn't have seen the owl. At the time Vane opened the red box with the yellow stripes and the blue star, Stella had been dead. Her body had been lying in Vane's drawing room. Yet Moon told him that her mother had mentioned Vane's owl to her. Since her mother couldn't have done any such thing, since Morland hadn't told her about the owl either, there was only one conclusion to be drawn—

*Moon had seen the owl with her own eyes.*

She had been inside the Villa Byzantine. She had gone up to Vane's study. To the so-called Pupil Room. She had actually picked up the owl and— Why in heaven's name had she killed Winifred?

Morland covered his eyes with his hands. What sounded like a moan escaped his lips. He shook and swayed. The shock was so immense, he wondered if it would bludgeon him into some kind of unconsciousness. It's all my fault, he thought.

He had been wrong to think her innocent. She had been to the Villa Byzantine not just once but *twice* . . . Stella . . . That morning . . . It had looked stormy . . . Stella had seemed preoccupied at breakfast . . . He had left . . . She and Moon had gone to the Villa Byzantine together. They must have done. Moon had driven her mother to the Villa Byzantine . . . In his old car. The *un*cool one . . .

207

Like Antonia before him, he went on filling in the gaps.

His old car – he should have got rid of it ages ago – his old jacket on the back seat – he shouldn't have left it there – the letters in the pocket – damned careless of him – he'd asked Moon to stop writing to him, though he had to admit he had been thrilled by the things she wrote – so damned liberating – never happened to him before, that sort of thing – so flattering – the praise she heaped on him – he should have destroyed those letters – why hadn't he destroyed the damned letters?

They watched his lips tremble, his face crumple.

Light of my loins, fire of my life – or rather the other way round. Sin and soul came into it, Payne did imagine.

Though it was doubtful whether Morland would have put it in any such Nabokovian terms.

# 36

# I Confess

'A folie à deux, eh?' Lady Grylls suggested hopefully.

'No, no, darling. They weren't in it together,' said Payne. 'Nothing like Laurent and Thérèse Raquin or the Honeymoon Killers or Bonnie and Clyde or the Macbeths. Poor Morland had no idea what his teenage inamorata had done. When enlightenment finally came – when he realized that she had killed not only once but *twice* – he broke down and wept like a child.'

It was exactly three weeks later, another grey afternoon, and he and Antonia sat in Lady Grylls' drawing room in St John's Wood, having tea.

'Stella signed her death warrant the moment she told Moon about Tancred Vane's samurai sword,' said Antonia. 'She described the sword in some detail. She knew Moon would be interested. Stella had been anxious to "bond" with her daughter, you see.'

'Moon decided she simply *had* to have the sword,' said Payne. 'Stella objected at first, saying it would be impossible to steal it and carry it back. Moon insisted that nothing could be easier. They would do it together.'

'How do you know all this?' Lady Grylls scowled. 'Of course you are simply frantic with brains, but you couldn't have deduced *everything* – could you?'

'No, darling. We didn't deduce everything. The girl confessed. The girl seems rather proud of what she has done. She is completely without remorse. A callous attention-seeking narcissist.' Payne shook his head. 'Once they arrested and handcuffed her, there was no stopping her. She wanted everybody to know what she had done.'

'The police had been keeping an eye on her and they got her as she was driving at breakneck speed towards a scrapyard somewhere in East London,' said Antonia. 'Her intention, on her own admission, was to strip the car of its plates and abandon it there.'

'Inspector Davidson let us listen to a recording of her recital – as a token of his gratitude.'

'He did? Highly irregular,' Lady Grylls said with relish.

'Well, he was jolly grateful. It was Antonia, after all, who alerted him to some of the facts and she also gave him an idea or two.' Payne reached out and patted his wife's hand across the tea-table.

'Tell me about the day of the murder.' Lady Grylls held up her cup. 'What happened exactly?'

'Moon drove her mother to the Villa Byzantine in James Morland's old car. Stella knew Vane wouldn't be in. He had told her he was going to the British Library. She had managed to pinch one of the front door keys. She sat in the back of the car. Morland's old jacket was lying on the seat beside her. At some point she seemed to pick up the jacket. Moon saw her bury her face in it.'

'That's how Stella found Moon's letters?'

'Yes. They were in a pocket of Morland's jacket. Apparently they were rather *frank* love letters. Short – but uninhibited. There were about ten of them, I think the girl said. Morland had kept them all, stupid old fool.'

'He is only a couple of years older than you,' Antonia said.

'He looks like the Ancient of Days compared to me.' Payne waved a breezy hand. 'Stella recognized her daughter's handwriting at once. By the time the car drew to a halt outside the Villa Byzantine, she had worked herself up into a dreadful state.'

'At first she said nothing – she must have been speechless with shock.'

'Moon described her mother as looking like a "dazed zombie". Stella unlocked the front door and they went into

210

the drawing room,' Payne went on. 'Moon took the sword off the wall and unsheathed it. She delivered a couple of blows, decapitating one of Vane's golden chrysanthemums as well as a curtain tassel. Clearly Morland was exaggerating her wrist injury!'

'It was then that Stella started screaming,' Antonia said, taking up the tale. 'She stood in front of the fireplace waving the letters in the air like a flag. She demanded an explanation. Had Moon been sleeping with James? Were they really lovers? How long had it been going on?'

'Moon told her mother to stop shouting, but Stella became even more agitated and vociferous. She said she wanted the whole world to know what kind of daughter she had.'

'Stella threatened to take drastic measures. She told Moon she intended to go to the police and report James, whom she referred to as a "perverted" type and "disgusting paedophile". This made Moon laugh. Stella said she would make sure James was put in jail for child abuse.'

'She had lived in England long enough to know that her allegations would be taken very seriously indeed,' Payne murmured.

'Moon explained to her mother, very calmly, or so she claimed, that it was she who had seduced James, not the other way round, after she noticed how he kept staring at her.'

'Stella called her a "shameless slut". She said she would take Moon back to Bulgaria.'

'She threatened to have Moon put in a "reformatory". These, Moon explained, are special units for delinquent teenagers, notorious for their harsh discipline. Her mother had used that threat before, Moon said, but now it sounded as though she meant it.'

'That's when it happened.' Payne pursed his lips.

'That's when the gel—?' Lady Grylls broke off. 'Goodness.'

'Apparently it all happened very fast,' Payne said. 'Moon had been holding the sword aloft. She admitted to having smoked a spliff earlier on in the car, so it all felt a bit like a dream. There was a thud as her mother's head fell on the floor and rolled towards the window. Then she saw her mother's body fall. Talk of lethal Lolitas!'

'Some of the blood went on Moon's clothes, but, as it happened, her brand new clothes were in the boot of the car. Morland had bought them for her,' Antonia explained. 'She changed into the new clothes and stuffed the jeans and the jumper she had been wearing into the Top Girl bag. She had worn her black gloves throughout, so she didn't have to worry about fingerprints. She left the house, got into the car and drove off. She dropped the bag in the river.'

'She didn't take the sword with her? After *everything*?' Lady Grylls said in some surprise.

'No. The sword had been contaminated with her mother's blood. She said she couldn't bear to touch it ever again. She left the car near the river, smoked another spliff, then wandered round London. She went on the tube where she was eventually picked up by the police.' Payne frowned. 'Am I missing anything?'

'She hadn't wanted to kill her mother. It simply "happened". She has already pleaded diminished responsibility. She is very clever,' Antonia said. 'It was all her mother's fault, she insisted. Her mother had no business to threaten her with the reformatory . . . I hope they keep her in for a very long time.'

'What about the handkerchief with the initials? MM, which was actually WW?'

'That, darling, is what I believe experts call a non-clue. Isn't that so?' Payne turned to Antonia, who shrugged. 'The handkerchief was important in that it alerted us to Winifred's part in the affair, but, strictly speaking, it did not constitute a *clue*.'

'Stella had a sneezing fit at Melisande's party. As she had no handkerchief, Winifred lent her hers,' Antonia explained. 'It was a silk handkerchief with the initials WW embroidered on it. Stella forgot to return it. She had been using it moments before she was killed. She took it out to wipe her tears, Moon said. She happened to be holding it in her hand when the blow fell. That was how the handkerchief got soaked in blood.'

212

'Why did the gel kill Winifred exactly?' Lady Grylls asked.

'Winifred was killed in mistake for Melisande,' Payne said. 'Stella had told Moon that "Miss Hope" was Melisande in disguise. Moon regarded Melisande as a rival. Melisande had been trying to poison Morland's mind against her. Morland had complained that Melisande had been ringing him, trying to get him back. Moon admitted she feared Morland might change his mind and go back to Melisande. At one point Morland had expressed misgivings about what he and Moon were doing. Moon said she wanted to make sure Morland stayed with her for ever.'

'She had been sitting in Morland's car outside Kinderhook on the morning Winifred set out to destroy the Prince Cyril biography. When she saw "Miss Hope" emerge and hail a cab, she started tailing the cab. She guessed "Miss Hope" was on her way to the Villa Byzantine. She had been looking for an opportunity to kill Melisande, she said.'

'She also said she meant to make it look as though Tancred Vane was the killer. She has an extremely inflated opinion of her intelligence and ingenuity.' Payne shook his head. 'She sounded impossibly smug on that tape.'

'Hubris leads to Nemesis,' Lady Grylls said sententiously.

'Yes, quite. By creating a second mayhem at the Villa Byzantine, the girl had also hoped to distract the police's attention away from her ... She left some notes for the police to find – she *is* manipulative – uncharacteristic emotional outpourings, quite convincing, apparently – she was innocent, but no one believed her – she related a childhood memory – some rigmarole about seeing a roe deer once and how it made her want to cry.'

'I suppose she is being assessed by all sorts of loony doctors?' Lady Grylls said.

'Well, yes. She likes that.'

'Do they really believe they'll be able to straighten out the kinks in her brain? More tea, Antonia?' Lady Grylls picked up the teapot. 'What's happening to Morland?'

'He is in a bad state. Looks a shadow of his former self. Emaciated – grey-skinned – wild staring eyes – brings to mind one of those warning posters the Department of Health releases every now and then. His sister Julia appears to have taken complete control of his affairs.' Payne paused. 'We caught a glimpse of the two of them going into the police station the other day. Julia is the unflappable kind. He had a stick and he was leaning on her arm. She has managed to get him a first-class defence lawyer.'

'Did Julia know what was going on?'

'She guessed,' Antonia said. 'Apparently, like me, she went to the Corrida Hotel herself and made inquiries. It had occurred to her there was something not quite fatherly about the way her brother kept looking at Moon.'

'Morland continues to deny that he and Moon were having an affair,' said Major Payne. 'The girl, on the other hand, has been eager to provide all sorts of embarrassing details – but everybody agrees she is a compulsive liar as well as a dangerous attention-seeker. That, I imagine, would be the line of the defence lawyer, so Morland might get away with it.'

'What about the actress woman? She is not dead, is she?'

'No. It seems Melisande has recovered from her break-down and is now working on a one-woman show called *Lizzie*. She says she's finding the work therapeutic.'

'I see. An autobiographical kind of show?'

'No, darling. It's about the life and times of Lizzie Borden, the axe murderess. By an odd coincidence Tancred Vane has started writing a book about Lizzie Borden. It is quite a departure for him, but he and Melisande have been paying each other visits and comparing notes, so romance may be in the air.'

Lady Grylls nodded. 'Another extraordinary affair – and one more feather in your collective cap. I've ceased to be amazed. Don't you ever get sick of sleuthing? No, of course not. Pointless kind of question. I expect you relished the symmetry, my dear?' Lady Grylls turned to Antonia. 'Two terribly obsessive love affairs, so intricately interwoven? I bet it appealed to your – what do they call it? *Sense of form*?'

Antonia admitted that the case had indeed appealed to her sense of form.

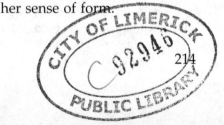